THEN CAME DARKNESS

A Novel

D. H. Schleicher

Then Came Darkness
Copyright © 2018 by D. H. Schleicher.

Cover Photo courtesy of Unsplash by Felix Besombes

This book is a work of fiction. Names, characters, places, and incidents either are products of the author's imagination or are used fictitiously. Any resemblance to actual persons, living or dead, events, or locales is entirely coincidental.

D. H. Schleicher
Visit the author's blog: TheSchleicherSpin.com
Official Site: ThenCameDarkness.com

Printed in the United States of America

First Printing: November 2018
Mabus Publishing

ISBN-978-1-729-42009-6

Thank you to Carla for your original round of edits, and to Joanna for putting on the finishing touches.

And to JB, whose arrival inspired me to finally put this out to the world.

PART ONE: WIDOWS AND ORPHANS

EPISODE ONE: ALONG THE JAMES RIVER

March, 1936

"One of these days I'm gonna kill somebody and mean it."

His hot breath rolled like fog into the cold space between their lips. Just a few miles south of the slip on the outskirts of the city where the water was shallow there was a small shanty town. It was here where Joshua Bloomfield learned of Samuel Kydd's whereabouts.

"He stays at the inn at the bottom of the slip," the smiling whore told him.

"You're sure of it?" Joshua asked her. Her warm bosom was still pressed against his chest as they lay in a tent at the top of a small hill. The smell of old grease and stale human odor lingered in the air while cheap whiskey lay on their breaths.

"I was with him last night. Said he missed his family. Asked him for pictures but he ain't got none."

Joshua's eyes wandered to the small tear in the top of the tent from which he could see late winter stars hung low in a clear black sky. His gaze then returned to her eyes. She started to laugh.

"Why you lookin' at me so funny?" she asked.

"Did he mention his wife's name?"

"Evie...Evelyn...or something. He was funny, too. You two friends?"

Joshua pushed the red-headed whore off his lap, stood up and clumsily buttoned his pants. He looked down at her as he grabbed his jacket off the dirty mattress.

"It is the fella yer lookin' for, right?"

"Oh, it's him alright." Joshua struggled with the buttons on his coat and then flipped his hat atop his head.

The whore looked at him starry-eyed and giggly. Her chest heaved up and down while one fat tit rolled over the top of her blouse exposing its milky whiteness. "You know I've been with all types...plenty of Jews, midgets, cripples, a Negro or two...but I ain't never been with a man who..."

Joshua reached into his coat pocket and threw two crumpled up dollar bills down on the dirt floor in front of her. "I've heard enough outta you. A good whore knows when to shut her trap."

The smile was smudged from her face as if his words were the violent brush strokes of a mad artist...like that painter she knew when she was young who had her model nude for him. She rolled her eyes, fixed her tits and blouse and shoved the dollar bills in between her cleavage. She longed for those days of her youth, lost now somewhere between her folds. Her once frivolous dreams were dashed on the banks of the James River along with her empty whiskey bottles. "You don't have to leave so quick like. It's cold out there."

"Sister, it's colder 'an hell in here."

"I got another bottle. Tell me how you lost your hand." Her eyes went wide upon her deduction, and she looked up at him, rosy-cheek, child-like. "Say...was it that Kydd fella? Did he have something to do with it?"

"You want me to stay and smack you around a little?"

"You don't have to be such a smart-aleck. Go on, you got what you wanted. Get the hell out." She pulled the musty blanket up around her shoulders and fell back onto the mattress. Her body shivered as Joshua disappeared through the flap in the tent. She lay her head down and dreamed of better days...in a warm parlor...with a record player...and a finely dressed man offering her his hand.

Joshua Bloomfield made his way through the mangy mangling of tents and shacks that lined the rocky shore. A light dusting of snow had fallen earlier in the day and still covered everything, and the thin icing over the river glistened in the pale moonlight. The stump at the end of his left arm ached as it always did in the cold. He kept it secure, hidden in his coat pocket, while his other arm gingerly swung as if it was a propeller pushing him up the steep incline leading back into the city towards the slips. He rose higher and higher above the river. To his right the rocks laid out beside him grew further away. To his left the rolling hills and gothic monuments of Hollywood Cemetery were frozen in the winter chill. He pondered coldly all the dead buried there in the icy ground, but the fire inside him longed for only one man to be dead.

He thought of the ghost stories he read Evelyn on those crisp autumn nights in the hills that were so far away now...the glimmering glass of the lake...upstate New York...so long ago. Would he even recognize her today? He could never forget the touch of her black hair, how soft it felt as he ran his fingers through it, brushing against his face, her warm brown eyes pleading, her red lips touching his cheek, kissing his ear lobe, his pulse quickening. Would she recognize him now, battered, bitter? The whore had said he was still handsome. The cemetery sank behind him. He was nearing the bottom, and then the landscape again rose above him. His legs were tired. For a moment, foggy-headed, he felt as if he was stepping up into the stars until he realized it was the lights lining the slip.

He walked up the steps onto the brick sidewalk where the city sprawled out before him. The inn was right there, a shabby little building on the corner, a place that advertised itself as a reputable establishment but housed a bar in its basement where tobacco factory workers enjoyed the sale of liquor by the drink and ladies of the evening were allowed to ply their trade. Joshua bypassed the lobby and walked down the alley to the steps leading to the basement. Music and the warm hearty laughter of drunken men stumbled out into the cold.

When he first heard it, Joshua thought perhaps he was in a dream and still back at the tent asleep with the fat whore warming his bones. But there was no mistaking it, even after all these years. It was that slow, warbling cackle that turned into a howl that could only be the laughter of one Samuel Kydd.

"Joshua Bloomfield!" he bellowed upon seeing the ghost walk through the door and approach him. "Surely this is a nightmare! How long has it been? Fellas, you won't believe it...this is that crazy bastard I've been telling you stories about. Jesus, Mary and Joseph...would you look at us now!"

Joshua had not expected this. Samuel was red-faced and swollen with drink, but he recognized Joshua immediately, as if it had merely been a few hours since they last spoke. Joshua walked up to the table where Samuel sat with a motley crew of drunkards, all of them smiling, laughing, unaware of the momentous nature of this little reunion.

"What brings you to Richmond?" Samuel asked casually.

"I heard about your poor mother. God rest her soul." Joshua looked not down, as someone might show respect for the dead, but straight into Samuel's eyes.

Samuel's face grew sour. He still had that youthful tenacity to change moods so quickly and easily even underneath that grey stubble and the wear of years of failure stamped across his face. He stood up before Joshua could sit down and placed his hand on his shoulder. He turned back to his friends, "Gentlemen, Mr. Bloomfield and I have much to speak about...I reckon you'll get along fine without me for a few moments while we step outside?"

The men grumbled. Some raised their drink, another tipped his cap.

Surprisingly quick-footed, Samuel stepped up onto the street with Joshua. He stumbled, though, when they reached the sidewalk, almost as if he wanted to run away.

"You wish to take a walk?" Joshua asked him.

"I can't believe you're here," Samuel mumbled loudly. Then he whispered hotly, "How did you find me?"

"I explained that already. I heard about your mother's death. I knew you would be down here."

"I've been down here for a while...when she first fell ill. She had no one else to care for her. I had to come down here."

"And Evelyn?"

Samuel smiled. He began walking down the path Joshua had taken to the tavern. His gait was clumsy. Joshua followed closely.

"And Evelyn?"

"She can manage the farm just fine. And the children are a great help."

"The farm?"

"Well, after things cooled down...we were able to settle in Milton. She inherited her uncle's farm. It's not much. Some cows...chickens. It's a good honest living."

"You went back to the hills. How convenient. And children? How many now?"

"God, what's it been? Thirteen years?" Samuel was beginning to lose his breath. He walked briskly. His exhales made fog in the winter night. Samuel turned back to see how close Joshua was and then almost tripped as he continued forward. "There's Edison...as you know. Almost grown. Ran the farm. More of a man than I'll ever be."

"Samuel, don't be so hard on yourself."

"Then there's Sally. She's eleven now. Takes after he mother with her moods, but she has my blonde hair and blue eyes...and freckles. Then there's Tyrus...he's about nine by now, but acts like he's thirty-nine."

"Such a lovely family. And Evelyn is well?"

"She's a great mother. I don't even know where to start, Joshua."

"You can start by telling me what happened to the old man's money?"

Samuel began to laugh and then cough. He stopped by the rocks along the water and spat. He stood to catch his breath and looked out over the James. "You didn't really believe what they told us, did you? The old man's secret stash? It was the ramblings of crazy people."

"You believed it enough then to kill him." Joshua stood a few feet from him staring him down.

Samuel kept his eyes on the water. "You know that was an accident," he said calmly.

"An accident worth covering up." Joshua wondered if Samuel saw the same thing he did when gazing into the water. Every night he was transported back to those hills...to the lake. They were in that rowboat, and the old man would be there under the shallow waters resting on his back on the rocks, a pool of blood around his head...the clear water turning crimson.

"Don't be a fool, Joshua. There was never any money. I swear to it. Just rumors."

"Yet you ran...and I was the one to take the blame."

"You think I ran off with the money?"

"You ran off with Evelyn."

"Can't we put this behind us? There is something I need to tell you. About Edison."

"What concern is Edison of mine?"

"I knew you'd say that. You don't deserve to know." Was Samuel weeping? Like a moody little school-girl he always was.

"Why haven't you returned to your family yet?"

"Oh, Joshua...you have no idea the situation I've made for myself here. There's a young girl...she helped care for my mother. I took advantage. She's pregnant now."

"That's the Samuel I know. You're a disgrace. You can't go back to those hills. You can't go back to Evelyn now. If only you had some money, you could take care of the girl and the child here and still go back to your family."

"Yes, if only..."

"Stop being a coy little twit. You never found it, did you? You couldn't find where he buried it."

"I told you there was never any money."

"You say that because you never found it...you were an idiot. You could never do anything right. Look at you now. The only thing you could ever find was a way to slip your snake into young girls' beds. But you know it's still out there...buried. But you can't find it."

Samuel wiped his face and then turned to Joshua. Samuel's blue eyes were pale and bloodshot, like cracked ice, his whole body swollen with piss and vinegar. "You're the fool who stayed. I did what any sane person would do in that situation. I took your girl and ran. And you actually think I was stupid enough to do that without any money in my pocket? You think Evelyn was the type of girl who would've stood for that? You were the idiot, Joshua. It all went exactly as I planned, don't you see? The only thing I miscalculated was that you lost only a hand. I'd hoped they would kill you."

Joshua stood there and took it all in, revealing nothing, his face like stone, like the rocks along the shore upon which they stood.

"Don't you have anything to say for yourself?" Samuel screamed. "I wanted you dead. Evelyn wanted you dead. You're dead to us now. You're dead to your..."

"Where is it then?"

"I took just what I needed back then and left the rest. I'm the only one who knows how to get to it."

"You lie. You could never keep a secret. Evelyn knows. She's not the type who would stand for that...you said so yourself."

"Evelyn knows nothing."

"Tell me where it is."

"You're insane."

Joshua took a step forward. Samuel flinched and stepped back, almost falling backwards onto the rocks.

"Don't come any closer," Samuel warned. He reached into his coat pocket and pulled out a revolver with his shivering hand.

Joshua leapt towards him and grabbed the gun. He took the handle and jabbed it into Samuel's right temple while pressing the stump at the end of his left arm into Samuel's chest. Samuel fell backwards onto the rocks and into the shallow pooling tide. Joshua had him by the neck with his one hand and was situated on top of him straddling his torso. He pressed his stump down against the top of Samuel's ribcage for leverage.

"Tell me where it is!" Joshua fumed.

"I was stringing you along," Samuel gurgled as Joshua loosened his grip so he could speak. "There never was any money! It was just a story."

"Tell me where it is!"

"Go to hell!"

Joshua tightened his grip around Samuel's neck. His hand was so cold. There was such heat emanating from Samuel's body, as if the tighter he choked his neck, the closer his body was to exploding right there underneath him. "Did you bury it on the farm?"

Samuel shook his head, "no."

"Did you bury it under the house?"

"NO!"

"Where is it, then?" Joshua shook his hand and bashed the back of Samuel's head into the rocks. "Tell me where it is! I've a right to take back what's mine! Tell me where it is!" He bashed Samuel's head around some more. There was blood trickling into the water. Joshua loosened his grip.

Samuel's eyes began to roll back in his head. "There is no money," he whispered between strained gurgling. "You'll never have her."

"Tell me where it is." The head against the rocks.

"You'll never have her."

"I'll fucking kill her. Where is the money?" Head. Rocks. Blood pooling.

"You'll never find it."

"I'll go your farm. I'll torture them until they tell me where the money is."

Samuel's eyes pooled with tears. "Leave them alone."

"Tell me where it is."

"Fuck you."

Joshua lowered his head as close as he could to Samuel's face. He could smell death coming up through Samuel's pores. He looked him straight in the eyes and told him, "I want what rightfully belongs to me. I will go to the farm and visit your family. If they are not there, I will hunt them down. I will torture them one by one until someone speaks. And if no one knows where the money is...I will kill them all. Now tell me where it is."

"No...wait...Edison..."

One last time. Samuel's head was dashed against the rocks. When Joshua finally lifted his grip, it was like letting a dead fish fall to the ground.

Walking away from the rocks he swore he could feel the old man's fingertips dance across his back. The moon seemed even lower now, as if it wanted to sprout legs and waltz across the James. In the past Joshua might have envisioned it as taunting, but now it seemed the moon wished to congratulate him. It whispered into his ear, a pale co-conspirator. "North...to the hills...the hills...the hills." Not even the fog from his own breath could cloud his vision. The path for Joshua Bloomfield was set.

EPISODE TWO: MYRA LONG TAKES THE TRAIN

Atlanta...a few days earlier...

Now playing. Anne Shirley in *Chatterbox*. Starting Friday March 20th. The Paramount Theater. Carole Lombard in *Love Before Breakfast*. Lombard's blackened eye was indicative of a different kind of love. The corners of the posters were pealing. The glue attaching the billboards to the wooden fencing atop the low brick wall running along the sidewalk stunk something fierce. When they first plastered the posters, the fumes wafted up through the open windows into all floors of the houses that sat behind the fence and the wall. Melted horses. It made Myra teary-eyed as she sat on the tattered chaise-lounge on the balcony overlooking the street. She thought of the horses she rode as a child. But those thoughts drifted out over the street along with her cigarette smoke as it was there that she imagined the large circular cutout in her perch to be the iris of a giant camera. All passers-by were looking up at her. She felt perfectly framed. In view. On display. No man would blacken her eye.

Myra wore an out-of-style fur-trimmed coat and hat, a costume, something similar to what that girl had worn on Fulton Street in his photograph from 1929. In the living room she struck a pose in the antique full-length mirror propped up against the wall.

She tried to capture that woman's image, that knowing look, that squint of recognition...the impending doom. She often wondered...had he captured that photograph before or after the crash? Had it been staged? Did he even know the girl?

Three days ago Myra had received the letter from her father, Dr. Horace Long. It was her private emotional stock crash. Looking at herself in the mirror, trying to annihilate the letter with her posturing, she wondered...how much longer could she stage this charade for her photographer? She had bought her ticket to New York City this morning. The train was to leave tomorrow. Her bags were packed. She thought of how much colder it might be up that way. Maybe she would take this coat and this hat. Maybe she would find that exact corner on Fulton Street and stand there with that knowing look. She often wondered what that girl was looking at, or who she was looking for off-camera. Myra knew she would only be looking for one person...that poor boy back home...buried now in the frozen ground on the side of the hill.

"I just don't understand the spell that this boy cast on you," the photographer said. "Was he like a brother to you?"

"I can't explain it," Myra told him. "You can't capture this in one of your photos." And as she told him this, she thought of that photo tucked into her suitcase. It was just a simple photo the boy from back home had given to her before she left for Atlanta. It was his school picture. It wasn't something this photographer could appreciate. It was something common and pedestrian...there was no art to a school photo. But there was a story in that boyish and mischievous smile...and there were the boy's words scribbled with a trembling hand on the back. A confession that was now Myra's secret.

"You're so beautiful," the photographer told her as the fur-trimmed coat fell to the floor and he took her in his arms. "I don't know if a morning can exist without your face to greet me when I wake."

"Please...there will be another girl's face...another morning in another city."

"But it will never compare to you."

"You can't change my mind. We're both too restless. We both have to move on."

Her photographer sulked in the twilight out on the small balcony overlooking the street...a cigar smoldering in the ashtray...a glass of gin frosting in the chill settling over the evening like a cold compress. Myra knew he was already imagining his next series of photographs. She called herself a taxi to take her to a hotel by the train station. By the end of the following week the apartment they shared would be empty. He will be in Mexico. The stench of melted horses will be but a bad aftertaste half-remembered. His Atlanta will be best known for those billboards outside the house. Anne Shirley and Carol Lombard, seemingly immortalized, the edges of their existence slowly peeling off the fence forever.

Myra Long, meanwhile, that following morning, had taken the train.

It the comfort and solitude of her sleeping car, she opened her jewelry box. The diamond studded cocktail necklace had the weight of a noose in her hands. It was heavy with memories of the boy in the picture.

"I'll buy the matching earrings next," his tremulous voice told her that night he presented her with the gift.

"But where did you get the money?" she asked. "I can't take this from you. What about your poor mother?"

He was struck mute, and she watched his Adam's apple as he took a hard swallow, the tendons on his neck tightening. She wanted to kiss him there. She knew he was hiding something. Winters harvesting ice from the lake could not have funded such an extravagance, and to give it to her, it was a scandal. He was just a boy of fifteen. She was a youth, too, in many ways still, but markedly older, though her soft skin betrayed her years and made her desirable to men and boys of all ages. She was leaving for Atlanta, and here he was without speaking, asking her to stay. To be his. He was already hers. She kissed him on the cheek as if sending him off to bed.

Myra had worn it only once, that night it was bequeathed to her. If it weren't for the contemporary nature of its style, she would've sworn it was a family heirloom. Where did he get the money to buy such a thing? Here on the train she felt compelled to feel its weight around her neck, its coldness against her skin. Memories of her boy from the picture tightened around her. She leaned back against the scratchy cushion of her seat and closed her eyes. She thought of his mother. The other children. She didn't want to see them. She opened her eyes, but a hazy sun glared in the window and drove her to shut her eyes again.

In warmer times, summer in the hills, she saw them in twilight. They were breathless from play in the woods, running out to greet her, the children drenched in smiles and clammy in their dirty clothes. That dog was attached to the youngest boy, always eyeing her suspiciously but in a non-threatening way. She could smell them still...kids and beast and trees alike. The grass. The lake. She would peck them on their necks and faces with kisses as they ran into her arms. The summer breeze lifted up underneath her dress as she straightened herself for him...for her boy...looking nearly a man now, too old for pecks and hugs. He would take her hand in his, his hand even at that age so much larger than hers, yet surprisingly soft and gentle in its grip. With the younger children and the dog leading the way, they made their way down to the lake. This time they did not stop on the shore. All spare for the dog...they stepped right into it. They did not stop. Deeper and deeper into the lake they went. And drowned.

Myra awoke gasping for air. In her dream she had been searching for light, but when she woke, she found darkness. The train moved now through the night. She heard outside her room the conductor announcing dinner was being served in the dining car. She could not succumb to the stranglehold. As it sparkled against the glass, the necklace began to lose weight. She stared out the window into the vast passing darkness. She had her future to think of. She imagined the sparkles in the glass becoming the checkered lights of Manhattan skyscrapers. She would be in New York City by morning. With newfound confidence she rose to her feet and straightened her dress. She checked her hair and make-up in the mirror. She was not picture perfect, but there was no photographer here, and this look would do. The necklace was gaudy, but it was hers now, and she would wear it proudly to the dining car.

It was not crowded. A few older couples, over-dressed and stiff, sat sipping cold soup and staring vacantly out the windows. Myra's shiny, flaxen hair seemed to glisten in its reflection in the window as she sat alone at her table. Her face almost seemed to disappear in the rushing darkness on the other side, and all that existed there in that window was the sheen of her hair, the sparkling diamonds of her necklace and the white of the tablecloth.

Myra noticed a man sitting at the last table on the other side of the aisle facing her staring in her direction. At first it appeared to be a leer, and she was startled. But then it seemed as if he was staring not at her, but at her reflection in the glass. He wore an unassuming dark brown derby hat and a dusty suit jacket. His white shirt underneath, unbuttoned at the top and without a tie, appeared musty but not unclean. When he realized she had caught him looking at her, he nodded and raised his cup of coffee to her with his right hand. There was a threat of a grin on his face. He winked as he placed the coffee cup down on its saucer and pulled from his inside coat pocket a silver flask. He uncapped it with his teeth, his left arm seemingly dead at his side, and poured a quick dash and then another into his coffee before quickly concealing the flask again. Myra smiled at him and raised her glass of coffee in his direction before taking a gentle sip. This time he gave her a full-on grin but showed no teeth. There was something ruggedly boyish about him, though he appeared to be much older than her...perhaps in his late thirties. He wasn't unattractive and presented to her in that one small exchange a sinister charm.

After dinner, they both retreated to the lounge car. Myra first, followed by the man. She rested while standing at the bar, leaning on the countertop and sipping a gin and tonic.

"Got on in Richmond?" he said to her, taking off his hat and placing it on the counter, revealing his slick jet black hair.

"Atlanta," she replied. "Getting off in New York City?"

"I suppose."

"Where are you from?"

He grinned as he sidled up next to her and motioned to the bartender for a drink. "The same as the little lady, here," he said. He turned to her. "My dear, I'm from all over."

"Well...where are you from originally then?"

He couldn't stop grinning. He showed a little teeth this time. There was a chip on his front tooth, but they were white, clean. He sucked air through them. "You might say I'm a bit of a traveling actor of sorts...why, I'm original everywhere."

Myra obliged him with a laugh. "Oh, you're one of those huh? I can tell from your accent you're not from down south."

"I would make the same case about you."

"New York."

"Me too."

She looked at him incredulously. "Upstate."

"What are the chances? Me too."

"Fenimore."

"Oh, no, no...much further Upstate. Almost Canada. You had me going there. Thought for a second fate was intervening right here on this train." He kept his left arm close to his side, seemingly hiding his hand in his pocket. With his right hand he lifted his glass to his mouth and titled his head back, taking it all in with two gulps. "You're probably too young to remember the prohibition days. Dry trains were no fun. That's why I got in the habit of carrying my little silver friend."

"Oh, and here I thought you were just cheap."

He mocked being offended and chuckled. He leered at her necklace. "Say, where's a lady like you pick up a piece like that?"

Myra touched it defensively with her fingers. "Wouldn't you like to know?"

"Traveling alone?"

"I wouldn't be standing here with you if I wasn't."

"A young lady like you, all up and down the country...Atlanta...New York City...you must have friends of all sorts."

"The only friend I see right now is you."

"Why I'm flattered. The name's...Daniel." He presented his right hand.

She could tell right then he was lying. "Lula Belle." She lifted her hand to him, palm down. He kissed it. His lips were coarse, chapped.

"Come now, surely that's not your real name," he said smiling, fatherly.

Myra smiled and pulled back a little. She finished her gin and tonic. He ordered them two more. They drank quickly.

"Okay, okay. I'm Myra," she conceded.

"Now that's better," he announced. "I'm Joshua."

* * *

Bloomfield had taken notice of her as soon as she stepped into the dining car. She looked lost in that dress and that necklace, like she had just stepped off a stage and expected to find herself greeted by gentlemen and drinks in a jazz club. Her whole demeanor was that of someone sleepwalking, voice tired from singing, eyes searching for respite. When she finally revealed her name to him in the lounge car...Myra...it didn't seem to match her appearance, but he knew she was being truthful. She looked like a woman who needed a distraction, and she was willing to be vulnerable. After three drinks she appeared to him to be aching.

"Do you have a compartment?" she whispered in his ear, her lips remaining close to his neck for uncomfortably too long.

"I'm afraid I'm in coach," he sighed.

She took his right hand in hers. "Follow me," she cooed as she led him out of the lounge car and through a stretch of passenger cars that seemed endless. He was transfixed first on her rump that moved up and down beneath the sheer dress, supple yet mournful in a way, as if it desired to be desired by better eyes than his. He worked his way up her back to her neckline and the clasp of that necklace. He wanted to snatch it off her right there and wondered how much it was worth, how much it would fetch him once he was freed from this moving prison careening through the night.

Finally they reached the sleeping car and stopped in front of what was presumably her compartment. Joshua broke his hand free from her while she placed her back against the wall. He placed his newly freed hand first on her thigh, firmly, taking in the silky feel of the fabric, the shape of her flesh beneath. He moved it slowly up and over her hipbone and was headed for the area right beneath her breast when she reached for his left arm to bring his other hand up to her face for a caress. A look not of horror, but of disappointment draped across her face when she found not a hand to touch her, but a stump at the end of his left arm. As his right hand then instinctually cupped her breast, she returned his favor with a slap across the face.

Joshua stepped back and was now up against the cold glass of the window. Myra's chest heaved as she placed her hands like a prayer to her mouth. She shook her head.

"I'm sorry," she said through the folds of her fingers. "You're very sweet."

"I'm no such thing," Joshua replied forcefully.

He knew that look in her eyes all too well, that look of disappointment followed by guilt and then pity, all within the same moment. A rage quickly rose up underneath Joshua's skin. He didn't need this from her. He only wanted to steal her necklace. Now he wanted to strangle her too. He suddenly saw fear in her eyes. Myra dove into her compartment shutting the door behind her. Joshua had lost his chance.

He returned to his seat and waited for the darkness outside to match the inside of the train. The world slept, but he sat there with eyes open, staring straight ahead into the muted blackness. The stench of the people around him fueled his rage. An infant awash in the odor of human filth and sour milk rested on its mother's fat greasy chest across the aisle from him. Other aimless, nameless, faceless vagabonds slumbered noisily around him, not having bathed for days, weeks maybe, wearing tattered and muddied clothes, stomachs growling, dreaming of second or third or fourth chances heading north on promises of work or reuniting with long lost family members, more nameless, faceless destitute drifters idling through life and praying for the sweet release of death.

Meanwhile, Princess Myra slept soundly in her private compartment comforted by her luxury and her pity.

Joshua found himself rising from his seat and floating like a specter through the passenger cars, his body casting no reflection in the windows as he moved. He found himself at the door to Myra's compartment, opening it, his left arm aching, his skin crawling, his right hand wanting to work its magic and wrap its fingers around her perfect, slender neck.

Myra lay there so peacefully. She must've collapsed right there on the seat, no bed turned down, still fully clothed with that necklace around her neck. Her head rested on a pillow and her hands were folded neatly in prayer beneath her cheek, her body resting on its side with her back against the cushion. The shade on her window had not been drawn and a low hanging moon cast a pale glow across her face and neck and shoulders. She appeared as a child would, so serene, so confident in its pity.

Bloomfield's right hand appeared as a claw in shadow form hovering over the sleeping Myra. As he inched closer, his whole body encroached on the light, and she was bathed in his violent shadow, drowning in his rage. But then he noticed something clasped between her folded hands. It appeared to be the edges of a picture and a piece of paper. Joshua's focus was lost and he slipped the items carefully out from between her hands. She shifted her body a bit and murmured something unintelligible, but she remained in deep sleep.

The picture was of a young boy probably not more than fifteen or sixteen years old. The boy's eyes and smile instantly pierced Joshua's rage, and it sank quickly and painfully into the pit of his guts where it turned into bitterness and regret. He knew that look. He had never seen this boy before, but he knew that look. He turned the picture over and written across the back was "Edison Kydd, 1935."

How could this be? His heart raced and the stump at the end of his left arm began to throb. The train raced in and out of a short tunnel briefly eclipsing the compartment in utter darkness, and upon exiting, Joshua suddenly caught a glimpse of himself in the window and was shocked by what he saw. He took a few steps back and out of the room, finding relief in the coolness of the hallway with his back against the cold glass. There was just enough light out there where he could read the handwritten letter. It was dated February, 25th 1936.

My darling Myra,

I write to you with a great heaviness of heart. Earlier this month, our dear boy, neighbor and friend, Edison suffered a most serious blow to the head in an accident while working out on the ice. My most esteemed colleagues at Haydon Hospital did everything in their power to lessen the severity of Edison's injury and revive him from the deep sleep in which his body had found itself due to the trauma. Despite their efforts and the prayers of all those around, his condition continued to deteriorate until it became clear that death was imminent. His dearest mother, Evelyn, wished to bring him home to the Kydd Family Farm so he could be surrounded by those whom loved him the most in his final days. There he found a most peaceful rest until his last breath on February 22nd, 1936. His body was later interred alongside his ancestors on the side of Haydons Hill. May you find some kind of comfort in these facts. Edison did not die alone, and his intentions towards you remained true and pure to his final days.

I will not muddy this sad announcement with talk of other matters. I will write you soon with talk of many things, and look forward to our reunion in happier times.

Your loving father, always.

Bloomfield was struck without breath. The letter and picture left his hand and floated down to the floor. He found himself clawing at his shirt, ripping open the buttons even further as if the article of clothing itself was the cause of his choking. He began to run through the series of sleeper cars and conductors' quarters until he found his way to the end of the train and outside onto the platform. There the cold night air filled his lungs and as the world raced by him and the sound of the train roaring over the tracks deafened him, he swallowed the darkness. Already over-full, he began to vomit gin and bile over the edge of the platform.

Once able to breathe again, he found rest outside and watched the sun rise over the east. His breathing ran in synch with the powerful forward momentum of the train, and he took solace knowing that like this train, he could not be stopped. He would find them. Evelyn. The other children. The money was out there. It was his. All he had to do was take it.

Joshua Bloomfield got off the train in Trenton to head west and then north up through Pennsylvania into New York.

EPISODE THREE: IN THE LAND OF TEMPLES

Six months earlier...

All children had their secrets. Some held them close. Others revealed them to anyone who would listen. Tyrus Kydd was no different. This morning, he thought of his secret and it brought him comfort. By the end of the day, it would breed in him a deep resentment towards the person he loved the most.

It was late September and the hills around the Kydd family farm were painted in varying shades of the sunset. The open swath of land, where generations ago trees had been cleared from the hills between Milton and Fenimore, was overgrown with thick green grass for grazing. The first frost was late this year, and during the day the air was still warm with memories of a recently deceased summer. Its ghost still whispered in the ears of bronzed children fooled by the sun beckoning them to be truant.

Tyrus raced through his morning chores before washing up and devouring breakfast. He kissed his mother goodbye, and with his bagged lunch headed down the hillside towards the road leading into town and the schoolhouse. But the light was funny that morning. Early fog had been burned off the hills and the sun's angle made crooked shadows of the branches from that great looming tree. Edison claimed once it was five hundred years old. It stood sentinel in the middle of the divide by that old crumbling wooden fence Pop had promised to fix every spring. The fence rambled up into the hills marking the property lines of the Kydd family farm and Duncan Abram's land. And Sue, Ty's trusty border collie, she just seemed to saunter calmly along the shade line. The shadows of the tree limbs seemed like psychic extensions of the dog's spirit begging its master...*please, for just one more day, stay here with me, for tomorrow, when it's cold, these shadows will cover the land.*

"You go ahead and stay here with that damn dog," Sally, his older sister barked from the edge of the road. "See if I care."

"Aww, Sally, don't be that way. Sue wants you to stay too."

"The hell she does. Go on, git." Sally had told him when she was ten and three-quarters that the day she turned eleven she would start cussin' and she bet him that ain't no one was gonna stop her. Well, Mom washed her mouth out with soap more than once since her eleventh birthday, but damn it, if she didn't keep on cussin' every chance she got, especially around Ty and Sue. But not around Edison. Nobody better cuss around Edison. Sally kept walking down into town.

Tyrus followed Sue up to that old tree. "You stay watch," he told her as he climbed the trunk and nestled himself into the crooks of the highest massive limbs with a perfect view of all the land. The entire known universe was laid out before him in a seemingly unending stretch of bright rolling morning glory. A gentle wind rustled the leaves overhead and below. Everything felt warm but crisped, as if one strong breath of cold air came rolling down from the highest hill, the entire land would suddenly be chilled and all the leaves would fall to the ground.

Tyrus' eyes became strained and tired as he stared out over the vast expanse and tried to see over the endless rolling mounds of earth and trees. Was the dust bowl out there? He had heard about in school and on the radio. His teacher's somber laments. The president's fireside chats. How close was it? Was it just a matter of shifting winds? Would it one day reach them? He felt protected here in these verdant hills. It was a land untouched by the great calamities that swept over other portions of the country, areas so large they could swallow these hills whole. Yet at night he would sometimes dream of a great dust, dark and smoked like ash, raining over everything. And he knew his mother shared the same dreams for when he would tell her in the morning about them, her eyes would grow wide with fear, and she would grab her throat as if she was choking.

"Don't be silly," she would say after collecting herself. "We're safe here."

His eyes lost focus and came back into focus with the sounds coming from the other side of the fence. He looked down and saw Sue still laying there in the high grass, but alert now and with nose, eyes and ears pointed toward the Abrams' barn. They both watched as Duncan Abrams led a horse around back. The horse walked slowly with great trepidation. It appeared to be limping and neighed in a defeated tone. Sue stood up and approached the fence. Tyrus climbed down the tree and joined her. He was close enough now that he could tell it was Myra Long's horse. It disappeared around the other side of the barn. Sue and Tyrus tracked along the fence to see if further up the hill they could see around to the other side.

A gun shot rang out and sparrows took flight from the tree in front of the barn scattering into the hills with the echo of the shot. Tyrus leapt over the fence and ran to the other side of the barn. Sue paced nervously along the fence line staying behind, yelping. Tyrus found Duncan Abrams standing proudly over the dead horse holding the smoking rifle at his side. His dark beady eyes shot out from under his hat and fixed themselves on Tyrus.

"Boy, why ain't you in school?"

"Still doin' chores," Tyrus lied instinctually.

"If I had known you been around, I would've showed you how to do this. You'll need to learn one day." He nodded his head and looked down on the slain beast, satisfied with himself. "Did right by this poor horse. Good clean shot. One time when I was about your age I watched my Grandaddy put a horse down. Had to shoot it eight times in the head before it stopped twitching and lurching. It was a horrible sight to see."

"Why did you do it? That was Myra's horse."

Duncan mused for a moment and stroked his scruffy white beard and mustache. "All you Kydd fellas be sweet on that girl. She ain't comin' back, ya know. This poor horse was old and growing lame. You can't let an animal live in misery like that. Gotta stamp out misery where you can."

Tyrus was suddenly overcome with a desire to cry and tears flowed down his cheeks. He was embarrassed, and his face grew red. He never cried in front of men.

"You've lived on this land long enough to know these things to be true. Ain't no use in cryin', boy." He shook his head. "Go on up to the house now and stop that blubberin'." He turned to the house which sat up the hill beyond the barn. "MA!" he bellowed.

Tyrus turned back to the fence and saw Sue poised to jump right over it. He shook his head "no" and with his eyes commanded her to stay there. He turned back towards the Abrams' house and saw Ma Abrams, as big as that barn, standing on that porch, apron on, beckoning him to come up. He ran up to the porch and she swept him up inside and to the kitchen.

"Now, now, I know you fancied that horse because it was Myra's," she said in her sweet, husky sing-songy voice as she dabbed away his tears with a dish rag.

"I'm sorry," Tyrus said.

"Ain't no need to be sorry. How old are you now?"

"Eight and three-quarters, ma'am." Tyrus' sobbing had subsided, but his voice was till weepy.

"Eight and three-quarters, my my. Have a seat now and calm yourself. It's perfectly natural for a boy your age to get attached to animals like that. Ain't no shame in sheddin' a few tears."

But it was more Myra that Tyrus was thinking of and Duncan Abram's pronouncement that she wouldn't be coming back.

Ma Abrams rustled around the oven some as Tyrus took a seat at the kitchen table. She slapped two huge biscuits down in front of him and a coffee cup filled with lukewarm gravy. "Eat. That'll comfort you. Make you grow big and strong like your brother."

Tyrus felt a little guilty. The lunch his mother had packed was still up in the tree, but Ma Abrams was not one to disobey. He ate ravenously as if he hadn't had a bite to eat for days. Between huge bites of biscuits, he said, "Is it really true Myra's not coming back?"

"Don't talk with your mouth full, child," Ma Abrams scolded kindly.

Tyrus swallowed his mouthful and before he had sense enough to realize his mouth was dry from the biscuits, Ma Abrams had placed a glass of milk before him from which he took a hearty gulp. "Sorry, ma'am. Thank you, ma'am."

"I know your mother taught you good manners. A woman doesn't keep a house and her children that clean without teaching her chaps good manners. Now ask me again, child."

"Is it true Myra's not coming back?"

Ma Abrams was at the kitchen sink gazing out the window as she began to clean the pile of dishes left over from breakfast. "Well, her father's still the town doctor, so I reckon as long as he's here she oughta come back some time, even if only to visit. I'm more concerned about the other people never coming back, all those city folk who used to come up into the hills for the summer in their fancy cars and rent cabins by the lake and ride their horses for which we provided board and care all year long. That's how we made our business, you know. And each year since the crash, fewer and fewer of them would come up, and they would stop paying their bills, and now we're stuck with caring for their horses on our own dime."

"So you just shoot 'em?"

"Come, child, you know it's not like that. That horse was old and its time had come."

"Am I gonna have shoot Sue when she gets old? She's almost as old as me."

"No, don't worry. That dog has a few good years left in her. And it's different for dogs...unless they grow rabid."

"I'd never shoot Sue. Not for nothing. Never ever."

Ma Abrams dismissed his declaration and went right on waxing about the troubles. "Your mother was a godsend when she sold us two of her cows, so at least we can make some money selling the milk to folks in town. We could never thank her enough."

"We only got one cow now. And Mom sold our sheep to the Robinsons. Just one cow and them chickens left."

Ma Abrams nodded. "I know. These troublin' times reach us all eventually."

"I know all about it. Will we turn into a dust bowl, too?"

"Oh, no, child. We're on God's earth here. This was the first frontier, blessed land. These hills will always be fertile, and no matter what comes of us, people will always have the land to live off of here, and we'll always have our neighbors. Your mother and I, we look after each other. You children will never want. You know, horse meat can make for a good stew. Why don't you come back when it's dark and I'll send some home for your mother?"

Tyrus felt sick to his stomach. "I ain't eatin' Myra's horse!"

"Aww, child, in these times we can't let anything go to waste."

"Will we have to eat Sue when she dies?"

"I reckon given the right circumstances, people will eat whatever they have to eat to survive."

"Even other people?"

"Hush, child!"

"I'm sorry." Tyrus stood up from the table.

Ma Abrams turned from the window and her dishes and wiped her soapy wet hands on her apron. She looked at the boy sternly. "I reckon you must have an awful lot of chores to do for your mother to have kept you out of school today."

"Yes, ma'am." Tyrus stood there looking down at his shoes.

"Go run along then."

"Thank you for the biscuits and milk."

"You're welcome. Now you come back when it's dark, ya hear?"

"Yes, ma'am." Tyrus turned sharply on his heels and then raced out the door.

Sue was still waiting for him by the fence when he came back. She scolded him with a few sharp barks as he climbed back over to her side.

"I'm sorry, girl," he said as he reached for the top of her head and ears but she backed away.

Still she followed him up further into the hills. He walked for a long time, to the far edges of their property in the north where over the fence he could see the sheep grazing on the Robinsons' land. He knew Sue missed them the most as she whimpered. They walked back down through the woods and by Gorey Pond before reaching the farm again. Tyrus checked on their one remaining cow and then threw the chickens some feed before returning to the tree. He climbed up and retrieved his lunch and then rested against the bottom of the massive trunk. He wasn't very hungry and gave half of his bologna sandwich to Sue, who gobbled it up ferociously.

"I won't never eat you, girl," he said as he petted the top of her head and behind her ears.

They both must've fallen asleep, and they awoke to the sound of Sally's voice.

"Mom saw you out here sleepin'," Sally announced proudly.

"I'm really gonna get it now," Tyrus lamented.

"Don't worry, I covered for you. I said you went home early not feeling well, and that you must've stopped by the tree to rest and fell asleep."

Tyrus' eyes beamed up at his sister.

"Don't get any wise ideas, smartass. I didn't do it for you. Mom hasn't been feeling well and I didn't want her getting any more upset over you."

Tyrus was deflated. "Thanks...I guess." He suddenly remembered Ma Abrams' command for him to return when it was dark for the stew meat. He felt sick to his stomach again.

"Well, what the hell's eatin' you?" Sally asked with her hands on her hips.

"Mr. Abrams shot Myra's horse. And now Mrs. Abrams wants me to come back later to fetch some stew meat."

"I've had horse before."

"I don't wanna do it."

"I don't understand why she wants to give it to us. Hasn't she given us enough already?"

"What do you mean?"

"Oh, you must've fallen asleep listening to your dumb radio show. She came over the other night with an envelope full of money. Gave it to Mom and said, 'I know you're not a religious woman, but we took up this collection, small as it may be, at church to help you pay your doctor's bill'. It was weird. I never say Mom cry like that. Edison practically had to catch her from falling to the floor."

"Doctor's bill? But Dr. Long is a friend. Why would we owe him any money?"

Sally shook her head. "Oh, you're such a child. Everyone has to make a living. Nothing's free. Especially these days."

"Oh yeah? Whadda you know about it?"

"Mom and Edison talk to me all the time about it. We try to shield it from you. We know how sensitive you are."

"Shut up!"

"Well, you gonna get that horse meat?"

"I'm not eatin' it!"

"You'll eat what's given to you." Sally enjoyed making definitive statements like that, trying to sound like their mother, like an adult. "Fine, baaaaby, I'll fetch it tonight. Now you better get inside and act sick. I'm not takin' the fall for you." Sally picked up her satchel off the ground and walked up the hill into the house.

Sue nuzzled her wet snout into Tyrus' hands. Inside Tyrus was fuming. He was going to let Edison have it when he came home from work. He pushed Sue away. "Go on inside!" he yelled at the dog. "Go check on Mom." The dog ran off, dejected. Tyrus climbed back up into the tree, sulking, and waited for his brother to return home.

Another hour passed before Edison came walking up the path to the house, tired and greasy from the long day working at the garage. An animated Sally greeted him on the porch and proceeded to point out to the tree from where Tyrus saw all. Sally went back inside the house and Edison marched over to the tree.

"Get down from there, Ty!" he yelled up to his kid brother.

"No!" Tyrus yelled back, arms folded, back rigid against the trunk, sitting with his legs stretched out and crossed as happy as he could be on the giant tree limb.

"What are you all sore about?"

"I'm mad at you!"

"Mad at me? Sally didn't mention anything about that. She told me what happened today. Whaddya mad at me for?"

"She tell you how I skipped school?"

Edison laughed and shook his head before craning his neck and looking back up at his brother. "Boy, no, but you just did. Man, if Pop was here..."

"I'm mad at him, too!"

"Oh, c'mon now, you can't keep actin' sore over that. He had to go take care of his sick mother...our grandmother! Wouldn't you do the same for Mom?"

"I'm not sore about that no more. I'm sore about what you and him been hidin'."

"You're talkin' crazy. I don't even know what you're talkin' about. What could we be hidin'? He ain't even here! Hell, I'm gonna level with you, man to man. I'm not sure he's ever gonna come back. You can't go around bein' sore at me for something I don't even know what you're talkin' about. And you can't go around bein' sore at him for runnin' off and doin' what he thought he needed to do. We need to stick together, you and me, you know that!"

"I don't wanna hear it! I've heard just about enough from people tellin' me other people ain't never comin' back here! I can't take it anymore...this place...without those people. You know the Abrams said Myra ain't gonna come back."

"Stop with that nonsense." Edison was about out of breath from yelling up into that tree. His neck must've been killing him. He lowered his head and looked around the hills.

"Myra ain't comin' back!" Tyrus yelled down at him.

Edison took a deep breath and arched his back. He cracked his neck and looked back up at his brother. "Our poor mother is in there right now cookin' your supper. You get down from that tree right now!"

"No!"

"If I wasn't so tired I'd climb up that tree and take you down. Go on and stay up there then."

"Fine, I will, thank you very much."

"Fine! Some brother you are. All we got is each other. You act like you want me to leave too."

"I wish you would."

Edison shook his head. "You don't mean that. When you're ready, you come down from there and talk to me like a man and tell me what's really on your mind. I swear I have no idea what you're talkin' about right now and I'm just getting' angry listenin' to your rantin' and ravin'."

As Edison walked away, Tyrus suddenly felt a pang in his stomach at the thought that Edison might one day leave too. He had never said such mean and hateful things to his brother. He wanted to throw up, but his resentment kept him firmly planted in that tree.

Night fell over the hills. Suppertime passed. He watched as Sally went across the fields to the Abrams' house to fetch the meat for what would inevitably be tomorrow night's stew. A soft welcoming glow came gently out into the darkness from the illuminated rooms of his house; the living room downstairs partially lighting the front porch, the light from his mother's bedroom seemingly pulsating. It was getting cold, and he was beginning to shiver there in his short-sleeves and knickers. He wanted to go inside and apologize to his mother for missing supper and tell her his secret so that maybe she wouldn't have to accept charity from the Abrams or from some church she didn't even go to. It seemed right then as he stared up through the darkened leaves at the first stars appearing in the night sky that even Sue had abandoned him by not coming back outside and waiting under the tree for him to descend and pet her. It was growing darker...colder.

He looked over at the Abrams house whose glow was obscured by the shadowy barn but from which he could see smoke rising up from their woodstove through the chimney. He wondered if they were already cooking part of Myra's poor old horse. He looked down the dirt pathway to the main road and saw nestled at the foot of the hills in glorious straight lines the streetlights in town and the spiked top of a distant steeple. He looked the other way back up into the deep hills and saw nothing but darkness. All he wanted to do now was climb down that tree, go inside to that warm glow, go upstairs to his bedroom and crawl into his bed and sleep...forget about all of this...the dead horse, Myra, his father, his secret, the descending cold blanket of darkness.

It was then that Tyrus saw Edison racing out of the house and down the pathway to the telephone pole by the main road. He frantically climbed the pole to make a call. Tyrus knew it must've been a call to Dr. Long. His mother must've been having another spell...serious enough this time to call on Dr. Long. Tyrus was petrified. He wanted to leap out of that tree and rush inside to his mother, but he was frozen stiff. He watched in static panic as Edison ran back inside the house. Dr. Long didn't live very away, just over in Fenimore, and it was only five minutes before his car pulled up alongside the road and parked at the bottom of the dirt path. He stepped out of the car, hunched over a bit from age, weary but determined, and climbed up to the house before disappearing into its violent yellow glow.

It was all of twenty minutes before Dr. Long exited the house and walked over to the tree. He carried not only his doctor's bag but also a blanket. He looked up into the tree searching in the darkness for any sign of a child up there.

"Tyrus, you best come down now," Dr. Long called up in a serious but caring tone. "Your mother had another seizure, but she's alright. She's trying to rest but is worried sick about you catching your death out here...first frost of the season I'd be willing to bet."

Tyrus could barely feel his arms and legs as he made his way down the tree. Dr. Long wrapped the wool blanket around him and escorted him back inside the house. There Tyrus felt as if he stepped into a fire, and it was like pinpricks of heat hitting his face and fingertips which were still exposed and gripping the blanket tight around the rest of his shivering body.

"Everything will be okay," Dr. Long assured him with a fatherly pat on the shoulder. "You best go on up to bed now."

Tyrus ascended the stairs as Dr. Long left. He could hear heated whispering coming from Edison's room, but it came to a sudden stop as he passed by the half open door and saw Sally and Edison sitting on the bed staring back at him begrudgingly. He stopped for a moment, perhaps to plead with them in his pitiful state, but then he remembered deep down he was still mad at Edison, so he quickly passed by and quietly entered the threshold to his mother's bedroom with his body still shivering and the blanket still shrouded tightly around him.

His mother sat upright in bed under the muted glow of the lamp by the window. The sheets were pulled up to her waist. Sue was on the bed with her, nestled at her side with her head on his mother's lap. His mother was stroking the dog's head and back, while the dog soothingly licked her hand that rested by the dog's head. His mother looked over at him with her soft brown eyes.

"Well, come on in," she said softly. "I won't break if you come closer."

Slowly Tyrus walked over to her bedside. He blurted out sheepishly, "I'm sorry about playing hooky and I'm sorry about missing supper and I'm sorry for making you worry when you're sick."

Evelyn Kydd smiled at her youngest child and with the hand that had been petting the dog, she reached out and caressed his flushed, cold cheek. "Oh, my darling Tyrus, what am I going to do with you?"

Tyrus sat down on the side of the bed and began to pet Sue. "She's such a good girl. Always there to help you."

"She is a good dog. You're a good son. Now why are you so mad at your brother?"

Tyrus sighed and continued to focus on the dog.

"Look at me, Ty."

He looked over into his mother's eyes. He wanted to cry but he held it in. He was too cold and too tired to cry now. "It's just that you had to sell our cows and our sheep and now the Abrams are offering us scrap meat and taking up collections for you at church, and you hate church, and I don't understand it all when Edison could make it stop."

"What are you saying, darling? You don't know what you're talking about."

"Edison could pay for everything if he wanted to. But he won't because he's not a real man and he's a liar."

"Oh, Tyrus. Where do you get such ideas? Your brother has been working very hard to help support this family since your father went away. He's still so young but he's already grown into a better man than your father ever will be. I don't mean to disrespect your father in front of you, but it's the truth, and you know I always strive to tell you children the truth no matter how much it might hurt. Edison is doing the best he can, but there are times when we just need to be thankful for those who would offer us help and accept it when it comes. I know you look up to your brother. You would be wise to want to be like him one day. I know you both can be better men than your father was."

"But, Mom, you don't understand."

"I don't understand what?"

Tyrus' heart was racing and he was starting to sweat underneath the blanket. He pulled away from the bed. He wanted to tell her his secret, but he didn't want to upset her any more than she had already been. "Never mind. I'm sorry."

"We'll talk in the morning. Just go to bed please."

Tyrus retreated defeated to his bedroom. He lay awake in the dark with his mind racing for some time until the door slowly creaked open and someone stepped inside. The lamp was turned on, and the glow blinded him for a moment until his eyes adjusted and he saw Edison standing there. His heart began to race. He sat up in bed as Edison took a seat on the side.

"Well, brother," Edison said, his voice suddenly sounding deeper than it had been, "here we are. Man to man. Let's get this out."

Tyrus gulped, collected his thoughts and nodded his head. He knew he wouldn't be able to sleep tonight if he didn't come clean about his secret.

"Okay," Tyrus began, taking a deep breath. "I know about the special gift...the necklace...you bought for Myra Long before she went away."

Edison nodded. "And..."

"I know where you got the money to pay for it."

"Oh you do?"

"The night Pop took us camping out by the lake...before he left for Virginia. You both thought I was asleep in the tent. And I was, but your voices outside the tent eventually woke me up. I heard what Pop said about the money. And I know he gave you some...as a taste, he called it. And I know you went and spent it on that necklace when you were supposed to help Mom with it. And I know the rest is hidden out there somewhere."

"Now wait. The money Pop gave me, yes I bought the necklace, but most if it went to payin' the bank money we owed 'em. Do you think I would let anything happen to Mom or to us? You think I would let the bank throw us off our land? And the rest of it, that's supposed to be our inheritance and I promised him, I swore to him, that I would not touch it until he died and that I would never let the bank or anybody else get their hands on it."

"But what if we need it?"

"We don't need it. I'm workin'. It's hard right now, but come winter when they need guys out there harvesting ice, I'll earn enough...enough to save so that we don't even have to think about touchin' our inheritance."

"Where's it hidden?"

"I don't want that burdenin' your soul. It's safe. No one can get at it except me and Pop."

"But you said yerself Pop might never be back."

"He might not come back to the farm...but he'll come back when he needs the money, and he promised he would always leave some behind for us no matter how hard times got for him. He swore we would be taken care of when he dies."

"And you trust him?"

"When he's talking about that money, yes I do. You don't know what that kind of money will do to a man...you're too young to understand."

"And he wasn't lying that night? He really showed you where it is? You've seen it all with your own eyes?"

"I know where it is."

"How much is it?"

"Enough."

"But what if you leave? What if you leave us and take all the money?"

"Hell, Tyrus, if a guy like Pop won't take it all when he leaves out of guilt over takin' care of his children, do you honestly think a guy like me would leave you and Mom and Sally behind and just take it all?"

"Hell, I know you wouldn't."

"Watch your mouth, Ty."

"You just said it."

"To show you I was serious. I won't never leave you and Mom and Sally. No matter what. That money is ours. In fact, if Pop ever did come back and tried to take it all, I'd fight 'im for it. I'd be willin' to kill 'im."

"Don't say that. Poor Pop."

"It's the truth. That's how much I love you. Pop, well, at least he loved us enough to only take what he needed at the time and leave the rest."

"Why did you buy Myra that necklace?"

"You would've done the same."

"You love her?"

"Yes."

"As much as you love Mom, me and Sally?"

"No, I could never love anybody that much. But I love her. The Abrams really said that Myra wasn't comin' back?"

"That's what they said."

"Awww, they don't know Myra. Myra will come back for me. In a few years I'll be old enough and we'll get married, you'll see."

"And what if she doesn't come back for you? You love her enough to go out there lookin' for her?"

"I suppose I might."

"Before you went and did that, would you tell me where the money is?"

Edison smiled. He reached over and tousled Ty's hair. "Clever man. Yes, yes I would."

"You promise."

"I promise. Now go to bed." Edison got up from the side of the bed and walked towards the door, turning out the light as he left.

Tyrus fell asleep, his resentment quelled, secure in his brother's word.

* * *

Evelyn, too, had a special affinity for that tree by the fence. Edison had gotten into his mind from a very young age that the tree was over five hundred years old, and even as he grew older and knew it to be untrue, he perpetuated the myth of the tree's age by telling Tyrus it was indeed five hundred years old. It wasn't nearly that old, but it was old enough. Family history held that it was only tree left standing on this swath of land by the first Temple to settle on the homestead in 1814.

And it was that tree that she dreamt of that night. Everything was bathed in a misty twilight. Evelyn was standing on the porch looking out at the tree. It suddenly lit up in an ethereal glow. The leaves aflame sounded as if they were screaming children, and the great branches cracked and splintered like brittle bones as the fire, bright blue and white, burned through them. The whole of the family farm, Abrams' land and all the hills beyond and the town below were illuminated by the burning tree.

A wind came over the hills with a lowly guttural boom, almost as if the mountains themselves were opening up and letting out the greatest of exhales. It blew down over the farms, and the burning tree was turned into a dark ash that whirled around in the gale and multiplied at an exponential rate until suddenly, this dust, like what she imagined must've been covering all of the Midwest, blew in all directions and blanketed the hills and her home and the town and the lake in a suffocating grainy soot which choked her until she woke up gasping for air.

Evelyn closed her eyes and could still see the images from her dream, the whole of the land turned to dust and now consumed by an otherworldly darkness. In the morning when she rose, everything was covered in frost.

EPISODE FOUR – FOUR WALKS

Evelyn didn't realize how much she would miss Myra until she was gone. She had been a great comfort to her over the years, like a little sister she had always desired to have. She thought of her often as the cold closed in over the hills, and she nestled in her favorite chair by the fire with Agatha Christie. They were mysteries they used to share and solve together.

However it was those summer nights at Horace Long's house that Evelyn recalled most fondly. Enjoying drinks on that sprawling back porch watching the sun set over the lake and disappear behind Sleeping Lion Mountain, the little ones asleep in their hammocks, Sue resting at their feet, Benny Goodman's "Moonglow" serenading them through the window from Horace's record player – the four of them sitting there, relaxing, dreaming – Horace, Edison, Myra and Evelyn – a family.

Yet there were flickers even in those moments of peace where Evelyn wanted to escape that makeshift family, and like electric currents connecting her to previous memories of wanting to wander, she would be sparked to move. Sometimes she would get up from her chair on the porch while the others were half asleep, and she would walk through the Long house to the front porch. She would look out past the front lawn onto the street, dark and quiet, the neighborhood asleep and dreaming, and she would think back to those days when she was seventeen and she stood on her parents' front porch in Albany and looked out onto a similar street.

It was summer then, too, the summer of 1919. She could still smell the street she grew up on in Albany, and it was not unlike the street outside the Long house in Fenimore...fecund earth underneath lush green grass, maple trees oozing sap, fresh paint on refurbished houses. There was life, not human, stirring in the night; a raccoon rustling in a metal garbage can; crickets chirping; night birds propped on tree branches, their little dancing legs like sticks against sticks, limbs tapping across limbs. Evelyn could hear her own heartbeat in this quiet cacophony, and it was her heart that skipped a beat when she first saw Joshua Bloomfield on one of his walks.

"Joshua!" she called out in a yelling whisper from the porch.

He turned and looked at the house, startled to see another person stirring in the darkness, but then he pivoted and kept walking.

Evelyn rushed down to the sidewalk and joined him in his stroll which had quickened, but soon slowed again, resigned to the fact he was no longer alone.

"I thought I was the only one," she said excitedly.

"I do this every night...almost..." he said softly. Joshua appeared nervous that someone had invaded a private space. It put Evelyn off for a moment, but she remained at his side keeping pace and determined to insinuate herself into his ritual.

"I love the way the leaves move over our heads...you know, the breeze blowing through them. I love how there's still a bite to the night, you know...a chill even on the hottest summer days. And all this life...the insects, the birds...this noisy quiet...it's so romantic, don't you think?"

Joshua turned and looked down at her, forced himself to smile, well, a half-smile at least. "We don't have to talk," he said as he took her hand. "We can just be...walking..."

Evelyn grabbed a hold of his arm, his pitching arm, and leaned in close to him as they continued their walk. She had wanted to do that all summer...touch his arm. She loved to watch him play ball. There was a barnstorming league of former major league players that came passing through town that summer, and they put up their best local boys to play against them. Sometimes, if a local kid was good enough, he might get an invite to join the league and travel with them all over the state, all over New England sometimes, even up into Canada. Joshua was that good. He mowed down those professional ball players. Evelyn's father, who was the editor of the local newspaper and took a special interest in covering baseball, had claimed he never saw anybody pitch like that. Evelyn was at all the games cheering with her father when Joshua took the mound and shut down the team of pros.

"You know, you might think because I'm just a girl I don't know what I'm talking about," she continued softly despite his request for no talking, "But you're really something special out there. My father thinks you could go pro. But I don't remember ever seeing you before...in school or in town or nothing...and you don't act like you're from around here."

"I'm from all over I guess," Joshua conceded.

"What does that mean?"

"I'm just passin' through."

"Wouldn't you like to be from around here? I see how you're looking at all the houses, into all those windows, wondering what it looks like inside. You're like me aren't you?"

"I don't understand."

"You look at each one and wonder if that's the one you want to live in one day. That's what I do."

"I don't want to live in any of these houses."

"Then what do you think about when you're out walking every night?" Evelyn felt a tension coil in his arm, his whole body tightened and uncomfortable, but she didn't want to let go. He didn't say anything, as if he was afraid or embarrassed to answer the question. Maybe he thought about girls. Maybe he thought about her. She wanted to calm him. She went on encouragingly, "Did they offer you to join the barnstorming league? Are you thinking about all the places you'll get to go?"

"They want me to go further upstate with them. All the way to Canada maybe if I keep playing this way."

"Does your arm hurt?"

"Naw."

"Good. I want to go with you. My father might send someone from the paper to travel with the league, and you know, they're going to need someone to cook and clean for them on the road. Take care of things."

"The road is no place for girls."

Evelyn was slightly insulted by the insinuation and disappointed that he wasn't keen on the idea of her traveling with them. "What do you know about it?" She let go of his arm and folded her arms across her chest as they continued to walk.

"I told you, I'm from all over."

"Well let's get married then and I'll go with you as your wife."

Joshua came to a sudden halt and put his hands out in front of her to stop her in her tracks. "Now wait just a minute, don't be ridiculous. We don't even know each other."

"Well, don't you like me? Don't you think I'm pretty?" Evelyn pouted.

"Hold on now. A lady doesn't ask a man to marry him. A man asks a lady."

"Well, now aren't we all prim and proper, *Mr. I'm-Just-Passin'-Through*?" Evelyn looked around the dark street as if a crowd of people was gathering. "I don't see any man or any lady standing here, so what's the big deal?"

"Yeah, maybe you're right. We're just two crazy kids who don't hardly know each other."

"Well, okay then. Maybe you could start by taking me out dancing Saturday night."

"Maybe I could start by slappin' ya." He raised the hand of his powerful pitching arm, mockingly, with a smile. Then he lowered it and placed it on her arm. He pulled her in tight, and placed his other hand on her other arm. They kissed, and it was like a burst of electricity that lit up the whole night.

Joshua let her into his private space, and Evelyn opened up to him all her secrets that summer. It was short-lived. Myra Long would become her secret keeper years later. As she stood outside alone on the front porch of the Long house, she wondered, if she and Joshua had passed by it on one of their midnight walks some fifteen years ago, would she have wanted to live here? Could it be a home? Her home now was in the hills outside town, and she worried that her mind drifted far too much while she watched the flames dance and cackle in the hearth. Winter was coming and it was far too cold for walks. Did her children do like she and Joshua did? Did Myra? Did they sneak out at night and go wandering into town, just taking it all in, the solitude...the dreams of a future, a home somewhere out in the darkness? Did Edison go on walks? Did Edison have a private space?

Mable "Ma" Abrams was very generous in Myra's absence, but her companionship was more akin to a mother's. And Evelyn didn't know how much more of Ma's home-cooking she could stand – always the biscuits and the gravy and a great multitude of sweets - avalanches of muffins, cakes and pies. She felt guilty when the thought crossed her mind, but she never wanted to end up looking like Ma – the size of that woman! The children loved it all, of course, but there were times when Evelyn questioned how often they were over there. The Abrams were so...*uncultured*. Simple folk.

Not like Evelyn. Yet so kind, too. But harsh. Judging. Evelyn could tell by the way Ma looked at her. And Duncan Abrams was an abominable beast of a man. Yet Evelyn couldn't deny that she sometimes thought it was good for Tyrus to go over there – maybe it would toughen him up. She worried about her youngest the most, and she would always be indebted to Duncan for showing the boys how to shoot and hunt. The only thing Samuel was ever good at showing them was how to pitch a tent on the lakeshore while drunk. She hoped none of the children would inherit their father's spirit for spirits.

The more Evelyn dwelled on it, the sadder she grew, and she wasn't sure whose heart broke more when Myra left – hers or Edison's. It was bittersweet to see him develop such a crush on Myra. He was so in love, from so early on, sometimes Evelyn wondered if it was at first sight. He must've been six when he first saw Myra...and Myra was fifteen -- just becoming a woman then. He had his eyes on her from the start. Evelyn loved watching Myra blossom into such a confident and free-spirited young woman. Myra's love for the children was always apparent, and those times when Evelyn was embattled by her epilepsy, Myra was always there to care for them. Evelyn could never thank her enough – and it would've been a sign of a cruel heart had she become jealous when Myra began to hold Edison's hand that summer – not like she held it when he was small – to guide him and protect him – but now it was to lead him – though there was no need to seduce him as he was already smitten and would've sold the world for her hand. Evelyn was never sure if Myra loved him the same way he loved Myra. She knew Myra loved him, but was there malice when Myra became complicit in his fantasy? If there was, Evelyn couldn't fault her. Yet she preferred to believe it was innocent – unlike her own actions.

Evelyn would be lying if she told Myra she thought it was natural – like it was some force that drew Horace to her. He was her doctor. He was a family friend. He was kind and lonely. Evelyn was tired and sick. They were both widows in a way. But what developed was awkward, inappropriate and needy. They weren't in love, but they cared for each other a great deal in their own twisted way. Evelyn never thought of herself as Dr. Horace Long's mistress. She always insisted he write up bills for the medical care he provided just like he would charge any other patient. He wanted to take care of her that way. He thought she was stubborn, proud. He wasn't wrong. But Evelyn would never allow him to treat her for free just because they spent a few tender moments together. She would never be *that woman*.

She could still see herself in the mirror, in his bedroom, sitting on what used to be his wife's chair, combing her hair. He stood by the bed getting dressed. Seeing him in the mirror behind her like that, struggling a little with the buttons on his shirt, slowly putting on his pants one leg at a time, hunched over, it was the first time she realized how much older he really was. He wasn't an unhandsome man, his hair white but still full, his face ruggedly aging. There was still something strangely dashing about him in his ill-fittings suits with his spectacles carrying his doctor's bag. There was a certain allure around a man of such skill who made house calls, but here it was she who made a house call to him. It had been his first night alone in the house after Myra took off for Atlanta, and he had convinced Evelyn to come visit him after the children were sound asleep. Another walk out in the moonlight. It would be the first and only proper night they spent together, their other moments of tenderness quick and fleeting and stolen in the daylight around corners, in hallways, hidden from sight, clumsy like teenagers still learning the ropes, embarrassed.

She remembered walking up to the Long house that night and feeling like she was coming home, but in the morning, in front of the mirror, watching him gct dressed, she realized this could no longer be. And after he had put on his shoes, Horace had the nerve to try and hand her money, knowing that she needed it now more than ever.

"This really needs to stop," she said to him matter-of-factly while looking at his sad reflection. "We have to go back to being doctor and patient. I can't leave my house and my children in the middle of the night like that anymore. I'm still a married woman."

"But we were always friends, Evelyn," he said. "Can't we just go back to that? And can't I be a friend offering you a helping hand? Like in the beginning when you first stepped off that train in Milton?"

"No."

And she thought she wouldn't be in this predicament, needing money, had she and Samuel not been so foolish all those years ago. It was yet another harmless stroll down Main Street in the fall of 1928. Evelyn could remember walking down the brick sidewalk, leaves crackling beneath their feet, their arms linked, maybe a part of her wishing Samuel was more successful with the farm, but in knowing that he probably would never be, forming the seed of her plan B. She wanted to open a diner on Main Street. She wanted to make her own money and have her own business, so that when he left town seasonally to find "other work" it ultimately wouldn't matter if he ever returned or not. She imagined they could serve eggs and milk fresh from her own farm, the one she had inherited from her uncle and was being spoiled by her lazy husband. When the kids were old enough, they could help out with the family business but in the meantime, Evelyn would do the cooking and manage the place, and maybe Myra could help waiting tables. She was such a pretty young thing, all the locals would eat her up. In that moment, she pretended to be in love with Samuel and to want his approval for her idea, which she had convinced him had been his idea all along. They walked up and down the street looking at all the other stores and businesses, at the few abandoned storefronts, and tried to imagine, "What would be the perfect spot for our diner?"

And there was a spot on the corner, a former lunch counter recently closed after the owner's passing. "I think that's our spot," Samuel said proudly.

"Do you really think we can do it?" Evelyn said. "Do you have any money saved from the work you did last summer?"

"You know I don't. I don't have anything. Not right now. I mean I can get something later but then this place might be gone. Someone else is gonna snatch it up realizing what a great location it is. Heck, you remember how busy that lunch counter was. Just imagine what we could do serving breakfast, lunch and dinner. So we can wait and take our chances, or we can just go down to the bank and ask for a loan. We got the farmland and the house as collateral."

Evelyn lit up. He had bought into it whole-hog. It seemed like such a great idea. So they took out a loan against the farm. And the diner was a success for a while, until next spring when Samuel disappeared for a month only to return with a mountain of gambling debt he raided the diner's coffers to pay off. Then Evelyn's epilepsy returned with a vengeance after having gone years without a major spell. Little Tyrus came down with a fever. Evelyn was unable to work. Medical bills piled up. Samuel skipped town again. Myra was eighteen and had just graduated from high school. She did her best to keep the place running, but it was unfair to expect so much from her. There was no one to manage the diner, and it had to be closed for a season. Evelyn fell behind in her loan payments. There was no income coming in. Her epilepsy worsened. The diner was dead. And now the bank owned the land and the house that had been in her family's name for generations. Samuel would come and go, immune to it all, it seemed.

Then there she was, years later, in no better spot, refusing money from a kinder, older man than her husband, who had in many ways as her family's doctor been taking care of her for years. In her mind, there was never really anything there between them, anything real or tangible, just fantasies probably conjured up on those balmy summer nights on the back porch listening to records like "The Very Thought of You". So she told him definitively that morning, "It's over, Horace. I'm sorry."

Myra had known about Evelyn and Horace's affair before she left. Evelyn had told her, even though she knew she had probably already suspected, and even though Horace had asked they keep it a secret from his daughter. But how could Evelyn lie to Myra? Myra knew everything. She kept all of Evelyn's waking secrets. She kept all of Evelyn's children's secrets. They hid so much from their mother now – Sally and Tyrus. Myra was no longer there to be the conduit through which they communicated. Maybe even Edison, too, was holding secrets, though it pained Evelyn to think he would hide anything from her. He was always such a perfect boy in his mother's eyes – so generous and strong and endless with his love and his affection. Evelyn knew she wasn't supposed to have favorites, but her oldest would always be special. He didn't have any of that bastard in him, and she always felt he was hers, just hers, all from her, all for her. She could see slivers of Samuel's sloth and avarice in Sally and Tyrus. She felt a need to tweeze it out of them, like splinters. She couldn't see any of that in Edison.

Could Evelyn blame Myra if she fell in love with him – her perfect boy? She didn't want to imagine that Myra's motives weren't clean. Yet the timing, so soon after Myra learned of her father and Evelyn, it seemed opportunistic. But maybe Edison was the one who made the first move. Would it be so odd for a teenage boy who assumed so much of a man's responsibilities over the years to act so boldly towards a woman he had grown up to love? Did Myra think Evelyn wouldn't approve? Maybe if Myra did return and granted Edison his wish, it wouldn't be so strange. It would be alright by Evelyn. She would never hold a grudge against Myra. And who better to take care of her special boy than the woman she had watched with such pleasure grow and mature, a woman she loved like a sister? But maybe this was a fantasy she shared with Edison. Myra was always meant to leave them both – it was written on her body. A different story. Myra's perhaps was the wandering heart. Maybe like Joshua, on her walks, Myra didn't imagine which house might be hers one day, but instead dreamt of houses and towns and people far far away from here, where nothing and everything might be hers.

Evelyn never tried to fool anyone. She was more than transparent about her and Samuel not being cut out for this life in the hills. They were romantics perhaps, but they were no farmers. They weren't ever much of a family either. Circumstances threw them together, and she tried to make the most of it. She thought he used their incompatibility with the land as an excuse to constantly leave it – and her. Like Myra, Evelyn didn't know if he would ever return. On the coldest of nights, when she longed for a warm body other than the dog's lying beside her in bed, she wondered if he was even alive. That bastard promised the children he would return, but she hoped they were all wise enough now to never trust a promise from him. Evelyn wondered, did Myra promise them anything before she left? Did she promise Edison anything? Did she promise she would share her bed with him when she came back? Or was she smart enough and kind enough to know you should never make a promise you have no intention of keeping?

It was now December, snow eternally on the ground and forever peacefully rolling whitely into the depths of the hills, shops on Main Street strung up with wreaths and lights, heralding a moratorium on the Depression through windows loaded with dolls and train sets and army men, not unlike a child's make-believe version of a darker premonition electrifying in Evelyn's mind. It was strange to think the Depression had been going on for as long as many of these little children had been alive. It was all Tyrus had ever known. It was all Sally could remember.

Evelyn strolled down the cleared brick sidewalks, linked to Edison's arm, careful in her steps, confident in his lead. She took great comfort in the strength of his arm, which had grown into a man's arm, a hard-working arm, an arm that protected the family like Samuel had never been able to do.

"Are you going to play ball in the Spring?" she asked her son.

"Hmmm...I dunno," Edison spoke pensively. "There's not really any money in it. I'll have to see what kind of work I can find."

"I wish you would. I don't want you giving up on your dreams. You could be like Lou Gehrig when you grow up. I think he's going to have his best season yet next year, don't you?"

"Awww, Mom, don't be silly. But we'll see. If I have the time."

She stopped them in front of the toy store and gazed in at all the dolls dressed up in fancy dresses, red and blonde hair curled like Shirley Temple, glass eyes of blue staring back at her. "Sally's too old for dolls now. I'd like to get her some books maybe. But I fear I can only get them each one gift this year."

"And what about Ty's birthday next week?"

"Ma Abrams will be baking a cake. We'll invite them over. Maybe Dr. Long, too. A little party. I'll cook his favorite meal. What is his favorite meal?"

"I wanted to get him something special this year."

"Oh, Edison, I don't want you spending all your hard earned money on silly gifts. I want you to save."

"I wanted to get him a real genuine mitt. That hand-me-down never really fit him and is about torn to shreds. I have enough, don't worry."

"He loves playing catch with you. He loves watching you play ball, too."

"I know. You wanna walk down to the lake, to see how much is frozen over already? Next month it should be thick enough to harvest ice. Just think of all the money I can make."

Evelyn, at 5 foot 4, leaned her head on her son's shoulder and pulled into him tight, using his height, which now had a good few inches on her, to shield herself from the cold air. In so many ways he was a man now, yet he probably still had another growth spurt or two left before he was done, and his face was still so boyish, smooth and with nary a stubble. He held her close and kissed her on the head. It was a confident and manly embrace, and she wondered if he had experience embracing Myra like that. Did he know the tenderness of lying with a woman? Did he use those strong arms to wrap around Myra after making love? Something deep inside told her he was still innocent to that carnal knowledge, but probably wouldn't be for long. But he did know what a broken heart was, and she could feel the fire of that aching inside him as he shielded her from the cold. They took solace in that brief moment window gazing and then continued their walk.

Edison was good. Evelyn had to believe that Myra was good, too. Myra had to be good enough for the both of them, for Evelyn believed she herself had forsaken being good the moment she jumped off her parents' porch to take that walk with Joshua Bloomfield. Myra had to be good enough to deserve Edison's broken heart. Evelyn refused to judge her.

That night she stayed awake well past midnight in her favorite chair by the hearth until the fire all but burned out and she could barely make out the words on the pages of the latest Agatha Christie novel. Sue had stayed with her too. Together they quietly marched up the stairs, Sue's nails click-clacking gently against the wooden floorboards. As she did almost every night, she and the dog peaked into each of the children's bedrooms to catch a glimpse of them sleeping. It occurred to her many years after that first night walking with Joshua Bloomfield and stealing inside of his private space, that maybe men like him went walking at night and peering into other people's homes in the dark because they were plotting to snatch people from their beds. It frightened her to think she once opened up herself to a man like that. In their bedrooms, her children were in their private spaces, safely asleep and dreaming, and she felt compelled to check on them, even as they grew older, just one last time, to make sure no one had invaded that protective space.

Tyrus' room was the last one to check, and the creak of the door must've startled him awake. He had always been a light sleeper. "Mom, is that you?" he asked wearily, raising his head into the sliver of light coming from the hallway.

"It's okay, Ty," his mother told him. "Go back to sleep."

"Is Sue with you? Can she sleep in here tonight?" It sounded like he had been sniffling a bit.

"Did you have a bad dream?"

"No, I'm okay."

Evelyn looked down at the dog which had been focused on the boy and was now looking up at her, asking permission to leave her side.

"Go on, girl" Evelyn told the dog, and Sue scampered into the room and jumped onto the end of Tyrus' bed.

Evelyn closed the door and retired to her bedroom. Lying awake in bed, she didn't know who to tell her secrets to anymore. She sometimes felt them welling up inside, like water, and a great deluge would come spilling out of her mouth and flood the house and the farm and the hills. And if she couldn't control the secrets she held in her waking hours, then what of the lakes of secrets she held when she was asleep...or when she was overcome by a spell...and she would have a vision of something horrific or spectacular? Those secrets could drown the entire world, and in the dead of winter they would be like glaciers gorging great deep wounds into the earth and leveling the hills she so hated and loved.

EPISODE FIVE – SOARING

February, 1936

G od damn it!
God damn him!
Son of a bitch!

Shit.

Damn it. Damn it. Damn him.

Sally wanted to hold a grudge against Edison. But she couldn't. Deep down she always knew he would leave them. She had a premonition. Like mother like daughter, they would say if they knew.

Sometimes Sally would sneak into her mother's bedroom and watch her sleep. She looked like a little girl, all curled up in bed under the covers. Sally wondered what she was dreaming about, and if she laid there with her, their foreheads touching, their measured breaths mingling in the warm space between their faces, could they share a dream?

God damn that little bastard. Tyrus was such a spoiled, clueless, little brat sometimes. She just wanted to slap him. The way Edison lavished him with gifts on his birthday and Christmas. The way he lavished gifts on all of them. Tyrus with his glove and his bike. She wanted to pop the tires on that bike the way he rode it around and around in circles in the driveway. Mother with her pearls. And Sally...the dress...and all those books. *Jane Eyre.* Sometimes she wished she was an orphan like Jane Eyre, though she never read past the first few chapters. She could never talk to her mother about those books. Her mother was too busy with those silly little Agatha Christie mysteries. In truth, she hated books. She preferred the movies.

But for all her cursing and her teasing and her torment, she loved them all...she guessed. Tyrus was too little to know it yet...but he had a heart so big it could crush them. And he lived inside it. And she worried sometimes, worried about things she knew weren't age appropriate, things perhaps she had uncovered in sharing a dream with her mother, in sharing her mother's anxieties. She worried that her little brother's heart was so big, there was a danger of darkness taking refuge inside it, and then his heart would turn black and devour everything.

And her mother...she just wanted to see her happy...to see her sleep like a little girl, to not worry...to feel secure, to feel proud and confident in her children's abilities to live out in that great big wide open world – the world beyond the hills...the unpredictable untamed world where dust storms blew and the tides changed and cataclysms tested the fortitude of those living in the midst of it all – tossing and turning and tearing.

And Edison. *God damn him Edison.* She loved him for his simple-minded determination...to love Myra...to support the family...to be strong...to be a man. He was focused in a way she never thought she would be. And there was no one who could've convinced him to not go out there on that ice.

Sally had a vision. Of a truck. Out in the middle of the wide expanse of the frozen lake. Her view was from the shoreline. The quiet was deafening. She couldn't even feel her own heartbeat, or hear her own breath. There was nothing but white icy expanse and Sleeping Lion Mountain looming in the background, enshrouded in a frozen mist, trees encased by snow and ice. And the truck...so far out there...almost undetectable. Everything was dead. Silent. And she knew in some way that this meant Edison was gone.

She didn't remember her vision until she was standing there on the shoreline, bundled up in her coat and scarf and gloves and boots, grocery bag in her hands. Her mother was at her side. They had come from around the corner when two men rushed by them outside of the grocery store and they, along with a small crowd, followed the men in a flutter down the slippery sloping street to the lake. There was heated murmuring and commotion.

"There was an accident out on the lake."

"Someone call a doctor!"

"Who was it?"

"What happened?"

"Someone slipped on the ice."

God damn it!

God damn him!

Son of a bitch!

Sally's anger, along with her heart, wanted to burst out of her chest when she saw that truck out there on the ice. It was clearer now than in her vision. And the silence was replaced with men shouting, boots sloshing in the snow, and women onlookers gasping for air, their speech frozen on their tongues, their eyes naked to the horror. She watched as the men ran out onto the ice and out to the truck where other men stood around giant blocks of ice that had been harvested and were preventing people on the shoreline from seeing what had transpired. The men were all looking down.

Her mother dropped her grocery bag into the snow and grabbed a hold of Sally's arm. "Tell me it's not him," she said in a defeated whisper.

"Damn him to hell," Sally said.

Her mother let go of her arm, took off her glove, and slapped her across the face.

Sally didn't flinch. She became frozen there in place, in time.

Edison had slipped out on the lake and fell backwards, his head hitting the edge of a block of ice. His skull cracked open.

Sally wanted to stay out there on the ice with him forever, her mother's stinging slap in pale comparison to Edison's head trauma...but a pain shared none the less. Her eyes moved to the trees along the shoreline. She longed for the warmer days of summer and playing in the woods with her brothers. She wanted to guide Edison's spirit there. Though he was still alive at that moment, and for prolonged days after, she knew he was already gone. And she wanted him to go deep into the woods. And wait. Wait for summer. Wait for them there.

* * *

Tyrus didn't understand it when Edison used to say, "She broke my heart." He couldn't imagine what it felt like. Was it like a hand wrapped around it, squeezing it until it popped? Was it like a weight slowly crushing it?

That night he learned what it meant. He was sitting by the fire with Sue resting beside him listening to his favorite new radio show, *The Green Hornet*.

"That's child stuff," Edison told him after he pleaded with his older brother to listen to it with him. They used to always listen to radio programs together, usually Edison the one excited about sharing in something fun with his little brother, initiating him into his world...where *The Shadow* ruled and knew what evils lurked in the hearts of men. That had been their favorite last year.

But things had changed between them ever since Pop left and Tyrus had confronted Edison about the conversation by the lake...and the money.

"Did you buy my bike with some of the money?" Tyrus asked him.

"I never knew you were capable of being so ungrateful," Edison said to him. He sounded like an old man, like suddenly this chasm had opened between them and aged them beyond years, beyond recognition.

"Why can't you just show me where it is?"

"I told you not to worry about it. Don't you trust me?"

"I do." But he lied. He didn't trust him anymore than he trusted Pop. And it made him sick. And sad.

And when Ma Abrams came knocking on the door that night, interrupting him from his new favorite radio show, she told him matter-of-factly, no sugar-coating, "We just received a call from Dr. Long. There's been an accident on the lake. Edison has been severely hurt. He's at the hospital. We're to stay here and wait for your mother and sister."

Ma Abrams cooked him some supper...soup and bread. But neither could eat.

"Is Edison going to be okay?" he asked her while the dog paced back and forth by the front door.

"I don't know, sweetheart. He's in God's hands now."

But Tyrus knew not what language she was speaking. She sat him down by the fire and they prayed. She was calm but her words sounded hysterical. Tyrus felt nothing. He must've fallen asleep by the radio, and Ma Abrams carried him up to bed. He remembered that warm feeling of being pressed against her bosom and rocked like a baby.

Tyrus woke up in the middle of the night shivering and alone. He tip-toed out into the hallway and peered down the stair case which was flooded by the soft glow of a low fire and the slow monotonous creak of Ma Abrams in the rocking chair. He walked past Edison's room and found it empty. He went into his mother's room and found her asleep with Sally. Sue rested at the foot of the bed. He climbed up under the covers on the other side of his mother and wrapped his arms around her. He felt warm and flushed now.

He felt a pain in his chest, like a hot poker, like his heart was pumping lava through his veins. He started to cry. He muffled his whimpers in his mother's hair. He didn't know what had happened, but he had a sense that he would never get the chance to talk to Edison again. Knowing his last moments with his brother were spent arguing about that money, he suddenly felt his heart break. Lava no longer flowed. His body, once tightly coiled, went limp, and he felt a tiny death slip over him as he fell into sleep in his mother's bed, uncomforted and lost in dreams.

* * *

I can hear you! I can hear you!

He wanted to scream.

Edison felt nothing. But he could hear them.

His sister's voice called him into the woods. He searched there for Myra, but he was blind. He didn't hear her. Only Sally.

They brought him home and laid him in his bed.

Sue talked to him and promised him everything would be okay. Sue would take care of THEM. She licked his face but he couldn't feel it. He could only hear the sound of her coarse tongue running across his dead skin.

He was hollow inside.

He was in two places yet none at all.

In the woods. The woods.

His mother crying.

"You can't leave me...alone...with THEM."

"But you have Sue. Don't worry." He wanted to tell her. She couldn't hear. Why couldn't she hear him?

And then Tyrus pleading with him. "You promised. You promised you would tell me before you left."

And he felt a darkness, like shadows moving across the hills, and he wanted to take Tyrus' hand and lead him away from it all. But he could only listen to the sobbing, to the begging.

He felt nothing.

Nothing.

Then soaring. High above the farm and the hills and the frozen lake and the woods. All those voices calling for him down below. But he was gone.

EPISODE SIX – THE UNKNOWING

"**C**ome here, child, let me take a look at you," Ma Abrams said.

Their mother was too distraught to help them get ready. She was downstairs in the kitchen with Dr. Long. "Oh, Horace!" she had wept upon his entrance. They were her first words in two days.

Tyrus didn't feel comfortable leaving her in the kitchen with the doctor. He had never heard her say the doctor's name like that before. Something about it made him feel uneasy. He instructed Sue to stay there in the kitchen, and she did so obediently, lying on the cool floor on her belly with her head on her paws. But Ma Abrams herded him and Sally upstairs. He didn't like Ma Abrams up there. He felt she was invading their private space...their bedrooms. She wasn't his mother. He didn't want her helping him get dressed. Why didn't she go help Sally pick out a dress? Why did Sally get to keep her bedroom to herself?

Tyrus didn't like undressing in front of anyone, especially some old lady whom normally he liked but was grating on his last nerves these past two days. He made her sit in the chair in the hallway, but the door was kept open half way and he could feel her peering in as he put on the suit. It didn't fit. The pants were too big. The shirt sleeves too long. The tie felt like a noose. The shoes would not work. He loosened the tie and popped open the collar of his shirt as he moped out into the hallway barefoot for inspection.

"Oh, Tyrus! Your poor mother is downstairs waiting for us and you're up here looking like you just got into a schoolyard fight." Ma Abrams shook her head disapprovingly. "And where are your socks and shoes?"

"Nothing fits," Tyrus said. "Can't I just go in my own clothes? I don't feel right wearing my brother's old clothes."

"Don't you have a suit of your own? You're mother doesn't have any Sunday clothes for you boys?"

"No."

"Of course she doesn't. We should've tried these on yesterday. I could've hemmed them."

"The shoes still wouldn't fit. I'd still have to go barefoot."

"You'll get frostbite if you go out there barefoot. Then Dr. Long will have to cut off your toes. Do you want to do that to your poor mother after all she's been through?"

"No, ma'am, of course not."

Sally came out of her room in a dress and coat and shiny black shoes. She stopped behind Ma Abrams for a moment, looked Tyrus over, and shook her head in disgust. "I'm going downstairs," she said quietly.

"Tell your mother we'll be right down," Ma Abrams told her.

"I asked Mom if we could bring Sue," Tyrus said, "But she didn't answer me."

"Stop it right now, child. We are not taking a dog to a funeral," Ma Abrams said.

"But Sue is part of the family! She was Edison's dog, too. And what if Mom has one of her spells?"

Ma Abrams began rubbing the area above her brow with her index finger and thumb while closing her eyes. "Please, Tyrus, just go back into your bedroom, put on the nicest clothes you have and meet me downstairs. I'm not going to play games with you anymore. The car is here and your mother is waiting."

"Please, Sue's gotta go."

"I'll ask your mother. Now go get dressed." Ma Abrams struggled to her feet and shuffled down the hallway to the stairs. "Life is too short," she muttered between labored breaths down the steps.

A few minutes later, Tyrus came galloping downstairs. He wore what he thought was the nicest thing he had: his baseball uniform. He put on his school shoes, though, and wore the nice overcoat handed down from Edison. The rest of the house was empty. He looked out the front window and saw the Abrams, Sally and Dr. Long out in the driveway by Dr. Long's car and Duncan Abrams' truck. Tyrus walked into the kitchen and found his mother standing over the dog. She looked to be in some kind of trance looking down at Sue. Tyrus tiptoed over, leaned against his mother's side and looked down at the dog.

His mother placed her hand atop his head, at first as if it were a dead hand, like she didn't know what to do with it. Tyrus wrapped his arm around his mother's hip and pressed himself closer against her. Her hand came to life, and she tousled his hair almost too playfully. Tyrus smiled.

"Sue is coming. But she has to stay in the back of Duncan Abrams' truck," she said mischievously.

"Ma Abrams will be so mad," Tyrus said triumphantly. He stepped aside and looked up at his mother.

Evelyn looked down at him and smiled. She took her hand to his chin and lifted his face to her affectionately. "I don't care what Ma Abrams thinks."

"I don't want her staying in our house anymore. And I don't want Dr. Long here anymore either."

"I know. Neither do I." She suddenly looked at him, curious about his attire. "You look like a mess, my son. But I think Edison would've appreciated it. He would've laughed at you."

"Thank you."

"How about you put on that nice ivy cap he bought you for Christmas...and your scarf? Out there on the hill in the cold, no one will be the wiser. It will be our little joke."

"Okay."

Out on Haydons Hill a narrow path in the snow had been cleared for the small group of mourners to make their way up to the Temple family crypt from the road. Sue waited in the back of the truck upon Evelyn and Tyrus' stern instructions. She watched the mourners intently as they carefully made their way about half way up to where the crypt had been carved into the hill. Among the mourners were the Robinsons, a group of ladies from the church which had collected money to help pay Evelyn's medical bills, and an Episcopal minister since Edison had been baptized as an infant despite as Ma Abrams' put it, "Their mother's ungodliness."

Tyrus stood towards the back, aligned with the threshold to the crypt while Sally stood up front with their mother. He wanted to keep an eye on Sue. He could see through the trees across the road the great frozen lake, and his heart dropped into his stomach realizing Edison's blood was out there somewhere. He wanted to cry, but it was too cold, and his eyes were painfully dry. He was filled with a great longing still...a desire to talk to his brother one last time...to say he was sorry...to ask him where the money was. He couldn't take his eyes off the lake.

He heard in the distance, as if he was at the opening of a cave and somewhere deep inside were the others, the minister say things in that same foreign language of Ma Abrams, like, "Our life here on earth is so brief. We're here one minute and gone the next. No one can know the will of God, but let us not question His taking of Edison at so young an age. Let us instead count our blessings and thank Him for what precious little time we had here with Edison."

He heard his mother crying, and Dr. Long telling her, "It's not your fault."

But Tyrus couldn't turn away from the lake and from the thought that his brother really was dead and gone. Finally, he couldn't bare it anymore, and he found his eyes looking up and down the walls of the crypt at the large masonry blocks stacked upon each other. Some of them looked loose. One near the bottom by the threshold almost appeared ajar. His heart began to hammer against his ribs.

Suddenly he felt Sue against his leg. He heard some alarmed murmuring from the church ladies. Tyrus barely had time to digest what was happening as a man's hand was on his shoulder and coaxing him down the hill. Duncan Abrams swooped in silently and guided boy and dog outside of the crypt.

"Wait!" he piped up as he stopped in his tracks. He turned around and looked up at Duncan Abrams who was sternly but calmly looking down at him. "Do they put things in the walls? I mean, can they hide things behind the blocks?"

"Boy, what are you going on about?" Duncan said. "The only thing they put in those walls are bodies. That's where they put the coffins. You've been to a cemetery before, boy, to this crypt even. What's wrong with you?"

"Oh," Tyrus said sharply. He realized Duncan didn't get what he was getting at, and perhaps that might be for the best. He would have to come back here...after the thaw...and see if those blocks could be removed...and if there were secret compartments back there...and if so...maybe...maybe...maybe not. "I'm sorry," he went on, trying not to get lost in his suspicions and fantasy. "I know that. I was just..."

"It's okay, boy." Duncan placed both hands on Tyrus' shoulders. It felt heavy but comforting as he prodded him down to the truck with the dog at their heels. Tyrus guided Sue into the back and then walked around to the passenger's side. Duncan helped him in and then closed the door behind him.

Tyrus' eyes returned to the lake. He wondered...had his brother just tried to tell him something? It was so quiet, and an overcast gloom hung over the frozen water and the hills. He listened. He heard nothing. Then Duncan's hearty breathing as he climbed into the driver's side of the truck.

"We'll go back to the house," Duncan said. "We'll lay out the food Ma made. Wait for the ladies to come back in the car."

Tyrus was uncontrollably in a panic and breathing heavily. He felt overwhelmed by his thoughts. He turned to Duncan while the old man started the engine.

"People keep saying everything is going to be okay," the boy said to the old man breathlessly. He wanted to cry again, but he didn't. He couldn't anymore. He could only panic. And wonder. "But I don't know. I don't know if everything is going to be okay."

Duncan pondered this outburst for a moment, stroking his ungainly white beard before placing his hand on the stick. "I don't blame you, son. I don't know either. Sometimes I think things will never be okay again."

"I don't wanna tell my mom. I need to tell her things will be okay."

"Yup, that's the manly thing to do." He put the truck in gear and jerkily pulled out onto the road. "This will be our secret. This unknowing."

Back at the house, long after everyone had left, including Ma Abrams, but only after the most adamant coaxing telling her, "You've done enough. Thank you so much. Please go home and get some rest," and Dr. Long had been driven out by Evelyn's cold looks, Tyrus found himself unable to sleep wondering about the crypt and what might lay hidden in its walls. Flushed with exhaustion by his racing mind, he wandered downstairs to find his mother and Sue by the fire, both woman and dog meditating on the flames while the boy's shadow danced across the walls before he settled in the chair opposite his mother.

"Does Edison speak to you?" he asked after a few moments, breaking the silence and bringing his mother's gaze to him.

"No," she said. "Does he talk to you?"

"No, I just thought maybe he was trying to tell me something today on the hill."

"Tell you what?"

"I don't know." He wanted to tell her about the money, how if he could find it he could provide for them and she wouldn't have to worry about anything ever again. He wanted to console her. He wanted to bring her peace like Edison had in the past. Make her smile. Make her proud. But he found his words inside his head fumbling, and he remained mute on the subject. "I'm going to find a job," he said.

"That's sweet, but you're too young. I don't want you worrying about those things. We'll be okay." She returned her gaze to the fire.

He didn't want to contradict her even though he didn't believe it, or even believed that she believed it. She said it because she wanted to protect him. He knew that. He wanted to protect her the same way. "Who's going to provide for the family with Edison gone?"

"My, how grown up you sound." She looked like she wanted to laugh but was too tired.

Edison didn't like this, her talking down to him, treating him like a child. "I can find work. Maybe with the Robinsons helping on the farm with the sheep."

"We don't need their charity."

"But we accepted money from the church ladies, and food from Ma Abrams."

Evelyn sighed. "I don't want you thinking like this."

"Life's too short for child's play. I'm ready to be a man."

"Don't you ever let them tell you life is short, Ty. Life is long and people do lots of things. Some of them good. Some of them bad. And sometimes these things catch up to people. And sometimes that takes a long time."

"But why do bad things happen to good people? Like Edison? Why was his life cut short?"

"Maybe what happened to him was something catching up to someone else."

Tyrus felt nervous. He felt that panic creeping in again, like it did out on the hill in Duncan Abrams' truck. He tried to swallow that panic down deep into his stomach and then said, "Did you do bad things, Mom?"

"We've all done things we regret, Ty. Even children carry their burdens."

Though she remained focused on the flames, Tyrus felt she was staring into his soul right then. It sent a shiver down his spine. When would this *thing* catch up to him?

This unknowing was like a huge hand around his neck, and it was tightening its grip. Feeling the breath squeezed out of him, Tyrus laid his head down on the arm of the chair and fell asleep.

PART TWO: BASTARDS AND BITCHES

EPISODE SEVEN – THE COMPROMISE

Albany, Fall 1919

"**I**s it better to be born an orphan or die a bastard?" Her mother was a battle axe. "That's the question you need to ask yourself, dear."

Her father was more thoughtful. "Indeed there are places for young ladies in your condition. And there are many families out there in need of a child to love as their own."

"The thought of those childless couples pains me," Evelyn said. They sat around the kitchen table in the wee hours of the morning. Coffee on the stove. "But it's not in my heart to be so charitable."

Mother went on. "If you keep the child, it will always be a bastard. If you give the child away, it will never know of its sad origins. It will be loved."

"You think I'm incapable of loving?" Evelyn asked.

"Clearly you thought you loved this boy, off to God knows where. I question, my dear, your definition of love, and your ability to ration it appropriately."

Father interrupted. "We're not unsympathetic to your feelings. We've always thought of ourselves as progressive. We saw you going to Mildred Elley. Independence if you wanted it. An educated, skilled woman of her own means. If you keep the child, you will lose that, as well as any respectable prospects for marriage. Then what will you become?"

"A child deserves more," mother said.

"We could always move. I've still my prospects in Chicago. We've always dreamed of living there. You could come with us. We could tell people you're a widow."

"You would fabricate such a lie for my sake?" Evelyn asked him.

"I would think not!" Mother exclaimed. "Father is not speaking rationally now. See what you've done to him?" She threw up her hands and walked over to the stove to fetch the coffee.

"I wouldn't want their fake sympathy," Evelyn said.

"Such a stubborn thing with so few choices," Father said. "Chicago is still an option. I could have more of a career out there – more upward mobility. And you, Evelyn, could have a fresh start. And you could move on knowing the child is cared for by a loving family back in New York."

"In times like these," Mother said definitely, "it's best to turn to the church."

"I'm not going to be shut away in a home for unwed mothers," Evelyn said.

Her mother looked like she wanted to throw the scalding coffee in her face. She was frozen in anger, and then walked over to father and poured him a cup. She had to hold herself up against the table, as if she was going to faint from disgust. Father gently placed his hand atop hers in a feeble attempt at soothing her nerves.

Evelyn looked at her parents coldly, her mother flustered and her father contemplative and lost. She couldn't imagine a passion between them. Did they ever love each other like she loved Joshua? Was it even love that she had felt for Joshua Bloomfield? From that first night she leapt from the porch and insinuated herself into his midnight walks, she had been the assertive one. Hell, she almost had him agreeing to marry her on the spot. And what followed was torrid, dizzying, both of them wanton and lustful. But no proposals of marriage came. Only more heated entanglements. Her hands slapping his face. Her nails down his back. His hands around her neck. Was this what making love was supposed to be? She knew no other way. He was all carnal knowledge. And she gave herself to him willingly. When she looked at other couples, she was proud. She saw no passion in their eyes, in their polite hand-holding, in their interlocked arms, when they danced cheek to cheek. Hers and Joshua's alone was on fire and boastful.

The fire was now in her belly, though Joshua was long gone and ignorant of the seed he had planted. Evelyn laid her hands upon her belly. She was not showing yet, but her parents would not let her return to school. She took a job at a popular lunch counter located just off campus of New York State College for Teachers, serving sandwiches and coffee and pop. Her parents may not have been able to imagine her beyond Mildred Elley, seeing her as a secretary at most, but she had envisioned herself here. Her customers were to have been her future professors and classmates. The boys her gentlemanly suitors. The girls her new best friends. Yet all she could think about was the fire, the touch of Joshua's hands, the feel of his body pressed against hers, inside her, the burning. It was invisible. The sweat on her brow appeared to have been from hard work. Unlike at home, no one judged her here.

This little bastard growing inside her. She knew it was a boy. He was like a light bulb inside her.

"Say, what's a pretty gal like you doing working at a grease pit like this?" It was a sharp, twangy voice. Like someone trying to sound like they were from around here and not somewhere way down yonder.

Evelyn remained focused on stacking the coffee mugs behind the counter and kept her back to the man. "Well, mister, it's a good honest living."

"Hey, I ain't no mister, lady." He laughed. It was like a warble. Cackily almost. Like he couldn't control it.

Evelyn turned around. Sure enough, he was just a kid like her. "And what makes you think I'm a lady?"

"Don't you recognize me?" he asked her with his face beaming. His face was a little shaggy, but not unkempt. His teeth could use some shining, but they were straight, and his blue eyes had this youthful exuberance, like he was on the verge of a great discovery and just couldn't contain his excitement.

Evelyn smiled and shook her head, befuddled.

"Maybe you remember me like this?" He jumped off his stool and posed like he held a baseball bat in his hand and he was at the plate ready to swing.

"Oh, yes...number nine? Right? Kydd?"

"Samuel Kydd! You betcha. And I never forget a pretty face like yours from the stands." He swung, imitating disappointment at missing the imaginary ball.

Evelyn laughed a little. "I remember you striking out quite a bit. But you had vigor."

"Yeah, well, you know how it goes. When it's someone like a Joshua Bloomfield hurling at ya,"

"Did you know him personally?"

"Well, you know, all us guys in the league knew each other I guess. I mean, I wouldn't say we were best pals."

"Oh." Evelyn took her rag to the counter and began to sullenly wipe.

"Hey now, I see. All you gals were sweet on a guy like that. He didn't break your heart now, did he?"

"Why, I would never! We didn't even know each other."

"Oh, I didn't mean to cast dispersions. Just an unlucky guy wondering about the luck of another guy. He sure would've been lucky to have had a gal like you. And, pardon my French, he would've been a God-damned fool to have left you."

"Thank you, that's very sweet of you."

"Let's suppose I take you out for a steak dinner tonight and show you just how sweet I can be?"

Evelyn's eyes went wide. She wanted to laugh. Men had flirted with her at the counter before, but never had someone been so unabashedly forward. He certainly did have vigor. She had to give that to him at least. "Dinner sounds lovely. I can meet you at seven. Outside, on the corner, by the library."

"I've got a car. I can pick you up at home."

"By the library would be just fine."

"Seven o'clock it is." He placed a dollar on the counter for his coffee and a generous tip. He snapped his fingers. "I'll be seeing you," he said confidently and strutted out the door.

Samuel liked his steak rare, like she did. He made her laugh. When she asked him where he was from originally, he was suddenly overcome with the affectation of a gentleman from Charleston, South Carolina – that exotic place where she and her parents spent a few weeks when she was eight visiting a doctor specializing in her situation – but alas, he was simply, "A young man from Richmond, Virginny, ma'am." He did impressions. He talked elliptically. He told tall tales of being a stable boy and spending his childhood traveling from racetrack to racetrack. He had friends and business acquaintances all up and down the east coast from Florida to Maine...Canada even. He dreamed of visiting Europe once the dust from the Great War had settled. He saw great opportunities on the border with "imports and exports, well mostly exports, things I wouldn't want to worry a young lady's mind about." He was looking for the next great thing. Maybe it was over there.

He kissed her on that first date, but awkwardly and earnestly like the boys she knew from school. He didn't work up the guts to take her back to his boarding room until the fourth date, and when he lay himself on top of her, it seemed mechanical, though she desired to please him. She wondered if this was what it was supposed to be like. Her stomach felt great pressure as he thrust himself into her. She winced, perhaps moaned even.

"I'm sorry," he said. "Am I hurting you?" He smiled. "Is this your first time?"

She smiled back at him, refusing to answer that last question. "Please, can we try with me on top?"

The thought of her astride him must've appealed to the stable boy in him, and they eagerly flipped over. From that point on, she was in charge.

A month later, she fell victim to a spell, the first in years, while at work. Flailing and writhing on the floor with schoolmarms blessing themselves over her and men at a loss for what to do, the bulge in her belly was apparent. At the hospital, it was Samuel who came to visit and held her hand.

"The doctor said the child is okay?" Sam asked.

Evelyn nodded. "Take me away from here, Sam."

"I may not be the smartest man, but I'm no hayseed. I'm good at math. And I know you were Joshua Bloomfield's girl."

"We've all had our parts to play, haven't we? I'm your girl now."

"I don't care that I'm not the father."

"Take me away from here and make me an honest woman."

Samuel smiled. "You'll need to be honest enough for the both of us."

They stole away in the night. And headed west. When she gave birth to her son in Syracuse, she and Samuel were husband and wife, and she named the child Edison. The light that had been growing inside of her for nine months had now been removed and shone on her world. Yet inside, there was still a fire. A fire in the darkness.

EPISODE EIGHT – IN THE DEEP

Summer 1920

Odette was a platinum blonde. Tall and meaty, but still svelte in a muscular way. Loud and boisterous. Demanding.

Evelyn was dark haired. Short and slender, compact but with generous enough curves especially after the baby. Soft-spoken. Commanding.

Samuel declared them "The Day and Night of Syracuse" and from the moment they met they were inseparable. Odette had a guy named Paul. They had a child a ways back, a boy, but had to give him up. Odette was pretty torn up about it, and she was more than willing to play nursemaid to Edison. It was a great relief to Evelyn who was isolated and away from her parents for the first time in her young life.

Paul was a bit older and had all kinds of cockamamie ideas about how he and Samuel could make money. "There's this old coot I know, up there on the border, rowing whiskey across. He needs help. We could turn this thing into a real operation," Paul would say. In subsequent stories, the old coot had a name...Phillip Bourget. There was talk of him being a distant uncle, you know, and that's how Paul knew all about it. Paul and Samuel had met at a speakeasy downtown. The ladies were introduced to each other the following evening on a double date.

There was an old dance hall across the way from the speakeasy, and the guys would sometimes take the ladies there for a spin. Evelyn dreamed one day of combining the two joints into one magnificent supper club, but she kept this dream to herself and spoke it only to Edison when he suckled on her breast in the early hours of the morning, her secret dreams safe in the amnesia of the dawn. The dance hall was popular with all types, but especially the highbrows who liked to get soused at the speakeasy and then stroll across the street to dance their inebriation away.

Odette and Evelyn loved it. Sometimes Odette would have too much to drink. Gin. She was hard to control. She threw herself on other men and made horrible comments. Paul would remain remarkably calm, though those who did not know him would sense a rage bubbling up underneath. People always steered clear of him. He was even bigger than Odette, and he was the one person who could restrain her. The next morning she would sometimes show up with a black eye. Paul was a teetotaler. A violent man of ideas and action. Samuel would drink too much, too, but he would never make a fool of himself in front of Evelyn. He would get all kinds of talkative, but then grow quiet and sleepy. Evelyn never drank in public. But she enjoyed a nightcap at home. A glass of wine with a meal, if they could find it.

One weekend when the men were away on a job farther north, the ladies decided to go to the dancehall without them. Odette had sampled the bathtub gin before going out. She was itching to dance and had been cursing about Paul all evening. It made Evelyn nervous. Edison was left with a neighbor. When they entered the dancehall the energy sent an electrical charge through Evelyn's body. A band was playing, people were dancing and laughing and talking loudly while a saucy lady, obviously of the bathtub gin drinking kind, sang about "a fire deep inside her soul" and "crying a thousand times" over a lover.

Odette saw him first, before Evelyn even had a chance to consider what was happening. Odette sized men up from behind, noticing the broadness of their shoulders, the way they arched their backs, the way they filled out a pair of pants and the scuff marks on the heels of their shoes. She was drawn to this one immediately, and letting go of Evelyn's hand, she rushed over to the gentleman and tapped him on the shoulder. When he turned around, she grabbed his arm and dragged him out onto the dance floor, but it was Evelyn's eyes that met his.

Joshua Bloomfield. Evelyn felt a tightening of her chest and throat, like her heart was expanding and choking her, beating like the quickened beat of her infant son when she held him to her chest. Joshua resisted Odette's advances and whispered something in her ear while eyeing Evelyn. He convinced Odette to walk with him back to Evelyn, and when Odette realized they knew each other and all of his attention would now be on her demure friend, she drifted back out onto the floor sizing up another gentleman or two. Odette was suddenly alone in a crowded room.

"Your friend is really something else," Joshua said to Evelyn as if running into her in a strange city far from where they last saw each other was the most normal thing in the whole wide world.

"Gin gives her courage," Evelyn said. "I'd like to think she means well, but I'm not so sure." She smiled at him, as if they were gossiping confidants.

She could tell he didn't want to talk. He touched her arm and then drew her to him. He caressed the side of her face. The music was moving through her. She felt like he could sense that and wanted to touch it. She saw floating sparks in her field of vision, and star bursts when she closed her eyes. She thought she might have a seizure, but when he kissed her, his mouth attacking hers, and his warm forceful tongue forcing its way beyond her lips, she felt a great release of energy. She allowed him to pull her into him, almost as if he was willing her whole body to pass through him, her back arching at the tip of his fingers pressing against her spine and holding her close, her head tilted back.

In the corner of her eye, as their lips parted, Evelyn saw Odette agape at the encounter. Odette was her closest friend and knew nothing of Joshua, of Evelyn's past...only that there was now Syracuse and once Albany. There was Samuel and Edison and no names before. Albany was a town of ghosts. Syracuse was full of life. Or at least so Odette thought – for she couldn't even imagine the life that could exist in the future when Evelyn would find herself in Milton. Odette could not see the darkness here in Syracuse. She could not see the darkness in herself and Paul. And she could not see that the light in Evelyn and Edison would need to set itself apart from that darkness lest they succumb to it, though that realization wouldn't be in time before the darkness found a way to stick to them. Odette would never realize the darkness had always been inside Evelyn, too, living in the shadows of the light.

In the opposite natural flow of the highbrows, Odette, a young man, Evelyn and Joshua made their way across the road to the speakeasy. They were exhausted and sweaty. Thirsty. Odette knew only lust. She ogled with jealousy and wonder the passion between Evelyn and Joshua. She longed to taste it, and only alcohol could wash away that desire. She heard her friend say to this beguiling man, "I'm married now. With a child. A boy."

"And where is your husband?" Joshua asked.

"Away."

He bought the four of them round after round of drinks. Odette had never seen Evelyn drink in public like that, but she soon became preoccupied with her man, really hardly more than a boy, but willing like a man. He was a friend of Joshua's, a young ballplayer. They were in Syracuse to play a few games before heading to Rochester. He was looking for a good time, and Odette was eager to oblige.

They brought the men back to their apartment building along the creek. Evelyn encouraged them to keep their voices down while they stumbled up the stairs and through the hallway to their apartment. While Odette took her man to her bedroom, Evelyn settled Joshua on the couch with a glass of whiskey. She then went next door to pick up Edison. She brought the sleeping infant back home to find Joshua with his eyes closed sitting straight up on the couch, the whiskey about to tip over. Holding the baby on her hip, she carefully took the glass of whiskey and placed it on the table beside the couch. Edison whimpered and wiggled. He had just begun teething. She dipped her index finger in the whiskey and then rubbed it on the baby's gums to soothe him. She carefully regarded Joshua, passed out, and then her child, exhausted and lowering his eyes lids. She saw no resemblance. She hoped Joshua would see none either. She retired to her bedroom.

It was a warm summer evening, humid and sticky. Evelyn felt no electricity through her body any more, only heat, like her blood could boil over right through her skin. She was restless in bed knowing Joshua was just outside her door. On the other side of the wall Odette and her friend were imitating the throws of passion. She tried to focus on the sounds invading the room through the open window of the night birds and locusts. Sadly there was no breeze. Edison was restless as well. She nursed him for a while, the alcohol eventually doing its magic for both of them, mother and child finally drifting into sleep, hot baby breath gently tickling her face, her hand secure over his tiny stomach.

Evelyn could sense the missing cadence of her child's breath in her sleep and it made her open her eyes. It was still dark, but she could feel the dawn approaching. The temperature had dropped slightly, and she found her hand resting on the cool sheet beside her and no sign of her infant son. She felt a presence in the room as she looked out the window and saw a fog rolling in over the water. She heard the creaking of the rocking chair, and then Odette's voice softly singing...

À la claire fontaine, m'en allant promener,
J'ai trouvé l'eau si belle que je m'y suis baigné.
Il y a lontemps que je t'aime, jamais je ne t'oublierai

Evelyn rolled over and admired Odette sitting there in the rocking chair in the clouded darkness, holding Edison so his head rested on her shoulder while she gently patted his back. Smoke came slowly rolling in over them like the fog outside, and it became clear there was another presence in the room. As Evelyn's eyes adjusted to the darkness and the figures became more solid, she was startled to find Joshua sitting in the chair by the door, smoking a cigarette and looking on at Odette with disdain, as if the tenderness she was showing was the symptom of some sickness, of rot. He looked back at Evelyn.

Odette abruptly stopped singing. She said to Evelyn sharply, "He was in here lurking. Watching you sleep. I heard the baby start to cry from the other room, so I came in and found him here, just watching you, letting the baby cry like that."

"I must've been dreaming so deeply," Evelyn said as she sat up and began to rub the cobwebs from her eyes.

The boy came barging through the door, half dressed, still drunk, satiated with sex. "There you are, my love!" he exclaimed to Odette. He wasn't drunk enough not to realize the graveness present in the room. Eyes saddened, he asked, "Oh, when will your husbands be home?"

Odette stood up and handed baby Edison to Evelyn. She laughed and turned back to the boy, hands on her hips, all her tenderness shed like a nightgown dropped to the floor. "My silly little man...there's no need to worry."

The boy turned to Joshua, who glared at him like a stern father. "We should get back to the hotel," the boy said. "Morning practice."

"I should think you're in no condition for any strenuous activity this morning," Odette said.

The boy looked dejected. He then wildly shifted moods and turned his eyes back from the floor and up to Odette and then over to Evelyn. "You'll come watch us play?"

"We'd love to," Evelyn said sweetly.

"Let's run out to the creek!" the boy shouted. "Watch the sun rise through the fog." His eyes traveled to the window and his spirit floated through it. "Breathe it all in."

"I think that's a wonderful idea," Evelyn said.

They found themselves on the edge of the water, barefoot in the dewy grass, still inebriated from the night, watching the sun rise from behind an old farm on the other side of the creek and burn through the mist that had enveloped them. The boy sat in the grass, Odette standing over him, quiet. Evelyn stood closest to the water, Edison asleep in the cradle of her arms, humming the tune of the French song under her breath.

Joshua kept his distance, meditating on his cigarette which was almost burned down to the nubs of his fingers. He wondered if he took Evelyn's baby and tossed it into the creek, would it just sink? How deep was the water? Whatever special something he and Evelyn still shared, surely it would drown. His hatred would have to freeze over the water.

EPISODE NINE – TO THE HILLS, THE HILLS, THE HILLS

Summer 1927

Sitting on the porch in the summer light with her baby asleep on her chest, Evelyn thought, how could she measure those seven years away from here...far away...but not far enough? Syracuse had seemed but a dream, something she remembered when she shot up in the middle of the night as if her heart had stopped and then started again. There was the sound of Odette's voice singing to Edison. The stealing away in the middle of the night. Samuel hysterical, mad. It was in that moment she knew he loved her.

"Evelyn, we must never come back," he told her that night.

They took so little with them, just a few bits of clothes and a swaddled infant, vagabonds they were, like when they had first left Albany for Syracuse. Was this going to be their way? She remembered thinking then there was a romance to a life like that...on the run...but from what? From whom?

"Paul and Odette are gone already," he said.

"Will we ever see them again?" she asked him, heartbroken to think her only friend would be alone with that beast of a man and she might never see her again.

"We can't. We can't let anything connect us to our past...to this place. We can't let Joshua find us. He'd kill me for sure."

"I don't know what happened to you all out there at the border, but I swear to you Joshua has no reason to follow us."

"I don't care if you were his lover still. That has nothing to do with THIS."

"What reason would he have to come searching for us if we left?"

Samuel looked down at baby Edison wrapped in blankets asleep in a basket. "You can't think of any reason why he would want to track us down?"

Evelyn knew where his mind was going, but she couldn't let him stay there. If they were going to be a family unit from then on, she had to stop his mind wandering to that thought...to the idea of Edison not being his. She never told Joshua that Edison was his son. She saw none of him in her baby boy, and she had to believe that Joshua did not suspect. She told her husband confidently. "I can't think of a single one."

"Then you let me do the thinking. We have to get gone."

Evelyn thought they would never return to New York...ever. After stops in Pittsburgh and Indianapolis, they eventually headed out to Chicago where her parents had moved. Her father helped Samuel find a steady job as a delivery driver for a local dairy. But after those brief good years, her parents passed away within weeks of each other and within weeks of her giving birth to Sally in the fall of 1924. A few years passed, lean ones, where Samuel lost his job as the delivery driver and began traveling...selling bibles and encyclopedias on commission all across the Midwest...or so he told her. He would come back after being gone for weeks at a time telling tall tales of all the people he met and the old friends he ran into.

In the fall of 1926 when Evelyn was as big as a house with her third child in her womb, she ran into some old friends while Samuel was gone a-sellin' books. It was at a lunch counter on the outskirts of Chicago within walking distance of the small untidy row home they rented. It was an anonymous part of town cut through by the railroad where most people were in transit and kept to themselves. And there they were, leaning at the end of the counter closest to the door through which Evelyn stepped in and lost her breath.

She almost didn't recognize Odette who looked smaller and meek hunched over the counter with her head down sipping on a cup of coffee. Paul looked drunk, as if he could barely balance himself against the counter. They looked like they just stopped in for the coffee...didn't have time to sit...to eat. And they noticed Evelyn immediately.

Odette looked up from her coffee and turned her head towards Evelyn, revealing dark circles under her eyes and a bruise on her left cheek. Her eyes widened as much as they could in her weathered state, but it seemed as if it was an act...like she had expected to run into her old friend from Syracuse here in the middle of nowhere Illinois six years after they last saw each other. She opened her mouth, but no words came out, as if whatever she had scripted for this chance encounter suddenly floated off into the ether, silent and useless.

Evelyn didn't know what to do but smile and open her arms as she waddled over to them. She and Odette embraced gently, Odette careful of the load Evelyn was carrying. Evelyn could smell whisky and cigarettes on her. Paul looked down on them, his face flushed and eyes bloodshot. All of his hair had turned grey. He mustered a half smile with his big, chapped lips, but said nothing.

"I cannot believe it," Odette exclaimed, back on script. "We were just passing through, waiting for our train...heading out to California, and here you are!"

"Samuel and I live here," Evelyn explained.

Paul began to cough, choking on a phlegmy unsettling laugh.

Evelyn tried not to look disgusted. She continued on. "We moved out this way to be closer to my parents some time ago...though they've both passed on now. Yet here we stayed...here we are."

"And look out you!" Odette said beaming while she laid her hands on Evelyn's belly. "And how is mon bebe, Edison?"

"Oh, he's wonderful. He's six now. In school today. And then we have a little girl named Sally. She's almost two. The neighbor is watching her to give me a rest. And now we have this little one on the way."

"Oh, Evelyn, this is so wonderful! How I wish I could see them both!"

Paul insinuated himself bluntly into the middle of their polite conversation. "And Samuel, where is he?"

"Oh, it's a shame you're here during his time away. He's a traveling salesman. On the road right now."

Paul coughed again. He cleared his throat. "Oh, I see! Good for him. And what of our dear friend, Joshua Bloomfield?"

Evelyn began to feel uncomfortable in Paul's presence.

Odette smiled and looked around, trying to change the topic and rescue her long-lost friend. "Remember, Evie, when we used to talk about owning a place like this? Chez Odette's! That's what we said we would call it, right? But it would be yours really. Oh, those, were the days, no?"

Evelyn smiled politely and nodded.

"Do you ever hear from Joshua?" Paul insisted.

"No. We haven't kept in touch," Evelyn said. "Haven't seen him since I last saw you two in Syracuse."

"Good, good. He was a troublesome man. I would not want to see you and Samuel involved with someone like that anymore. So a traveling salesman old Sammy is now, eh?"

"Yes...bibles...encyclopedias. That kind of thing."

"Big sellers, these books, I imagine. My, my, it sure is funny how long six years can be. I bet you two crazy kids were livin' high off the hog when you left Syracuse. And now...look at you..." Paul snorted. "...*here*."

"It's not so bad," was Evelyn's instinctual retort. Who the heck was he to look down on them? But then she wondered what he meant by them living "high off the hog" after Syracuse. "And I'm not quite sure I follow you."

"Psfth...the way you two ran out of town so quick...on the make...with all that dough. Poor Old Man Bourget. Poor Joshua." His eyes widened and his upper lip crumpled up in a sneer. "*Poor me.*"

"I don't know what you're talking about. We left with nothing. Just some rags. Me, Sam and Edison. I don't know what happened to you guys up there. But we were running for our lives."

Paul slapped his hand loudly on the counter and started to have a fit of coughs between desperate and violent laughter. His eyes began to water. Odette placed her hand on his shoulder. "Please, baby, calm down. Don't make a scene."

Evelyn stepped back from the counter. "On your way to California, huh?" she said shaking.

Odette looked over at her while still trying to comfort Paul in his fit. She smiled, the way a mad person or an idiot would smile. "Oh, sure, Paul's got prospects out west. Oh, how we wish you all could come with us!"

"It really was great seeing you, but I just remembered I forgot to give Sally her medicine before I left, and the neighbor doesn't know. Poor baby has such a cough. Must be something passing through. I'd invite you back, but I don't want you all to get sick. And you've a train a catch, right?" She stepped further and further back towards the door. She almost wanted to weep. "Oh, Odette."

"Evelyn, wait!" Odette cried out, but she became completely engulfed in Paul's fit and couldn't break herself free of him.

Evelyn fled the scene and raced home. She had never been more afraid in her life. She felt like that wasn't the Odette she knew. It was some gross specter of her former friend. And Paul...she never doubted he could kill a man...but now she felt certain he wouldn't think twice of killing a woman...or a child. And even more than that mortal fear, she feared most that Joshua Bloomfield might not be far behind them.

Three days earlier a notice had come in the mail from a lawyer back in New York stating that her uncle had passed away and left to her his house and farm in Milton, a quiet hamlet nestled in the hills between Syracuse and Albany. She hadn't known yet what to make of it, if they should even dare go back to those hills, even if only to sell the place. But now she thought maybe that was the safest place for them...hidden in the hills so close to their past haunts, yet such a seemingly unlikely place to hide, the last place where anyone would come looking for them. Nobody knew of Milton...of her uncle...of the farm. She had her neighbor pick up Edison from school while she stayed home with Sally and packed what she could of her children's things into two small suitcases. They couldn't be packed too heavily. Edison would have to carry one, and she another, with a baby on board and Sally on her hip. Oh, how pitiful they would all be getting on that train headed east.

She wrote two letters that night. One was to the lawyer stating her intentions and that she was on her way, which she had her neighbor promise to give to the postman tomorrow. The other was to Samuel, telling him where they went and to come follow them as soon as possible. This too she left with the neighbor, such a kindhearted old woman, who promised to give it to Samuel as soon as he returned from his travels. In the morning, she went to the train station with her two suitcases and two children. There on the bench squeezed tightly with her sad-eyed babies and old luggage, she read the newspaper where it stated an unidentified French Canadian man was murdered last night just a few blocks from the station in a brawl at an ill reputed speak-easy. The suspect escaped before being identified. The dead man must've been Paul. It had to be Paul. She wondered if he had killed that thing calling itself Odette before he went out in a rage, and if her body was yet to be found. Maybe in a happier life the real Odette was on that train to California. Evelyn's train, headed in the opposite direction, arrived just as she shuddered at the thought of Paul and Odette's demise. She discarded the paper and held Sally tight. Edison looked at her stoically and placed his hand on her belly. "He'll be born in a new home," he said confidently.

"In the hills...oh, you'll love them, Edison. I promise."

And just like that, they were gone again...this time to the hills, the hills, the hills.

But not before a layover somewhere in central Pennsylvania where they were to catch a train that would then take them north to Milton. The stress of the journey wore down on Evelyn. She felt too weary to finish the trip, and they spent two nights in a cheap hotel. She felt progressively worse, feverish and achy, but she couldn't bear to spend another night in that horrible stuffy room staring at the dingy yellow wallpaper while poor Edison played Daddy and tried to quiet a wailing Sally. The poor child never said a word of complaint. He was a great comfort to her, and she was determined to complete the last leg of their journey for him. She wanted to see him swimming in a lake in the hills. She wanted to see joy on his face again.

"We go now?" he said in the fog of that morning while caressing her flushed cheek and brushing the sweat-soaked hair from her forehead.

"Yes," she said. And she felt a second wind lift her from bed. Edison had already dressed himself and the baby. He had even gone downstairs to the kitchen where they filled Sally's bottle and made him some eggs and toast. After dressing and packing, Evelyn slogged herself and her troops downstairs. Shocked at the sight of her, the kindly old man at the front desk helped them across the street to the train station. "Don't worry, I'll be fine," she told the man. "Someone is waiting for me there."

The old man looked down at Edison and said, "You take good care of your mama." He gave him some money and a candy bar.

At the station in Milton, Evelyn barely made it off the train and almost passed out on a bench along the tracks. "Take Sally's hand and go over to the counter. Tell them to call this number. The lawyer will fetch us." She handed Edison a piece of crumbled up paper from her coat pocket.

How many miles? How many homes? How many loved ones lost? To find herself in Milton. With three children now. Tyrus was born some time later, after her fever passed, thanks to the care of a Dr. Horace Long, a good friend of the lawyer who came and fetched them at the station. He was kind enough to put them up at his own house in Fenimore, the town next door to Milton. There he and his daughter, a beautiful girl of fifteen named Myra, nursed Evelyn back to health and looked after the children.

"Why didn't you take me to my uncle's house...to my home?" she asked him when she was well enough to measure time and her voice from the sickbed.

"Oh, dear," Dr. Long said cautiously. "We couldn't put you up there in your state. The place needs some work before it can become livable again. But it's a beautiful plot of land, Mrs. Kydd.

And there are people who have been looking after the farm. The Abrams – Mabel and Duncan. Good people. Willing to help fix it up until your husband arrives. And we'll help, too."

"But why? Why would you all want to help me?"

"You're a Temple by blood. You're part of this community. And look at you! And your poor lovely children. Who could turn you away?"

So many kind people. Could she measure the passing years in kindness? She had relied for so long on the kindness of strangers. The old lady who lived next door to her outside of Chicago. The old man at the hotel. The lawyer. Dr. Long and his daughter. And now these Abrams whom she hadn't even met yet. She was lucky, she knew. Especially considering all the horrible ghosts that seemed to follow her. She had made many choices in life. Some bad. Some good. But she knew coming back to these hills was unquestionably good.

There was just enough money left from her uncle's meager estate to fix up the place right before the worst of winter fell on the hills. Evelyn and the children, with help from the Longs and the Abrams who lived on the farm next to her uncle's, were able to move in before Christmas. It seemed then they hibernated until spring. She had never remembered sleeping so much. Tyrus seemed to have suckled the life blood from her. And Edison and Sally were so very sleepy in the cold mountain air, like they had stumbled into a fairy-tale land just before bedtime and could barely keep their eyes open. The crackling of the fire. The frost on the window panes. The howling wind rolling down the snow-covered hills. It was all so very very much like a lullaby. And all that time...no sign of Samuel. Had he suffered the same fate as Paul?

In the spring, Duncan Abrams, who like a bear seemed to have hibernated all winter long while his wife Mabel cooked day and night for Evelyn and the children, came thundering up the steps with a manic border collie.

"This bitch," he said, "had a litter of pups. I'd like to give one to your boy, Edison. She can tend your sheep, too, when she is grown. I'll train her and the boy." And then there was Sue.

But still no Samuel. Had Joshua found him outside Chicago and killed him, just as he had feared all those years ago when they fled Syracuse? Could she measure these seven years in fear?

And in the twilight of a warm spring evening, she and the baby and the puppy and Sally and Edison and Myra went down to the lake in Fenimore. It was just as she dreamed. The last throws of sunlight descended behind Sleeping Lion Mountain, and a muted ethereal glow descended upon the shore. Their faces were warm, wide-eyed and happy. Barefoot she swung Sally around and around. "Fly, baby-girl, fly!" she called out, and Sally squealed with delight. Sue nipped at her ankles as she spun dance-like in the tall grass and baby Tyrus cooed happily in his basket under the tree to the soft signing voice of Myra sitting on the blanket beside him.

Edison, shirtless and shivering, splashed in the shallow clear water of the lake and looked out at the sun setting behind the lion's back. His feet molded themselves to the still ice-cold rocks. He felt a solid footing here. He felt like this was home. At last. He brought his arms in close and folded them over his chest where he rubbed his hands up and down his arms, smiling, teeth-chattering. He turned around and looked back at the others playing on the shore, and it pleased him. Evelyn saw him in this moment, and she could see he loved the lake. He loved his sister and brother. He loved his dog. He loved Myra. But he missed his father. There was that longing and heartbreak in his eyes even as happy as he was right then.

Finally it was summer. 1927.

The longest day of the year. Hours after supper and the sun still wouldn't die. Evelyn sat on the wicker rocker on the front porch with baby Tyrus resting on her bosom. Sue never left her side when she had Tyrus with her, and the animal slept quietly at her feet with one eye open on the road down at the bottom of the hill. Evelyn got the feeling this puppy, which had grown so fast into a dog, thought that baby was hers. Edison and Sally were somewhere on the other side of the screen door in the bowels of the house playing. And that's when in the hazy gloom of the unending day, he appeared like a little splash of darkness down at the bottom of the hill having wandered in from god know's where. Sue sparked to attention and let out a few tentative yelps. She growled.

"It's okay, girl," Evelyn said to the dog. She sat up in the chair and held Tyrus tightly to her chest. The baby wiggled a little, unnerved by his mother's quickening heart, but remained asleep. Sue stood up and trotted out to the middle of the stone path leading up the hill to the porch. "It's okay, Sue," Evelyn said again.

The man walked up to greet the dog. He leaned over and slowly put out his hand. Sue growled and then took a few careful steps forward to sniff the man's hand. The man laughed as the dog began to lick his hand and then he looked up at the porch and took off his dusty hat and held it over his heart. He hadn't even a single bag with him. Just the dirty clothes and dusty shoes he wore. "Well, well, well," he announced broadly, "Looky what we have here, old girl! Looks like I'm gonna be a god-damned farmer!"

Evelyn shook her head in disbelief as she stood up and walked to the top of the steps. Inside the house the scamper of little feet reached the level of a cacophony before stopping dead on the other side of the screen door. Bright, cheery eyes peered out longingly at the reunion. "Come outside, Edison, and hold your brother while I tend to your father," Evelyn said calmly. The screen door creaked open and out slipped two small, warm and eager bodies. Evelyn turned around and gently placed the sleeping Tyrus into his big brother's arms. Sally clung nervously to Edison's waist. They stood there stunned as their mother ran down the steps. The dog spun around confused by its owner while the man ran up to his wife and embraced her.

"No more wandering...no more gettin' gone," Evelyn said hotly into his ear as they held each other tight and he lifted her slightly off the ground, swinging her around once while the dog yelped and danced around them. He gently placed her back down on the ground and broke the embrace. They stepped back and took a good look at each other.

"Paul and Odette are dead," he said.

"And Joshua?"

"He was never even close."

And Evelyn wasn't sure right then if Samuel was lying or ignorant.

EPISODE TEN – PLAYING HOUSE

Spring 1936

In Milton and Fenimore you either worked for the regional Haydon Hospital system or were a farmer. Unless of course you were a Haydon – then you owned the hospital system and most of the farms and had the grandest of mansions, a naked neoclassical behemoth known as Haydon Hall, nestled in the wilderness on a swath of land that overlooked the wide frozen lake and gave you a clear view straight into Fenimore nine miles away while you spent your winters in Florida. In late March, the ice flow still covered most of the lake, but the shorelines were thawing and water was flowing which meant the Haydons would be returning and all the gentry of the county would soon be attending their annual Spring Ball on the mansion's grounds. To outsiders in recent years it seemed an affront to the state of affairs across the rest of the nation, and almost crude considering the dwindling tourism in the area and the suffering that caused those living in the shadow of the Haydons, but it was tradition and the natives wouldn't have it any other way. Besides, even those who suffered still saw these hills as untouched by the outside world and protected from the Depression. They, as well as Haydon Hall, were to be cherished in good times and in bad.

Thanks to Horace Long, the Haydon's family doctor, Evelyn was able to secure a temporary job preparing the mansion for the

Haydons return. She found comfort there working among the other men and women busying themselves about the sprawling house as the vast, drafty rooms seemed physical manifestations of the emptiness she felt at home with Edison gone. There were no other children or a dog nipping at her heels here. The other workers looked on her with pity, as a widow of sorts (they spoke in hushed whispers concerning the whereabouts of her husband) but they didn't hound her with questions or attempt to console her over the tragic loss of her eldest son. There was too much work to be done, and here in Haydon Hall Evelyn could face the emptiness she felt head-on and brush it, scrub it or wash it away as if it were dust, grime or dirt.

Sally had begged her mother to let her come work with her, as she felt as empty and lost as Evelyn without Edison, but Evelyn wouldn't allow it. She couldn't bear to have Sally in that house. It was her refuge, and if Sally was there sharing the emptiness, she would be a constant reminder of Edison. Evelyn wanted the void to herself. Sally would have to find another way to cope.

"You need to focus on school now. And help take care of your brother," Evelyn explained to her daughter.

"I hate school and Tyrus can take care of himself," Sally proclaimed, arms folded across her chest as she stood in the doorway of the kitchen, her back rigid against the frame.

Evelyn was preparing supper. "My decision is final, young lady."

"Are you going to let Tyrus work for the Robinsons this summer?"

"Tyrus will play baseball."

"Tyrus isn't Edison." Sally was too flippant to want to take back those words. She continued. "He isn't as good. Might as well let him work. And me, too."

"Why don't you go see how Ma Abrams is doing? If she's feeling any better. She might need some help around the farm."

"Around the farm? Ain't got nothing left to tend around the farm. Neither do we. Everything's dead or sold to the Robinsons." Sally threw her arms up in disgust, stepped into the middle of the doorway and faced her mother, her hands now on her hips. "Don't you wanna hit me now for givin' you sass?"

"Go read a book. I'll call you when supper is ready, but until then leave me be."

Sally was infuriated. "Don't you know Tyrus has been runnin' all over town with that little colored girl?"

Evelyn turned from the dough she was kneading and looked at Sally sternly. She wasn't sure if Sally even knew what that turn of phrase usually meant. To a child, running around was just that...running around. In the adult world, it was what she knew her husband had been doing for years when he traveled. She didn't want her children living in that adult world. "You don't think I'll know about it if one of my children gets in trouble?"

"You don't know anything!"

Evelyn took two quick steps towards the door with her right arm raised ready to strike Sally right across the face. Sally flinched instantly and took two steps back, but Evelyn suddenly felt faint and almost collapsed to the floor. She held herself up on the edge of the counter.

"Mama?" Sally cried.

Sue was there, nuzzling Evelyn's legs and herding her towards the kitchen table where she sat down. The dog propped its front legs up on her lap and began to lick her face.

"Tell Tyrus to call Dr. Long," Evelyn said.

"But that's where he is. At Dr. Long's house with that stupid girl."

"Ty isn't home yet?"

"No," Sally cried. "See, you don't know anything." She stepped forward into the kitchen and pushed her way in between the dog and her mother. She wrapped her arms tightly around her mother's neck, while the dog frantically tried to work her way back into the embrace. "Don't worry. If I squeeze you maybe the spell won't be so bad this time."

"Sally, why don't finish making supper?" Evelyn pushed her away.

Sally wiped the tears from her eyes and nodded her head. "Okay." She walked over to the counter.

Evelyn stood up slowly and walked to the doorway. She sat down on the floor in the threshold with Sue pacing around her. Just before she went into the throws of a small seizure, she thought about how she couldn't wait to be in the echoing bowels of Haydon Hall tomorrow, lost in that cold anonymous desolation...away from all this...from all these needy things around her.

* * *

Tyrus hadn't given much thought to Mostlee Weathers, the new girl in his class that year. There had been a little colored girl in Sally's class the year before, a bright sassy thing who challenged Sally's status. They got into some serious fights, hair-pulling and rolling around in the dust and everything, but eventually they became friends, and Tyrus was pretty sure that's who taught Sally all those new swear words she liked to sling around now. That girl left, though, when her parents shuffled off to Buffalo.

As there only ever seemed to be one colored kid at a time in Milton-Fenimore Elementary, Mostlee Weathers was now the token, but nobody paid her much attention. She sat quietly in the back of the class, minding her business, only speaking when spoken to. She didn't wear the typical country smocks like the other poor little girls. She always wore dresses, like something you would see a little girl wear in the movies – city clothes, Tyrus presumed. She had big eyes that always stared forward and her hair was always pulled tightly back and tied into two thick, nappy braids with big, white clips on the end. She was pretty in a way, he guessed, but he didn't pay her any mind apart from the initial noticing of her arrival.

That was, of course, until he returned to school after Edison died. She calmly walked over to him out in the schoolyard while he sat alone underneath a tree with his back against the trunk and his knees pulled up under his chin. She handed him a white letter-sized envelope. It was the first bit of contact he had with any of the other kids since returning earlier that week, and it was the first bit of contact he had ever had with Mostlee Weathers. She was cool and confident standing over him in her little dress and light overcoat in the dead of winter. He was surprised she wasn't shivering. His nose was running.

"I'm sorry about your brother," she said.

Tyrus took off his gloves and opened the unsealed envelope. Inside was a dried red rose. He knew people gave flowers at funerals and planted them on graves, but he wasn't sure what this was supposed to mean. He looked up at her and mustered a weak, "Thank you."

"Wanna walk home from school together?"

He didn't have time to ponder this before he said, "Okay."

"Then it's settled." She gave a nod of her head, turned and walked briskly away.

On the walk home they didn't speak. Mostlee lived in a hotel with her mother. Tyrus had never met someone who lived in a hotel before. It seemed exotic to him.

At the foot of the sidewalk in front of the hotel, Mostlee said to him, "It's okay that you don't want to talk yet. We'll talk when you're ready."

"Okay," Tyrus replied.

And from that point on they were inseparable. Eventually a whole lotta talking came with the walking and mostly it was Mostlee talking at first. And it was hard to get her to stop, and she talked so fast. The colder it got, the faster she talked. To keep warm, Tyrus supposed. But it was alright, because he liked to hear her talk in her sing-songy way, relaxed and with an accent she hid when she spoke her few carefully measured words at school. She and her mother had moved there from the big city – New York City. Harlem. Her mother had been a singer, and her father was her mother's manager. When he died last year, her mother couldn't sing anymore – like physically, she lost her voice. She was so heartbroken she lost her voice. So they moved out here where her mother took up cleaning houses for all the doctors and administrators who worked at Haydon Hospital.

And they started going into those houses on their increasingly rambling walks home. Mostlee timed their "tours" with her mother's schedule, always knowing which one she had just been in. They would sneak into the empty houses, so quiet, so clean. Mostlee would run her finger across the edge of the finely polished dark wood furniture.

"Look," she would proudly say while holding up her finger. "No dust. Doctors like their houses clean."

They would walk around the houses like cats, careful not to touch too much, aware of every creak their footsteps made on the floors. But there was a ritual. If there was a record player, and there always was, Mostlee would inspect the records.

"Pfphhh...boring white folks music," she would always say and then smile at Tyrus.

And they always took off their boots in the master bedrooms and then jumped up and down on the beds. But they were quiet about it. They didn't giggle. It didn't feel right to do so. They just smiled and spun around until they collapsed onto the soft sheet covers. They would bury their faces into the pillows, taking in the deep smell of clean linens. And then they would carefully smooth out the beds, put on their boots and leave.

One day in the early spring when the winter chill was loosening its grip, they took a long walk into Fenimore. They came upon Dr. Long's house, and Tyrus was startled when Mostlee ran up the walkway to the porch.

"What's wrong?" she asked as she turned around and looked back at Tyrus still standing on the sidewalk.

"I know this house," he said.

Mostlee was surprised by this for a split second and then this fact excited her. "Well, great! C'mon then – you can show me around."

For years the Long house had been like a second home to Tyrus, but today it felt like stepping into a stranger's home. He felt queasy being there. The last time he was there was last summer with Edison. He was even more careful with his steps in here. Mostlee was instantly drawn to and studying the pictures on the walls in the living room and atop the fireplace mantel.

"Is that your mom?" Mostlee asked as she stopped in front of a picture from a few summers ago of the whole family standing on the back porch with Dr. Long.

"You can see the lake from out back," Tyrus said trying to change the subject.

"You were so little," Mostlee laughed. "Cute." She gulped. "And your brother..."

"I don't feel good about being in here."

"Oh my god, is Dr. Long your Daddy?"

"No!"

"I'm sorry." She moved around the room admiring the other pictures. "Where is your Daddy?"

Tyrus shrugged his shoulders. "I dunno. Maybe dead. Dr. Long is my mom's doctor. She gets these spells...seizures."

"Epilepsy? Our neighbor in Harlem had epilepsy." She stopped in front of a picture of Myra Long standing in front of the house. "Wow...she's beautiful."

"My brother was going to marry her."

Mostlee turned around and looked at Tyrus standing in the middle of the room. He was shivering. "Oh," she said.

"She lives in New York City now. She writes to us. I'm gonna marry her one day."

Mostlee's eyes grew wide and then shrunk. "Ohhh."

Tyrus couldn't stop shaking and his eyes grew misty.

Mostlee ran over to him and hugged him. Despite all their time spent together, it was the first time they really touched each other. It was a quick, hard hug. Mostlee stepped back. "Show me the rest of the house."

"There's a great Victrola in the other room." Tyrus was composed and eager now. He hadn't cried. Not since Edison's death.

Flipping through Dr. Long's records, Mostlee remarked with her head shaking, "More boring white folks music." She slapped the last record down on the shelf, spun around and smiled. "But Mama will take care of that."

Tyrus didn't know what she meant by that, but he soon would.

EPISODE ELEVEN – THE PICNIC

The rain started in the west over the hills and swept down into the lakes and lowlands. It came down in undulating sheets as if the hands of giants were holding the ends high up in the dark sky and shaking them out in preparation to hang them on the line to dry. One could scarcely see through the downpour, and there was a great rumbling coming from Sleeping Lion Mountain.

But then it all stopped, and the world grew silent and clear. Sally found herself on the shore of the lake and all of the water had turned red like blood. She felt a presence lurking over her as if someone was watching her from behind. She turned back to the woods and saw a dark shape approaching. Then there was a hand upon her throat.

She woke up with an animalistic yelp, and then realizing she was in her bedroom safe and sound she calmed herself and tried to shake the dream from her mind. She was sweating. It was warm and stuffy in her room. It was May and the thaw was in full effect. She walked to the window and drew back the curtains. She cracked the window and in blew fresh morning air. Looking out over the farm and the hills there was mud everywhere and she swore she could hear the murmurs of melt water rushing down the hills in mini torrents washing the grounds clean. The morning glow projected itself from behind the house where the daylight rose and bathed the hills soon to turn from brown to green. But Sally couldn't shake the feeling of that dark shape watching her, grasping for her throat. No amount of thawing could rid her of that chill.

Things still felt like a dream later that day on the boat ride to Haydon Hall. The Haydons had invited the families of those who had worked on the house for the past two months to a picnic on the Saturday before the more upper crust Spring Ball. The last of the ice flows had melted the week earlier, and it was quicker to taxi by boat from Fenimore out to the Haydon Hall grounds than to take the winding back roads snaking around the perimeter of the lake.

Evelyn had expected a fight from Tyrus about wanting to take Sue or putting on the new spring suit she had bought him, but he gave her no grief. Stepping out of her bedroom in her new spring dress, she found him in the hallway standing in front of the mirror fixing his tie.

"You look nice," she said. And she wondered who he was dressing for. Surely there was manipulation afoot...or had her baby boy turned into an adult over the course of a few weeks? She feigned pride and smiled.

"Thank you," he replied politely as if speaking not to his mother but instead to a teacher or a much older woman of authority.

They walked down the stairs together, and there she expected to find Sally prepared to give her some sass, but her daughter sat on the couch sullenly waiting for her as if she was still half asleep. The three of them walked down into town and to the pier, quietly, properly, with the air wrapping warmly around them and the sun beating down on their pale skin. For months following Edison's death they had to stare out at that frozen lake, but the water was sun drenched and glimmering now. Looking at it now, it would seem absurd to imagine a truck parked out in the middle of the vast expanse and death so white and naked smothering everything in sight. They stepped onto the boat confidently as a family unit as if they had conquered that lake. But in a way, too, it was as if Edison had never existed, as if any memory of him had also thawed and was now just one of the countless drops of water that made up the lake, anonymous and flowing continuously into one body.

It pained Evelyn as she took her seat, looking around at some of the other people she had worked with at Haydon Hall, none of them dressed as nicely as she and her eerily well-behaved children. They exchanged pleasantries and introductions. None of these people had ever known Edison. She felt his memory and spirit had been drowned in the lake and would never be recovered. She regarded her children pensively. Sally sat across from her looking out over the water. Tyrus had gone to sit at the ferry's bow, his gaze turned towards the mountains. All three of them, apart...politely away from the other people. Condemned to their private thoughts and daydreams. Evelyn had never felt more alone.

Haydon Hall appeared like a castle on a hill as they approached the shoreline and the Haydons' private dock. Tyrus and Sally had never seen it up close like this, as from land it was hidden away from the road by a long, snaking private driveway and the woods around it. It was positioned at an angle atop the hill so that the front and back of the house were visible from the boats as they came up to the dock. Its most striking feature was the grand portico and Grecian columns in the front. It was like something from another world...from one of the fantasy novels Edison used to read to Tyrus when he was little. For a moment, he was lost in a childhood reverie and imagined they were explorers coming upon a strange land and Haydon Hall was some ancient ruin of a bygone civilization.

On the shoreline there were picnic tables lined up. The Haydons' full-time hired help were there ready to serve the guests, but the Haydon family was not yet returned from Florida. They were due midweek. Instead they had sent emissaries from the hospital to play host for these seasonal workers who had prepared the house.

They came down from the grand house in their smart suits and dresses and greeted the little people coming in off the ferry. Tyrus was disappointed to find Dr. Long was not there among them.

Evelyn paid no attention to her children who disappeared into the encroaching and overly amiable crowd. The other children began running up and down the grounds laughing and playing, burning off months of cabin fever and marveling at the grand mansion. After some more pleasantries and introductions, a few of the doctors recognized Evelyn from the time Edison spent in the hospital before being sent home to die and offered their most professional condolences. Evelyn found a quiet place out at the gazebo near the dock where she smoked a cigarette and stared emptily out over the lake. The sun at its height now over the cloudless sky created a shimmering on the water that was near blinding.

Tyrus found his way into the house, which was bound by an unspoken rule that it was off limits. But as he had discovered during his domestic adventures with Mostlee, nothing was off limits. The massive and cavernous rooms downstairs were still cold and airless. The furniture was uncovered and the floors polished and clean, but it was still enveloped by a feeling of being unlived in, like a museum...or a cemetery crypt. Tyrus imagined he had tunneled his way through a secret passage underneath the Temple family crypt up on Haydons Hill and had discovered a secret cave system inhabited by furtive creatures never before seen by man. He walked carefully and hushed, almost holding his breath, around the caves, feeling as if he was being watched by creatures hiding from sight.

Tyrus exited this reverie when he came upon the grand central staircase which he ascended to the upper floor. He wished Mostlee was there with him to explore the bedrooms. He wondered if they kept a record player up here. Or a radio. He entered one bedroom, a child's room, and looked out the window at the grounds and the lake. He saw the distant figure of his mother standing by the gazebo alone. He scanned the grounds for his sister but couldn't see her. He then looked out over the water and tried to imagine where Haydons Hill was on the other side. It was warm enough now to enact his plan and go back to the Temple family crypt. He had only ever been there by car, and it seemed such a long ride back in February when they went to bury Edison. How long would it take to walk there, he wondered, or to ride his bike? And would Mostlee come with him? Could he trust her with his suspicions about what might be hidden there in the walls of the crypt?

Tyrus crossed the hallway into another bedroom, a grander one with a four poster bed canopied by white fabric and a bearskin rug in front of a fireplace. The window there overlooked the front grounds which gave no evidence of the revelry out back. There were a few cars lined up in the drive, and another one approaching.

Aha! A spy! The enemy! – but no, he recognized the car. It was Dr. Long's. Out of the back seat came Mostlee dressed in her nicest wears, and from the front came her mother, Lillian, and Dr. Long. This was his first time seeing Lillian Weathers, as she was always in another house when he was with Mostlee, but even from afar he could tell she was a woman of great refinement and beauty. She wore a dress like he imagined Myra wearing in the city, and her hair was done like that of a famous jazz singer he had seen a picture of once. She walked with her arm linked to Dr. Long with an air of class that seemed out of place in this wilderness. He couldn't imagine her cleaning houses. But he could imagine her living here in this one, her voice filling the caves with music. And Dr. Long looked younger in her presence, his hunched back straight and proud. It was funny, when Tyrus was with Mostlee he felt older, yet it seemed like when Dr. Long was with Mostlee's mother, he became a young man again. Or a proud man at least.

Tyrus was so lost in watching the three of them come up the stone pathway to the front doors that he didn't realize someone had snuck up behind him. Sally leaned on the windowsill and startled him.

"Hey," she said moodily. "I see your little friend has arrived. Is that why you got so dressed up?"

"Shut up," Tyrus lazily retorted, still in a hushed tone, as if cave creatures were listing in.

"I can't believe Dr. Long would allow himself to be seen in public with THAT woman."

"She's his maid."

"Oh, brother, you're so naïve. How many men do you know bring their maids to a party dressed like that?"

"I don't understand what you're saying."

"Just like our mother. You don't understand shit. Why do you think Dr. Long never comes around anymore?"

"He's busy. Working. He's never home either."

"Ha! You should know! He's out cavorting with HER!"

"What does ca-cavorting mean?"

"Oh, geeze, you are an idiot! C'mon!" She grabbed his arm and took him downstairs. "Dr. Long used to cavort with Mom. You should realize that at least," she said galloping gleefully down the steps, fully awake for the first time today. They just missed Dr. Long and the Weathers pass through the main atrium and out back. They ran outside.

Sally and Tyrus descended into the crowd. They ignored the advances of other children on the sidelines shouting from them to come and play. They maneuvered their way casually and with great care through the adults. There was a definite murmur amongst the other doctors and their wives about Dr. Long's companion. Dr. Long, Lillian and Mostlee had found their way to the front of the crowd, close to the shore, a bit away from the others, but not as far off as the gazebo where Evelyn still sulked.

"Beautiful day, isn't it?" Dr. Long said as he breathed in deeply the fresh air, put one hand on his hip and the other atop his head to keep his hat from blowing off in a sudden breeze off the lake. There was still a crisp bite to the air despite the abundant sunshine. He turned and saw the Kydds approaching. "Sally! Tyrus! So wonderful to see you. I miss having you around the house."

Sally smiled politely as they sauntered up to the three while Tyrus made a quick furtive look over to Mostlee who winked at him, complicit in the secret about their home invasions.

"I'm going to get some lemonade, would you like some, Dr. Long?" Sally asked the doctor graciously.

"I am a bit parched, than you so much, my dear." He turned to Lillian who had been staring off at the lake with her back half-turned. "Lemonade, darling?"

Lillian turned around, even more stunning up close and responded with a smile and a shake of her head "no."

"I'll be right back," Sally said as she darted off leaving Tyrus alone with them.

Lillian approached him brazenly and leaned over and placed her hands on Tyrus' cheeks. He was a bit taken aback and feared she was about to pinch them, but she caressed only and smiled. Her teeth were gleaming white and she had her daughter's same big eyes, but her skin was lighter, a creamy caramel, and she smelled intoxicatingly of flowers and sweets. "Dear child, you must be my Mostlee's friend she has been telling me so much about." She stood up straight and looked him over, her hands now on her hips.

"You can talk?" Tyrus blurted out.

Mostlee giggled.

Lillian laughed. "Of course I can speak! What silly stories did Mostlee tell you about me?"

"Only that you're beautiful, Mama," Mostlee chimed in as she sprinted over to Tyrus and stood uncomfortably close to him.

"Is your mother here?" Dr. Long interrupted.

"Yes, sir," Tyrus said. "Here she comes now." He pointed to his mother approaching from the gazebo.

"Why don't you children run along and play now?" Lillian suggested as she turned and gave Evelyn the once-over with her eyes. She held her hand to her forehead like a salute to shield her eyes from the sun.

Tyrus wanted to stay, but Mostlee took his hand and led him away to the shade of the trees on the fringes of the grounds...away from the other children...away from everyone. He turned back to get a quick glimpse of his mother, her smile forced and her body tense, as she was introduced to Lillian Weathers. There seemed to him then to be an infinite sadness inside his mother, and he wasn't sure if there would ever be anything to take it away. Mostlee had let go of his hand now, and he walked under the shade of the great trees to the edge of the lake. He picked up a small stone off the ground and skipped it out across the water. The stone danced atop the ripples and then finally sank to the bottom of the lake like his feelings.

"My brother taught me how to do that," he said wistfully.

Mostlee walked over to him, took hold of his arm and rested her head on his shoulder. "Mama and I moved into Dr. Long's house," she said.

Tyrus sighed. His eyes were itchy from the pollen swirling about the hills. He thought of Myra Long and Edison. He brushed a sniffle away from his nose with the back of his free hand. He and Mostlee just stood there quietly, solemnly. Closer.

EPISODE TWELVE – THE STUFF IS HERE

"This is real music," Mostlee said as she lowered the black disk onto Dr. Long's Victrola. Upon the music starting, Mostlee began doing a little dance, pointing her right index finger up in the air and wiggling it as she moved her feet and slowly turned her body in a circle timed to the music. She smiled and tried to hold back a laugh when her eyes met Tyrus, who stood there sullenly.

"If I can't sell it, I'll keep sittin' on it," the woman on the record sang.

"C'mon, boy, tap your feet at least," Mostlee said to him, her head bobbing and her hips shaking to the music.

Tyrus blushed. He didn't know what the woman on the record meant, but it seemed wrong.

"Oh, you're no fun," Mostlee said. "Ain't you ever heard REAL music before?"

"Who is this?"

"Georgia White."

It was June. Mostlee and her mother were now comfortably and permanently ensconced in Dr. Long's house. Today, the mailman delivered a package from the city, a large box full of all of Lillian Weathers' records along with a few new ones courtesy of her friends back in Harlem. Mostlee tore into it recklessly after she and Tyrus saw it sitting up on the porch as they approached from their walk home from school that day. It was unseasonably hot. School would be out for summer soon.

"I'm thirsty." Tyrus said.

"Well go pour yourself some lemonade then, see if I care." Mostlee dismissed him, still wrapped in her little dance, enraptured by the music. But then she had one of her split-second changes of heart. "Wait! Better yet...let's driiiiiink..." She looked around the room, Dr. Long's study, and her eyes honed in on the bottles of liquor atop the bureau against the wall. "THIS!" She leapt for a fancy lookin' bottle that looked like a giant bottle of perfume to Tyrus. Inside was an amber liquid. She turned to Tyrus. "Get us some glasses, will ya?"

"I don't know about this," he whined. "I don't think Dr. Long will be happy if he finds out we tasted his..."

"Horace won't mind, silly! And we're not gonna just taste...we're gonna drink!"

She ran back over to the Victrola and switched records, pulling another one out of the big box still half-wrapped in brown packaging paper and that she had Tyrus lug into the study after she tore into it on the porch moments ago.

"Was I drunk? Was I happy? And did my mom give me hell." Georgia White proclaimed sweetly on the scratchy record.

"You're mom will give us hell if she finds out," Tyrus offered, slowly getting into the music and suddenly relating.

"Go get us some glasses...and some ice already. Geeze!" Mostlee moved her body to the music. She wanted to mimic her mother, but there was still something awkward in her movements. She was till learning the ropes...still years from being a woman.

Tyrus disappeared and then came back a few minutes later carrying two glasses filled with ice, the type of glasses his mother and Dr. Long used to drink from on those long summer evenings out on the back porch. He placed them down on Dr. Long's desk.

Mostlee had already taken the cap off the bottle of amber liqueur and sauntered up to the desk with a devil-may-care attitude inspired by the music. She poured carefully into both glasses until the syrupy liquid covered the ice. She put the bottle down on the desk and picked up her glass and smiled at Tyrus.

"Cheers!" she said to him.

Tyrus took a deep breath and picked up his glass too. He said something, eager and natural, that he fondly recalled his father having said on many occasions. "Bottom's up!"

They toasted and then brought the glasses to their mouths. Mostlee sniffed the liqueur, like almond syrup, before taking just a sip. Meanwhile, Tyrus threw his all the way back in a few big gulps, barely tasting what made its way quickly down his throat that created a cold burning sensation. It's how his brother had taught him to take medicine. He winced and made a sour face, then shook his head as if he was drying out his hair after a swim.

Mostlee giggled and took another sip. "You like it?"

"It's terrible!" Tyrus cried.

"Let's dance!"

They put their glasses down on the desk and Mostlee stretched her arm out to Tyrus who took her by the hand. He didn't even know how to dance, but they swung around childishly and laughed and stretched out their arms and pulled their bodies in closer and then farther away again and again. After the song ended Mostlee poured him another drink, which he downed in the same fashion as the first, while she continued to sip from her original pour. She went over to the record player and put on another song. It was the fastest one yet.

"*Close the windows and lock the door. Take the rug up off the floor. Hey, hey, let's all get gay. The stuff is here.*" Georgia White sang in gloriously mellow excitement.

"What stuff?" Tyrus asked with a giggle, his face flushed now and sweat starting to form around his collarbone.

"This stuff!" Mostlee said raising her glass. "Hey, let's get the rug up off the floor!"

They hurriedly got down on their knees at the edge of the area rug and began to roll it until they uncovered the hardwood floor beneath it. They stood up and kicked off their shoes and then began sliding from one end of the floor to the other, the rolled up rug on one end and Dr. Long's big comfy leather chair on the other end as their buffers. They slid, grabbed at each other, pushed each other, swung around, danced and laughed until Tyrus slid right across the entire floor in his socks and fell into the big chair. Mostlee leapt across the floor and collapsed into the chair half-on top of him. He pushed her off him, both of them laughing uncontrollably and now snug together in the chair.

Tyrus felt his heart racing and his whole body was flushed with warmth. They both calmed down a bit curled up in the chair with Mostlee snuggling up against him. It was too hot, he thought to himself, but he couldn't push her off and her head rested on his shoulder. He felt butterflies in his stomach, fluttering at first, and then furious and tumultuous as if he was going to be sick. His head felt as if it could float away from his body.

"I'm tired," Mostlee cooed.

Tyrus breathed heavily, in and out. His eyelids grew heavy as his heart started to slow and his stomach settle. Mostlee cozied up against him, her warm breath on his collar. They fell asleep wrapped in the music, the buzz and the lazy afternoon heat.

This dream started with just a feeling...a feeling that his mother was gone. He wasn't sure if she was dead. Just gone. And he saw his father as an old man struggling up a tall flight of brick stairs, holding his feeble body against the railing, careful not to slip on the brightly colored fallen leaves draping over everything in sight.

Tyrus was standing at the foot of the steps by the lake, and he felt cold watching his father struggle from one step to the next. Looking up there were shocks of yellow and orange and amber on the trees looming down on them. A fierce wind blew in from the lake and Tyrus folded his arms tightly in over his chest, shivering from the cold. A loud, distant rumble came from the hills behind him. It almost sound like a growl...or a lion's roar. He smelled fried chicken.

Tyrus opened his eyes and sat up. He found himself lying atop the covers on the bed in Dr. Long's spare room where he had taken many naps as a little boy. It had been a long time since someone had carried him up to bed in this house. There was still a bit of dim light coming in through the windows. Across the hall he could see into Myra's old room where Mostlee was asleep atop the bed covers. He looked at the bottoms of his socks; they were filthy and grey. He looked down over the bedside and saw his shoes neatly placed on the floor. The smell of chicken frying in the pan wafted up the stairs and into the dusk soaked room. His stomach growled. He felt famished.

Tyrus hopped off the bed and slipped on his shoes. He slowly walked down the stairs suddenly remembering what trouble they got into this afternoon and fearing what retribution might be waiting for him down there. He stealthily glanced into the study, but saw no one there and the rug carefully put back into place. He walked through the living room and dining room and then stood at the threshold to the kitchen where Lillian Weathers, dressed down and in an apron, busied herself at the stove flipping over the golden brown chicken in the pan. He felt nervous as this was his first one-on-one encounter with Mostlee's mother.

Lillian must've sensed the boy's leering but cautious presence behind her. She turned around and smiled lightly at him. "Well, well, well..." she trailed off before returning her gaze to the stove and her back to Tyrus. "You don't have to worry. I won't tell Dr. Long that you got into his booze this afternoon." She motioned her hand to the half full glass on the counter, one of the same glasses they drank from this afternoon, filled with the same amber drink. "He won't notice anyways. I have a taste for the same stuff." She forked the chicken in the pan and carefully lifted it out of the grease and then let it rest on some paper towels. She put the fork down on the counter, turned off the burner, wiped her hands on her apron and turned around to face Tyrus again. She reached for the glass and brought it up casually for a sip. "So are you staying for dinner?"

"Yes, ma'am," Tyrus replied with his head down, still shamed by his behavior and the fact that he passed out and had to be carried like a baby upstairs for a nap.

"Doesn't your mother miss you?"

Tyrus shrugged his shoulders.

"No matter. We're always happy to have you." The window above the sink behind her was open. It overlooked the back porch, and the sound of wood beams banging against each other could be heard. Lillian rolled her eyes. "Was HE here when you two got home from school?"

"Who?"

"The man Dr. Long hired to fix the porch."

"I don't remember. I don't think so."

The two of them of made their way to the back door and peered out through the screen at the commotion out back. The man was stacking wooden beams at the foot of the porch. Lillian was still holding her glass, and it was at Tyrus' nose level as he stood beside her. The sweet pungency of the liquor was enough to make him sick. He still felt a little foggy and couldn't really make out the features of the man through the screen. Music from the other room filtered out into the hall and through the screen into the outside world. A sad angry man wailed about how his woman should *"Do like the millionaires do"* and put herself on the market..."*and make a million too."* The slow horns and cadenced strings told of something foreboding...forbidden.

"It's going to be a hot one this year," Lillian remarked into the still air, seemingly at no one at all, as if she was unaware of the child by her side. "Guess he thinks it's smarter to do work at twilight. Fool's gonna go blind or hammer a nail right into his hand."

The man continued to work in the encroaching darkness unaware of the people watching him through the screen door. And then something – or better yet, the absence of something – revealed itself to the onlookers. Tyrus squinted to get a better look lest his eyes were deceiving him.

"Would you look at that?" Lillian gushed in a hushed tone, her free hand suddenly on Tyrus' shoulder, her delicate fingers trembling like startled dancers above his collar bone and at the edge of his neck. "Ain't never seen that before. A one-handed carpenter."

And that sad, spooky music spilling out into the twilight seemed to take flight and fill the hills. Back at the Kydd house, on guard at the top of the front porch steps Sue waited with forlorn conviction for her boy to come wandering down the road. Meanwhile, her owner peered out into the twilight from behind the screen door. Evelyn sighed at the sight of her son's bike, seemingly abandoned and collecting dust leaning against the house. Behind her in the kitchen her daughter cooked dinner, but it was otherwise an empty house.

Soon, though, the music knew all that hollow dusk would be filled with a darkness that would make all souls nostalgic for this empty space.

PART THREE: FIRE AND DARKNESS

EPISODE THIRTEEN – THE MOUND

J oshua Bloomfield was born in 1899 in some nameless town on the border of New York and Vermont. His mother said it was in the dead of winter, but later when they lived in the swamps of New Orleans, she claimed he was born at the height of summer – when the world was hot and gold and ill-tempered. Memories of his early childhood were vague. He had some sense of Montreal – his mother always following the trail of his father – of a language neither he nor his mother spoke or ever cared to learn – of cold winters and sleeping by the fireplace alone. When he was seven he remembered an endless train ride all the way down to Louisiana, which for him at the time seemed like the end of the world where one's feet sank into the marshes and bodies were swept away into that great gulf of water at the end of which he imagined a waterfall cascading into the darkness of empty space.

Joshua's mother was the cook at a bordello in Storyville. From the time he was seven until he was twelve they shared a house on the outskirts of the city – more like a shanty – with a Haitian gravedigger who toiled away in the city's only cemetery where they still buried people six-feet under. Joshua remembered that old fat whore who took up to being his nanny telling him stories of how in the olden days bodies and coffins would wash up into the streets any time there was a flood, so they started burying the dead above ground in tiny little stone monuments and mausoleums.

But this gravedigger dug against the tide. "Like ovens," the Haitian would say to him. "Burn you up inside. Like hell. I bury people in the ground."

"How do they stay down? Not wash up in the floods?" Joshua would ask him.

"You weigh them down. With rocks and stones."

The Haitian played baseball, and he taught Joshua how to pitch after watching him throw punches in a brawl with some neighborhood street urchins over his mother's honor. At night the Haitian would skim dirt off the tops of fresh graves and bring it back to their yard in a wheelbarrow. In back of the house he used the soil to build a pitching mound atop which Joshua practiced after the sun went down, pounding pitches against an old tin roof propped up against the fence, the rhythmic and increasingly powerful sound of the tattered balls hitting the malleable tin in the hot, humid stank of summer nights. In a normal neighborhood it would've kept folks up at night, but in their neighborhood most were plying their trades into the wee hours of the evening leaving Joshua alone with his thoughts, his mound and his developing strength.

His life was harsh but predictable and routine then. He found comfort in that. He found comfort, too, in the new girls who took up shop in the bordello, always sweet smelling and dressed in the finest French lingerie, like little painted porcelain dolls.   His muscles, stamina and confidence made him appear older than he was, and the girls were happy to use him for practice when they arrived. He was maybe eleven when they first took notice of him in that way, and he was all too eager to oblige them. He learned as much about sex from them as he did about baseball from the Haitian, and by age twelve those were the only two things that mattered to him. He drank, smoke and brawled, too – but those were just for fun. He was serious about the other two things.

One night he came stumbling home drunk from the bordello to find the Haitian beating his mother. He took a knife and stuck it deep into the back of the Haitian, between his ribs, a pool of thick blood quickly turning the Haitian's white shirt red. The Haitian was even drunker than Joshua and he stumbled away from Joshua's battered and bloodied mother awkwardly grasping for the knife in his back, blood dripping all over the carpet.

"Everything you know, boy, I taught you!" the Haitian cried out, his eyes white, hot and bulging.

"You're not my father," Joshua said calmly, the anger like steam in a teapot already released through that quick thrust of the knife into the Haitian's flesh moments ago.

"When you find your father, and you do this to him, you'll think of me."

"Get out of here or I'll cut your throat."

The Haitian, crippled and bleeding, wandered hopelessly out into the night. Days later his body was found in a gutter a few miles away with his throat slit. A man with a knife in his back apparently made for easy prey, especially with so many enemies abound.

A few months later Joshua's mother died of syphilis, but not before telling her son that she had received word that his father was in New York, near the Canadian border. "You should find him," she said. "His name is Philip Bourget. Tell him about me."

He remembered in that moment something from his early childhood – when they must've still lived somewhere in New York. "There's a great waterfall near here," his mother whispered to him, "And at night if you listen closely when all else is quite, you can hear it." The roaring of the rushing water, he thought, racing to flow over the edge of the cliff...into nothingness. He thought up there must be the other end of the world. But all he could hear at night were the sounds of baseballs hitting the tin roof...the constant, rhythmic pounding of each pitch...getting stronger and stronger. And he knew that sound would drive him north. To Niagra maybe? His quest would be sprawling. He would learn patience.

That's when Joshua started walking. And hopping trains. And taking up odd jobs where he could as he made his way north. He was serious, but charming, and was always able to pass for older than he was. He cut down on the drinking and smoking and brawling...and for the most part, even the whoring, though some gals were just asking for it, and he had to oblige the ladies where and when he could. He was focused on his game and his plan. At fifteen he started joining local teams wherever he laid down camp. He was always able to blow them away with his fastball. Nobody asked where he came from after they saw him pitch. Most towns were happy to have him, and later on many had lost their young men and star players to the draft. But Joshua Bloomfield was able to avoid the Great War by never staying in one place for too long – he had no birth certificate, no home – he might as well have been a ghost. His goal was to eventually get invited to join a barnstorming league, his travel paid for, his search honed in on specific points on the map along the way. He thought he could track down his father this way. All he had was a name and a few sorry letters from old acquaintances of his mother – but he knew his father was up there somewhere – he could sense it. And at night, as he got closer north, he began to imagine the roaring of the rushing water. He could sense the darkness. And he wanted to push his father into it. He believed in a kind of fate. And his father's was to fall into the darkness.

In the summer of 1919, he found himself in Albany, New York where he played with Samuel Kydd and he met Evelyn Temple. He was startled by her precociousness, but he found something morbidly nostalgic in her aggressive chattiness that reminded him of the young girls at the bordello who first showed him the ways of the world. During that summer, he took no care with her innocence. They fucked. It was glorious. But it was primal, and his intention was to toss her aside just as those young girls had tossed him aside in his youth when they then went on to please paying customers.

That kind of fate that he believed in – brought him to Syracuse in the summer of 1920, and there, lo and behold, was the little girl he tossed away – Evelyn, now a wife and mother, a Kydd. In just one short year she had changed so much. She was even more alluring now, and the trysts that followed were of a romantic sort, forbidden and carried out with great planning, caution and care. On some nights when Evelyn was able to leave the baby with Odette, and Paul and Samuel were on a late-night job, Joshua would drive her out to the lake, and they would just lay there on a blanket in the cool grass, the autumn wind caressing their skin in the calm twilight – crickets serenading them with their last breaths before the chill settled in. His hands would run through her black hair, and he would read to her from the book of ghost stories that old fat whore had given him when he was seven and lived in New Orleans. The whore used the ghost stories to teach him how to read. He was gentle to Evelyn then...gentle like that long dead whore was to him when he was alone and scared and a little boy. But when he ran his fingers over her skin, she shivered, and he wasn't sure if it was his touch or the stories that chilled her.

Joshua saw it as fate, too, that she was married to Samuel, for it was Samuel and his friend Paul who had grand dreams of bringing whisky down across the Canadian border. He knew it was there his father must have been. And when the name first crossed Paul's lips...Phillip Bourget...Joshua did not believe in coincidences.

Though she knew nothing of his past and his plan, Evelyn did everything to dissuade him from getting involved in that "dirty business" with Samuel and Paul.

"It's okay for your husband to do this, but not your lover?" Joshua asked her while they lay in bed in his cheap hotel room after lovemaking

"But you have a talent – a gift – another way to make a living," she pleaded with him. "The Yankees will have scouts in Binghamton, and if you don't go with the team, you'll miss your shot."

He imagined that she had some crazy notion of him going to the Major Leagues – and then maybe she would divorce Samuel and marry him. But she didn't understand. Playing ball had always just been a means to an end.

Joshua went full in with Samuel and Paul on the deal, and they met with Old Man Bourget in Canada, just across the border at a brawly bar where brawny loggers drank their troubles away. When Samuel and Paul had gone out back to piss, Joshua had his moment. He asked Philip Bourget if he had known his mother. The old man looked at him strangely, and when their eyes met, Joshua could not see any of himself in him.

In his phlegmy French accent, Bourget said with a smirk, "Mademoiselle Bloomfield is probably the type of woman everyone here knows." And he laughed, and then slapped Joshua on the shoulder while sloppily downing his mug of beer. "Oh, now, mon fils, no sense of humor?"

Joshua did not smile. He pulled out from his coat pocket a picture of his mother, from when they first moved to New Orleans, when she was still young and somewhat beautiful and had no time for her boy, whom she would leave with the fat whore with the penchant for ghost stories.

The old man regarded the yellow photograph and then pushed it away. "See, she was a whore?"

"She was a COOK."

"So many years ago. Who is to know?"

But Joshua could tell by the way that Bourget looked at the photo, the recognition in his eyes, the furrow of his brow, that he knew her at one time. Knew her well. Joshua asked, "Paul is a relation of yours?"

The old man snorted. "How do you say....allegedly?"

And Joshua put it in his mind that he would one day kill all three of them.

In the row boat that night sat the old man at the stern, Samuel in front of him, the cases of whiskey in the middle, then Joshua and Paul at the bow. It was colder than they had expected. The men could see their breath before them, but the generous spirits they enjoyed before loading the boat warmed them. Everything was crisp and dark and crystal clear like the waters of the lake...only their cadenced breaths fogging any line of sight. As they approached the wooded shore line and the shallows, the boat rocked and the two men in the rear stood up. There was a commotion, and before Paul could steady the boat and Joshua stand up to see what had happened, there was a splash.

Old Man Bourget had fallen overboard, and he had landed in the shallows on his back with his head dashed against the rocks. His blood quickly muddied the clear water.

"Jesus Christ," Samuel muttered while inhaling through his nose. "I thought he pulled a knife," he said on exhale through his mouth.

Paul, the diplomat, stepped out in the shallows and regarded the old man, lifeless under just a few inches of water. "It was an accident. The old man was drunk." He lit a cigarette.

Instinctively Samuel and Joshua hopped out of the boat and helped Paul steer it to the shore line about ten feet away. On the other side of the brush along the shore was a dirt road and Paul's car. Joshua had the sinking feeling that there was some other plan...between Samuel and Paul. He turned around to get one last glimpse of the old man...maybe his old man...an old man he thought only he had the right to kill. He had been robbed of his fate. Stupid Samuel. An accident.

The men quickly and silently unloaded the boat's cargo into the back of the car.

Samuel was noticeably shaken. "What are we going to do about the body?" he asked staring out beyond the boat at the dark corpse lying in the shallows, the waves gently lapping up over it. "I know, I know, I'll tie some rocks to it...take it out in the boat...somewhere deeper."

"You weigh them down," the Haitian's voice rattled in Joshua's skull.

Paul and Joshua leaned against the side of Paul's car, sharing a cigarette, gazing out over the shore and into the phantom waters of the lake. Samuel picked up some rocks and scurried out into the shallows back to the boat where he dumped his load.

"Samuel...here!" Paul tossed him some rope he had grabbed from the back seat. The distance was too far. It landed in the water. Samuel frantically grabbed for it, and then lobbed it into the boat. He began to struggle with the body. "Just hop in and drag it out with you," Paul barked at him, like an impatient father giving direction to a stupid child.

"Shouldn't we help him?" Joshua asked.

"His accident...his mess. We go and take this to the club."

Joshua and Paul got in the car leaving Samuel behind. Paul didn't turn on his headlights until they got to the main road.

"Why would the old man pull a knife on us?" Joshua wondered aloud.

"Pfphhh..." Paul smiled. "Who knows? Maybe he thought we were going to try and take his stash?"

"His stash?"

"You heard the stories, no? Old Man Bourget's secret stash? Tall tales. You know."

"Philip Bourget was my father."

Paul took his eyes off the road for a shocked moment to look at Joshua who remained cold and firm, staring ahead at the dark macadam unfolding before them. "You don't say?"

"If that old man left any money behind, by rights it would belong to me."

"Like I said...tall tales. We got this stash...liquid gold, eh? And maybe if Samuel is any smart he'll pick up a few more cases and the money we paid Bourget for this load on his way back before anyone shows up at Bourget's cabin. Why not play ball? This is no life for you. You take your share and run. You take Samuel's wife and run." He started to laugh.

"How far is Niagra Falls from here?" Joshua had a notion to throw baby Edison into the raging water. Samuel had robbed him of his chance to kill his father, now he wanted the chance to rob Samuel of his fatherhood.

"You are a strange one." Paul shook his head. "If Bourget was your father...then that makes us...what...cousins? It's dangerous to do business with family."

In the morning, Joshua would be the only one left in Syracuse. And Bourget's men came looking for him when they couldn't find Samuel or Paul. Apparently more was missing than just the money they paid him and the whiskey. He realized soon his biggest mistake was not killing all three of them out there on the lake, though he regretted, too, not fleeing the night before. He would pay for this mistake with his left hand. Taking away a man's livelihood was more pleasing to the Bourget gang than taking his life.

But no one had counted on Joshua Bloomfield's patience. And just like he had found Philip Bourget...one day he would find Paul...and Samuel...and then he would take what was rightfully his. And like the rhythmic sounds of his pitching, like the mound created from the restless soil skimmed from the top of human remains, like the blood pooling on a dying Haitian's shirt or in the glimmering water of a lake in the hills, like corpses not properly weighted down bobbing to the top in flood waters...so rose the darkness inside him that he imagined devouring the entire world.

EPISODE FOURTEEN – THE CARPENTER

Odette couldn't stop talking before he killed her. Sitting in the car like that, stopped on the side of the road, on that hill overlooking...was it Pittsburgh? As if they were a newly married couple on vacation...driving cross country, taking in the sights, innocent. It was easy to find her after killing Paul in Chicago. And here they were, just a few days later on the run together.

"The way I see it," she said. "You did me a favor...taking care of Paul like that. He always had been such a beast of a man." She talked in a peppery, loose way. He had recalled her having a harsh French accent when they all lived together in Syracuse. But that had all faded away...or maybe it had just been put-on. Like she was an actress. A lousy one. She sounded more ignorant now. "But you can't be serious about wanting to track down Evelyn and Samuel. Oh, if I could just see them now...she always had been so beautiful. People used to call me a handsome woman. Can you believe that? *Handsome!*" And Joshua just wanted to wrap his fingers around her thick, mannish neck...but could he get them all the way around? Could he squeeze the life out of her? This handsome woman. "But Evelyn...well, you know. Please...oh please." She turned to him misty eyed and red cheeked and placed her hands atop his one hand. "Please just leave her be...leave them be. They've got two children now...another on the way. They're doing nobody any harm. Can't you...can't we...just go about our lives...together...and forget about them?"

Joshua had been staring forward gazing down at the lights of the city below, but now he was turned to her, looking her in the eyes, struck by what she had said. She pulled her hands away suddenly. "I thought you hadn't seen or heard from them since Syracuse?" he said to her.

"Oh, Joshua...you have no idea how close you were. I hadn't seen them...and then...it was like fate, you know...we were passing through Chicago...and there she was...in a diner by the train tracks...pregnant...and...and..." she trailed off suddenly regretting what she had said.

"I need some air." Joshua stepped out of the car. He waited a moment before stepping around the back of the car and to the passenger's side. He opened the door and dragged Odette out by her hair. Her French accent was suddenly back, "Please, Joshua, I loved her! So did you, no? Please! Do not do this!" He took her to the edge of the hill and spun her around to face him.

"Are they still in Chicago?"

Her face was swollen and streaming with tears while her hands folded and pleaded with him as if bounded in prayer. "I do not know. Please, Joshua...we can find them together."

Joshua's knife was drawn and he jabbed it quickly into her chest, just below her left breast. It was quick, deep, in and out. He pushed her over the edge. He was surprised by how quiet her body was tumbling through the brush...tumbling and tumbling down until out of sight.

Chicago had been the closest he had been to them...until now. Nearly ten years later...Samuel's body left behind in the shallows of the James River outside of Richmond. And now he was on a train headed into New York where he was certain to find Evelyn.

When he arrived in Milton by bus at the end of March, snow still covered the ground. He was directed to a boarding house...a hotel some called it...a cozy place on a cozy street. Reasonably priced. He asked the proprietor where a man might find work.

"You come up here from the city?" the man asked. He was middle-aged, balding, wore suspenders but chewed gum like a kid.

"I'm from all over," Joshua replied.

The man eyed him suspiciously, though he hadn't thought anything of it when Joshua paid him four week's advance on rent just moments ago. "Naw, you don't look like one them tent city folks. Sometimes they find their way up here lookin' for work without one cent on 'em. Thinkin' they can just squat out by the lake. We don't take too kindly to that."

"I just go where the work takes me."

"I can abide by that. Well, ice harvesting season's done past...can't imagine you could've done that with your...condition and all. Plus there was a bad accident out there last month. Poor kid. Cracked his head right open. Died a few weeks later. Got people all jittery about the whole operation, ya know? Not exactly sure what kind of labor you can...*handle?*"

"I can handle my own just fine."

"Well, when the thaw starts, there's always folks lookin' to fix up their houses for the summer. I don't suppose you're a carpenter?"

"I've tried my hand at everything."

The man smirked, thinking it a pun, but Joshua just stood there stone-faced, leaning on the front desk gazing out the front door, a tooth-pick in this mouth, his body turned away as if he wasn't even talking to the man behind the desk.

"Well, I suppose someone new in town might get to know some folks through church. Just a stone's throw from here. You could meet some fine people on Sunday. People who might need...a *handy man.*" He chewed his gum and couldn't help but smirk some more.

"I don't suppose you know where a man might get a drink around here?"

"Just a stone's throw from the church. Head out here and make a left, you can't miss it. You could make friends there too."

"Thanks for the advice. I could sure use a drink."

"Nectar of the gods...I can abide by that, too. Welcome to Milton."

Joshua tipped his cap, placed his toothpick on the counter and marched out the door. He made no small talk at the tavern. He just listened. Maybe someone would say her name. He wondered if these men knew her. Knew her at all. *Knew her like that.* Evelyn. Fate had brought him here to her. But he would be patient. Let things happen as they may. He had waited this long already.

He went to church on Sundays. He sat in the back. He sang not the hymns. He appeared pensive. "A thoughtful man," he heard the old ladies chatter about him as they walked by on their way to their reserved seats in the front pews. He asked some of the other men in the back about work. They knew of none, but if he was patient, there might be something soon after the thaw.

He walked around town. He got to know it. Main Street. The road into Fenimore. The rambling snake of macadam around the lake. One day he walked it. Nine miles around. In the cold. The cemetery on Haydon Hill. The Temple name on a crypt. Eveyln's maiden name. Her name back when he just fucked her. Before she married Samuel. There was still ice out there in April. You could row out to it if you wanted. He pictured that boy from the picture on the train...Myra's picture...of Evelyn's boy...Edison. He pictured him sprawled out there on the ice. The blood from his head steaming in the cold air. He thawed his bones at the tavern.

"Wasn't that kid a Temple?" a drunk man asked his friend.

"Naw, he was a Kydd. The kid was a Kydd."

"Who the hell are the Kydds?"

"They're the Temples," another man chimed in.

"The kid's mother used to run that lunch counter in Fenimore. She was a pretty little number. Husband never around."

"You mean that's the same Kydd?"

"She's a Temple...that Kydd lady. Born a Temple. But bad luck musta struck her when she became a Kydd."

They were like a chorus.

"Didn't that Long girl work at the lunch counter?"

"Mmmm...now there was a pretty little number. Fancy girl. Ran off to New York City. Poor Doc Long."

"Poor Doc Long! Ha! I heard he had that Kydd lady. He was more of a husband to her than that no-good souse of a husband. Where the hell has that Kydd fella been anyhow? I'm not sure I would even know him to look at him." Suddenly they all stared over Joshua's way. "Hell, this stranger could be him for all I know anymore!"

"Rest assured, fellas," Joshua said while raising his glass of beer, "I ain't the man you're lookin' for."

"I don't even know who we're talkin' about no more. But that poor kid. Still can't get over that. Good ballplayer, too. That poor Kydd kid."

"To the kid!" Joshua held his glass in the air still. They all did, and then they all took a slug in unison.

"Did you know the kid?" one of them asked.

"No." Joshua slipped his quarters on the counter and then took his leave.

Joshua stood frozen outside the tavern underneath the streetlight. Darkness was all around him, and he held onto the lamppost, breathless, lest he lose all his composure right there. He walked back to the hotel and into the fire-lit warmth of the front sitting room. The proprietor was there, not chewing gum like he did all day, but enjoying a cigar, a newspaper freshly read and neatly folded on his lap.

"You look like you're in quite a way," he said kindly. "Have a seat by the fire. Enjoy a cigar. On the house."

Joshua was afraid if he tried the steps he would fall over. The cigar would settle his stomach. He took a seat in the parlor. The man lit a cigar and handed it to Joshua. He took a few hearty puffs and relaxed. He felt like he could fall asleep right there. A blast of cold air came in as a pretty, light-skinned colored woman and her young daughter passed through the front door. They had clothes fancier than Joshua was used to seeing on colored people. The little one, in braids, stopped at the foot of the step and looked on the men in the parlor.

"Good evening, gentlemen," she curtsied flippantly and smiled.

The proprietor smiled back at her. "There's my sugar!" Her mother shooed her upstairs.

"Where's that uppity colored lady work?" Joshua asked the man.

"Here and there I suppose. Cleaning woman. Nice people. Daughter told me once in secret she used to be a jazz singer. Sure looks like it could be true. God knows what she's doing here cleaning doctors' houses. Probably runnin' from her old man. And mind what you say. We all get along just fine up here." He regarded Joshua quizzically. "You from down South?"

"I told you I'm from all over." Joshua slouched in the chair and closed his eyes, the cigar dangling from his mouth.

"Though there is plenty of gossip about her and Doc Long. Spends an awful lot of time cleaning *his* house...if you catch my drift."

Joshua opened one eye. "You don't say?"

The two men sat in silence for the rest of the evening, finishing their cigars.

The next day Joshua began following the colored woman on her rounds, careful in his stalking. She had three houses on her route. The last house was in Fenimore. And it was there she stayed until she came back to the hotel at night. This must've been Dr. Long's house. After a week, she stopped going to the other houses and just went to this one. Her daughter starting coming to this house, too, after school he supposed. And she would sometimes have a little friend, a white boy. He watched them from afar, not able to get a close look. He wondered if this was Dr. Long's son, though he was puzzled why he hadn't seen him before this became the cleaning woman's exclusive job.

One night in May he had supper at a small diner down the road by the stoplight. He walked back down to Dr. Long's house in the twilight to see if the colored woman and her daughter were still there. Just as he approached, the kids came galloping down the steps of the front porch. Joshua casually stepped off the sidewalk and behind a hedge a few houses down. The children passed. Then he heard the woman and Dr. Long come out of the house. They were smiling and laughing.

"It's been so long since I've been to a picture show," he heard her say. "Such a treat."

They hopped into Dr. Long's car and drove off. This was Joshua's chance. An empty house. He slipped in comfortably through the front door. The lights were still on. He saw the pictures in the living room. Evelyn. Edison. The good doctor. A little girl. What had Samuel said her name was? Sally. And then he recognized the youngest boy as the little friend of the colored girl. Tyrus. He had his father's same sly smile. And the beautiful young woman he meant to strangle on the train. Myra. It felt suffocating inside the house. He stepped back out onto the porch into the darkening twilight. He breathed in the fresh spring mountain air and made his way up the sidewalk to the stoplight.

At the corner under the light, Joshua saw the two children. They were holding hands innocently and standing on the curb. The little girl pecked the boy on the cheek. They let go of each other's hands and the little girl made her way down the sidewalk towards Joshua while the boy crossed the street and headed towards Milton. Joshua tipped the brim of his hat low so as to shadow the top half of his face, but the little girl looked up at him as they brushed past anyways, recognizing him perhaps from the hotel where they both once stayed. Joshua didn't want to lose sight of Tyrus Kydd in the encroaching night.

The streetlights of the quaint little town guided his way. He kept pace, three lamps behind so as not to let the child sense he was being followed. There were a few others out walking babies or sweethearts, heading down other streets, but it was otherwise eerily silent. A chill was settling in. The little boy stuck his hands deep inside his shorts' pockets and his body clenched up as the cooling breeze came down from the hills. Just the sound of the boy's shoes on the pavement, the brisk movement from the darkness between the lamps into the next light. Joshua walked lightly, timing his steps with the boy's so that the sounds seemed as one...or as echoes against the hills...the boy still unsuspecting he was being followed.

The walk was long. Eventually the child turned down an unlit side street off the main road and began an ascent up a dirt path into a hillside lit by the warmth of two farm houses separated by a rambling fence. This was the boy's home. This was Tyrus' Kydd's home. This was where his mother Evelyn could be found. It was like something out of a child's fairytale...everything nestled so peacefully into the hillside, safe from the darkness below. Joshua stood at the foot of the path at the bottom of the hill, the ink of night blotting out his figure. Halfway up the hill, the boy looked back pensively to see if anyone had been behind him, but it was too dark to see anything down on the road. As he stepped up onto the porch a light came on and the front door opened. Through the screen door Joshua caught a glimpse of her...the long dark hair...a modest but pretty dress...eyes briefly glancing out into the darkness down the hill. The screen door opened and in the boy crept and disappeared behind the woman into the warm light.

Joshua stood frozen as Evelyn stared out into the night. He suddenly felt a presence behind him...a menacing growl. He glanced over and saw a border collie bitch standing her guard, bearing her teeth. She let out a quick, sharp bark between the growling.

"Sue!" Evelyn shouted out into the darkness. "Get in here now!"

The dog barked again and then charged up the hill to the porch and was shooed in through the door. The door closed and the light went out.

That Sunday Dr. Long showed up to church looking for a carpenter. "The place is flush with them," the old biddies laughed. "So good to see you, Dr. Long. You should come by more often."

After the sermon, as the congregation exited, Dr. Long took up to negotiations with the men who normally gathered in the back with Joshua. Patiently he waited until the crowd dissipated, and then approached Dr. Long as the doctor was heading back towards his car.

"I heard what those other men were offering," he said to the doctor while tipping his cap to him. "I got but one hand, but I make do. I might take a little longer, but I'll fix that porch of yours for half what they would charge you."

Dr. Long looked Joshua over. "You from around here?"

"Just lately, Doc, but those old ladies will vouch for me. Been coming to church a good month now. Just looking for some honest work. It's a nice town here, and I wouldn't mind staying on for more than a spell."

Dr. Long took him at his word, and before long Joshua was toiling away building a new fancy porch so the Doc and his pretty colored girl could enjoy their night caps in the coming summer evenings staring out at that beautiful lake. One day when he came over to start work early, he thought it was an empty house again, so he went inside to look at Edison's pictures once more. He found the little colored girl and Tyrus asleep in the doctor's chair in the study. They had taken to drink. He carried the girl up to bed first...into what he presumed had been Myra's room. And then he took the boy up and gently laid him down in the room across the hall. He stood in the doorway a good while, regarding the boy soundly sleeping. The boy had Samuel's coloring of hair and the eyes, but he had some of Evelyn's more refined facial features. Joshua couldn't help but think that when he was in Chicago tracking down Paul and Odette, he had been so close...he could've killed this child while he was in his mother's womb. Hell, he could kill him right now, his neck so small, one tight grip could choke the life from him before he had even the chance to wake.

But what really got Joshua thinking was how much this boy didn't look like Edison. No, he was surer of it now than ever. Edison looked like *his* father...not Samuel.

EPISODE FIFTEEN – TICK TOCK

Horace Long had a gold pocket watch on a gold chain that kept perfect time. It had been given to him by his wife's father after he had asked the man's permission for his daughter's hand in marriage. Horace intended to give it to the man who would eventually ask for Myra's hand, though with his free-spirited daughter off searching for adventures he wondered if that day would ever come and he would grow nervous and then sour watching the seconds tick away on his beautiful, shiny heirloom.

The Kydd boys had loved to see it when he pulled it out of his pocket when they were little, as if he was revealing to them a piece of stolen treasure...perhaps from a pirate ship or a bank robber's stash. He would dangle it over the child by the chain, holding it high in the air and the boy would jump up and down trying to grab it, his little eyes glistening at the sight of the gold. But as soon as each boy reached an age where they could easily snatch it from his hands, the pocket watch lost its luster. He had thought maybe he would give it to Edison as he was reaching an age when he would appreciate such a priceless piece handed down from man to son, but he never had the chance to before Edison died. And Tyrus was now in that in between age...rambunctious and indignant one moment...shy and combative the next...but mostly sullen. The watch had no appeal to him now.

And so whenever he looked at the watch and listened to the perfect measured ticking, it brought to mind sad thoughts of a daughter who might never marry, a dead boy he thought of as a son, and a foolish little boy who was now mimicking his own mistakes...slothful around the house, separating himself from Evelyn, falling in love with a colored girl. It became a wretched thing to him. And so he kept it hidden away in his desk in his study, the sound of his life slowing ticking away muffled in the darkness of a drawer full of old papers.

* * *

Time was slipping way too quickly for Joshua Bloomfield. Work on the porch was nearly complete. While he plotted how to insinuate himself back into Evelyn's life and find the money, he maneuvered a longer stay working at Dr. Long's house. The doctor was pleased with the work he did on the porch and agreed to let him stay on to do some landscaping and few other odds and ends. Today was the day he was to paint the porch, but it was too hot. It was a cloudless sun-scorched day, and gazing out onto the glimmering lake from the foot of the porch it was hard to imagine this vast body of water had been a solid block of ice earlier in the year. Joshua's eyes squinted painfully as he took off his hat to wipe the sweat from his brow. It was then that he heard the anxious, rhythmic sound of a rubber sole hitting wood at the top of the porch. Joshua turned around.

There sitting in a chair at the top of the porch was Tyrus Kydd swinging his right leg back and forth so that the sole of his shoe hit one of the wooden beams of the railing that Joshua had recently repaired. Joshua hadn't realized it was already that time of the afternoon when the children arrived home. The boy looked warm and tired and bored all at once.

"How long have you been sitting there watching me?" Joshua called up to him harshly.

Tyrus sat up, stopped swinging his leg and shrugged his shoulders.

"Where are your parents?"

"How do you know she's not my mother and Dr. Long my father?" Tyrus said, referring to Lillian Weathers.

"She's a Negro and you're a little lily white boy. Do I look like some sort of idiot to you?"

Tyrus appeared shocked and a little embarrassed. "No, sir."

Joshua stepped up onto the porch and hovered over Tyrus, his shadow all but eclipsing the boy's view. "Where are your parents?"

"My mother's at home."

"And your father?"

Tyrus paused and knotted his brow, searching for the appropriate answer. "I don't know. He could be..."

"He could be what?"

"Dead." He pulled his bare knees up to his chest, his shoes resting on the edge of the chair, his arms now folded around his legs. "I hope he's dead." He burrowed his face into his knees.

"That's a horrible thing for a son to say about his father." Joshua stepped away and then turned around to face the lake again and leaned against the railing.

Tyrus stood up and took his place next to Joshua leaning against the railing. His arms couldn't reach completely the top of the railing so he could fold them over the wood like Joshua did, so he just stood there with his fingers gripping the rail and his eyes high enough to ponder the still waters of the lake. Joshua could feel the warmth of the boy next to him. He looked down at him briefly and noticed the taut tendons of the child's neck.

"Did you ever wish your father was dead?" the boy asked.

Joshua noticed now more than ever the streak of Evelyn in this wretched child...the desire for physical closeness...the shameless inquisitiveness.

"I don't even know you, son," he said back to the boy sternly. "Didn't your mother ever tell you not to talk to strangers?"

"You're not a stranger. I've seen you working out here. I know you followed me home." He seemed to be looking up at Joshua and saying with his eyes, *it's okay, I'm as interested in you as you are in me.* "How did you lose your hand?" the boy blurted out.

Joshua clenched his teeth and placed his hat atop his head. "Someone thought I owed them a debt."

"What's a debt?"

"Someone thought I took their money." He turned to face the child and held his stump up to the boy's face. "This is what can happen when you hide from someone something that belongs to them."

"When you owe a debt?"

"Yes."

"I don't want to owe anybody anything."

Joshua was taken aback by the boy's easy declarations, as if he just went though life asking questions without consequence and soaked up all the answers to draw instant conclusions about how the world worked and how he wanted to fit into it. It brought an uneasy smile to his face. "You figure out how to do that, boy, and you'll be a free man."

"*Tyrus!*" Lillian Weathers called sharply from inside the house. "You leave that man alone and come inside now!"

Tyrus sighed and backed away from the railing. "Gotta run."

"Where's your little friend?"

"Mostlee's not feeling well. Came home and went right up to bed. I'm gonna go read her a story."

"A scary story?"

Tyrus paused and smiled, "Of course."

Joshua regarded him carefully, but didn't smile back. He tipped his hat and leaned his back against the railing. "Run along then."

The boy turned and ran into the house.

Joshua followed a few minutes later. Inside it was cooler and musty. The curtains had been drawn to keep out the sun and there was a large, noisy metal fan in the hallway blowing dust and air all over. Joshua stepped around the fan and stood in the cool threshold of the kitchen. Lillian was standing there in her comfy summer dress with her back against the sink fanning herself with one hand and holding a chilled highball glass half-filled with whiskey and melting ice in the other. She smiled lazily at the sight of him standing there staring at her.

"Did you want me to fix you a drink?" she said.

"Water would be just fine, sister," he replied.

"Suit yourself," she finished her drink with a quick motion and placed her glass in the sink. She drew a tall glass from the cupboard above her and filled it with water from the spigot. She casually walked over to him, hips swaying, feet seeming to glide across the linoleum, and handed him the glass. "Say, where's a fella like you come from anyhow?"

Joshua paused to take few long gulps of water. "*Tsth – ahhh.*" He looked Lillian up and down, thought for a moment, and then said, "Louisiana."

Lillian eyed him suspiciously but playfully. "I don't believe you."

"Believe what you will, sister." He raised his glass and tipped his hat. "Thanks for the water nonetheless." He stepped backwards into the hall.

"Wait!" Lillian chimed. She was over at the kitchen table now fiddling with her purse.

Joshua stopped and returned to the threshold. "*What?* Did you want me to ask what the hell is a trifling colored woman like you doing playing house with this poor old white doctor?"

Lillian's eyes widened and her lips tightened. "No – I was going to say that I need to go to the drug store down the street to fetch medicine for Mostlee."

"I'm not watching those kids."

"They can watch themselves." She picked up her purse and clutched it to her side. "I was going to say that you could feel free to help yourself to anything in the kitchen. I thought you might be hungry." Her once loose body had clenched tight now.

"Much obliged."

She moved to pass him in the threshold. He put his hand up almost touching her shoulder.

"You don't have to be so rude," she said to him.

"Just observing is all. Didn't mean any harm." He put his hand down and let her pass.

She stopped in the hall on her way to the front door and turned back to look at him. "There's leftover chop steak in the icebox." She stood there awkwardly for a moment waiting for a "thank you."

"Don't think I don't have your number, sister," Joshua said to her.

Lillian fluttered out of the house.

While finishing his glass of water, Joshua took a leisurely stroll through the first floor eventually finding his way into Dr. Long's study. There he admired the dusty books and the liquor collection and the Victrola. He placed his empty glass on top of a doily on a side table and then walked over to the large mahogany desk atop which an array of loose papers was spread. He ruffled through them. There appeared to be one from Myra.

My darling father...

But then he noticed one of the drawers slightly ajar and peering from the inside appeared to be something shiny and gold. He opened the drawer and pulled out a gold pocket watch on a long gold chain. He held it up and admired the piece until he heard the sound of feet in the hallway. He thought twice about snatching the watch but dropped it back into the drawer. He picked up a collegiate ring that sat atop a decorative medical book, admired it quickly, acted as if he was about to drop it in his pocket, and then put it back in its place instead. He then turned to find Tyrus standing in the doorway.

"You should learn to be quiet when spying on people," Joshua said.

"I wasn't spying."

"What happened to the story?"

"She was asleep. Does Dr. Long owe you a debt?" Tyrus asked.

"You shouldn't go poking your nose in the business of adults."

"It's okay. Take it. He won't miss it. He never wears it."

Joshua left the ring in its place and moved to exit the room. In the doorway he paused and touched the boy on the shoulder, instantly regretting this. He could feel the boy's shoulder tense under his firm grip. He removed his hand and walked down the hallway and out of the house. He marched back to the hotel on an empty stomach with the watch and time tick-tocking away as his mind became fevered with schemes.

Tyrus was a child full of secrets. Joshua would use the boy to find the money.

EPISODE SIXTEEN – FIRE

The first day of summer...

Tyrus floated down those steps on a twilight breeze and the lake spread out before him like a sheet of glass. His father was there standing at the edge with his back to him. Breaking through the glass was Judge's Rock, which only appeared at the height of summer when the water was lowest. A rock that used to be the peak of a mountain, Edison told Tryus once, but he knew it was just a tall tale. The Indians used to meet there, in the olden days, when the water was always low and the chief would pass his judgment on the people brought before him. This is what the Abrams said. It seemed plausible. But now it just peaked out of the water, a reminder of both the permanence and impermanence of this place. And Tyrus's father turned to face him, but it was not his father's face on this ghostly man. It was the carpenter's. Tyrus couldn't look at him and moved his eyes out over the glass and towards Sleeping Lion Mountain whose great rolling hills seemed to be moving. Gun-fire, quick, almost motorized bombarded the mountain.

The sounds of the guns became muffled and turned into the familiar watchdog bark of Sue off in the distance. Her warnings came galloping through the open window into Tyrus's bedroom and he sprang from his slumber, slid across the floor barefoot to the window and lifted it all the way open to lean his body out in the still half-light of predawn. It was barely 5 am, but it was already warm. From his window he could see up the hill towards the Abrams' house. There was a fancy black car parked at the foot of their driveway and Sue could be seen pacing back and forth on her side of the fence separating the properties and barking up a storm.

"Quit it, girl!" Tyrus yelled in a whispered tone from his window. He didn't think she would hear him, but she did, and quickly looked back at him. Flippant, she turned back towards the Abrams' house and continued her yelping.

Flustered and worried this racket would wake his mother he hastily threw on a shirt and knickers and grabbed his shoes. His patented barefooted tip-toe running got him out of the house where he slipped sockless into his shoes and ran towards the bottom of the fence to head Sue off at the pass as two men, a fat one and a skinny one, in brown suits came marching down from the Abrams' place to the opening in the fence so they could cross over into his yard.

"Hello there, son!" the skinny one called out breezily as he took off his hat. "We'd like to speak to your mother."

"That's a fine dog," the other man said crustily as Tyrus put his hand out to signal to the dog to stop charging the men. Sue slowed to an angry saunter and quit her yapping. There was some biteless growling underneath her new found calmness. She sidled up beside her boy.

"It's far too early, mister. Can't disturb Mama's beauty sleep." Tyrus was adamant.

"Ah shucks, I'm sure your mother can chance losing a bit of shut eye. Won't take but a sec, son, just let us on by." They brisked past him, the crusty fatter man tipping his hat on the way.

By now Sally was on the porch still in her nightdress and sleepy-eyed. "Sue, Tyrus, get in here!" she called out, confused by the men approaching the porch.

"Good morning, little lady," the breezy skinny man said as he lead the way right up the steps. "Would you mind fetching your mother for us? We have a bit of business with her. Won't take but a sec."

Neither boy nor dog listened to Sally and they both made their way up to the Abrams' place to investigate what happened there. There was a weight hanging over the house like a stale heated fog. Tyrus entered stealthily after ordering Sue to stay on the porch, and it felt oppressive inside the dim home, which after passing through the kitchen, appeared to have been turned upside down. A huge bed sat in the middle of the sitting room. All of the other more room appropriate furniture was pushed to the fringes against the walls. In the bed a giant sonorous hump of a figure barely gave off any signs of life other than those heavy breathing and gurgling sounds, and beside the bed in a small chair sat Duncan Abrams with his head down as if he were asleep, looking like a shell of the man who had driven Tyrus home from Edison's funeral.

There was a rotten human odor hanging in the air that Tyrus associated with guilt. He suddenly felt terrible for not having seen the Abrams for so long. He couldn't even remember when he last was in the house – there was still snow on the ground then. He knew Ma Abrams had been sick, but he had no idea it was this bad. He had been idling away at Doc Long's with Mostlee for far too long now he realized, acting like a mere boarder in his own house, unaware of the pain and suffering of those who loved him up on the hill.

"Duncan?" he called out weakly with a lump in his throat. "Mister Abrams?"

Duncan's head shot up and he eyed the child with a deep sigh. "What are you doing here, boy?"

"Who were those men?"

"They're from the bank."

"They're up at the house tryin' to talk to Mama."

"Can't stop 'em. They're comin' for us all."

"Is Ma Abrams dyin'?"

"Boy, where you been?"

"Tell her I'm sorry."

"There ain't no tellin' her nuthin' now. But she knows. She knows." He looked at the hump of dying flesh lying in the bed and then over at the boy. "She'd scold you for not wearin' your knee socks right now."

Tyrus' heart was pounding. He felt dizzy. He wiped away a bead of sweat that had come down his forehead and traveled around his eye to his cheek like a tear. "It's too damn hot."

The old man just sat there and nodded and then returned his gaze to what was left of his wife, gently taking her hand in between his and holding it at her side. "By the door there's my rifle. I taught you and your brother how to shoot with it. I'd like you to have it. I think Ma Abrams and Edison would like that."

Tyrus nodded, pivoted, and ran out of the house, grabbing the rifle by the door on his way. Sue nipped at his heals, and he marched to the fence at the point where he had a clear view to the porch and through the screen door into the house. The fat man was standing just outside the door. The skinny man was just inside presumably talking to his mother.

Tyrus was small for his age and the rifle almost seemed as long as he was tall. He positioned it like Duncan had shown him, the back of it held against his thin shoulder. He pointed it right at the fat man's hat. But then a turkey vulture came up from behind the house and buzzed over the space above the land between the two properties. Tyrus found himself pointing the rifle up into the sky and firing. The kick-back almost knocked him down. With a shot of adrenaline he kept his composure, dropped the rifle at the fence and started running for the road. He didn't stop to look at the reaction from the fat man on the porch or to see if he hit anything or to see if Sue was trailing alongside him. He just ran.

And ran. And while running he suddenly wished he had asked Duncan how far it was to the cemetery, to Haydons Hill. He suddenly wanted to tear that crypt apart. Move all the stones. Find his father's hidden money. And he wanted to take it and keep running. Far far away from everything, from everyone. Before he knew it he was in the center of Milton and the sun was up, full and cruel and casting hot gold over everything.

He walked slowly, catching his breath, taking in the sounds of the early morning, of the song birds, of windows opening and screen doors slamming. He walked past the hotel and boarding house. He later passed by a house with a beautiful garden out front. He picked out some flowers that he rustled into a makeshift bouquet. He turned down another road and saw a kid's bike turned over in the front yard. Not a soul around. He thought about the bike Edison bought him and how it was abandoned back at the house. He felt guilty and casually picked up the bike and began walking with it. A little bit further down he hopped on and began peddling with the flowers he had intended to take to the cemetery now discarded in ceremonious fashion along the sidewalk as he peddled faster and faster. He found his way to the road that snaked up into the hills and around the lake. He knew Haydon's Hill had to be along this route, and he began his lonely trek uphill along the side of the road.

Haydon's Hill appeared like a group of squatting soldiers on the right side of the road standing sentinel over the lake on the left. A few lonely headstones scattered the borders, worn and titled in the ground, before the more formal rows of graves met in the middle with monoliths, obelisks and crypts scattered amongst them. A small dirt path curved up from the road. Tyrus abandoned his bike by the foot of it, the path being too steep to peddle, and he made his way up into the center of the hill with the trees providing shade from the increasing heat. He walked solemnly and carefully, his head buzzing a bit from hunger, his throat parched and his legs aching from the peddling. He regarded the headstones as he passed, reading the names of the dead. There was one small stone shaped liked a pendant atop a square base, worn and partially dripped with white as if the tears of angels had eroded it. The family name, MABUS, was carved into the top. Then... *Our Willie. Died Oct 23, 1871. Aged 1 Yr.* He thought how puzzling and cruel the world must've always been.

He came upon the family crypt with TEMPLE plastered atop the doorframe, itself being shaped like a small temple with a triangular roof of stone atop and rectangular body burrowed into the side of the hill. He walked up the slight incline and approached the door partially ajar with leaves and dirt piled up at the foot of the opening. He pushed it open, the door being heavier than he imagined, and a shot of cooler stale air enveloped him as he stepped into the dark chamber. His eyes adjusted and just enough light from outside allowed him to read the names against the back wall where the bodies of family members he never knew laid in eternal rest along with his beloved brother. He looked for the loose stone by the threshold he had remembered from the day of the funeral. It was still there, slightly angled and jutting out from one side. He knelt down, the stone floor hard and cool against his knees, and began to jimmy the stone from its place. It came out quite easily, but behind it there was nothing.

A man's voice suddenly shot through the doorway. "Young man, just what do you think yer doin'?"

Startled, Tyrus jammed the stone back into its place and shot up and turned towards the door. Standing there was an old, thin man leaning on a shovel.

"Visiting my brother's grave, mister," he said nervously. He pointed to Edison's name over on the far wall. "Edison Kydd."

The old man eyed him suspiciously. "What chew doin' with them stones?"

"Nothing, mister, I just saw it was loose is all."

The old man seemed satisfied with that. "You here alone?"

"Yes, sir."

"You ain't with that other man I saw?"

"No, sir."

"Strange man. Strange to have two people rustlin' around up here this time of morn'. You look right hungry, boy. Didn't they feed you no breakfast?"

"No, sir."

"Well, say your peace here if you want, then follow me." The old man turned around and stepped back down to the dirt path.

Tyrus walked over to the far wall of the crypt and ran his fingers over his brother's name engraved in the stone. "I'll be back," he whispered. He made a sign of the cross because he didn't know what else to do and then walked out of the crypt and followed the old man down to a small stone house overlooking the road. Inside there were two rooms, one with a cot and an old dresser and stacks of books piled up against the walls, the other full of all of the tools of the gravedigger's trade with a small stove on the right wall and an old wooden table with two small chairs in the center. Atop the stove were a pan partially full with scrambled eggs and a few strips of bacon and another pan with coffee that looked like motor oil.

"Sit down," the old man said as he tended to the stove.

Tyrus sat down on one of the wobbly wooden chairs and tried to position himself at the table. The old man slapped the pan down on the table and handed him a fork. Famished, Tyrus dug in. The eggs were cold, but tasted good enough, and the bacon was dripping with congealed grease, salty and tough, but he didn't care that it wasn't crisp like Ma Abrams would make.

The old man regarded him trying to ascertain the child's age. "You drink coffee, boy?"

"Yes, sir," Tyrus said with a full mouth between chews. He lied.

The old man poured some of the thick black liquid into a chipped cup and placed it down next to the pan. "Ain't got no milk nor sugar."

Tyrus picked up the cup and took a huge gulp. He grimaced; it was bitter and felt like he swallowed some dirt. The old man smiled and shook his head. Tyrus considered the sludge in the cup for a moment, and decided it was manly to finish it. Moments later the pan of food and the cup were empty, Tyrus' head was buzzing in a good way and his stomach felt full. He sat there for a few moments, his head swimming with thoughts, and he suddenly felt exhausted.

"If you're tired," the old man said, "you can lie on the cot for a while but then you best be on your way."

Tyrus stood up and shuffled into the other room where he collapsed onto the dirty, musty cot and fell asleep instantly. He awoke to his stomach growling, the coffee not settling too well. He wasn't sure how long he had been out. He walked outside and found the old man further down the dirt path sitting in the grass on the side of the hill gazing through the trees on the other side out into the lake. Tyrus quietly sat down beside him. The old man was drinking water from a canteen and passed it to Tyrus without a word. The water was warm, but still tasted good after that coffee and it helped settle his stomach some. He passed it back to the old man after nearly drinking it dry.

"Strange for a boy to be up here by himself visitin' family," the old man said.

"That other man you saw...did he have one hand?' Tyrus asked.

"What an odd question. I don't right recall noticin'. I take it yer a boy with an active imagination."

"Thanks for everything, mister, but I better be going."

"I guess you better be." The old man gave a nod as Tryus stood up and made his way down the dirt path to where he had left the bike.

Renewed and refreshed the boy peddled back down into town, coasting along most of the way downhill. Milton was more alive now. He peddled through some kids playing stickball in the street. The pitcher eyed him suspiciously, but then there was a woman hollering at the kids to come in for lunch. It must've been about noontime. Tyrus made his way towards the lake and to that special spot at the end of a side street where there was a little spread of thick grass shaded by tall trees and a bench overlooking a steep decline down into the water. A wide set of steps had been built off to the side descending down into a small boat slip and cove from where you could see Judge's Rock if the season was right. Tyrus planted the bike down at the top of the steps and walked down into the cove. Halfway down the steps he heard crying, and then he saw her...Mostlee was sitting on the edge by the slip, her feet dangling over the water. Her head was down and her shoulders heaved up and down with each sob.

Tyrus continued his descent slowly and then came up beside her and sat down, placing his arm gently around her shoulder.

"How'd you know where to find me?" she asked between epic tears.

"Luck, I guess," Tyrus said.

Mostlee sniffled and brushed away her tears with her arm. She calmed a bit with Tyrus sitting next to her. "I wish you could always be there to find me."

"Why can't I be?"

"Dr. Long threw me and Mama out of the house last night!"

There was suddenly a commotion on the street, a gaggle of kids buzzing and approaching. "Hey, see, I told ya! That IS my bike!" They heard one kid yell.

Tyrus and Mostlee stood up and made their way up the steps. The group of kids he had seen playing ball were coming down the street. The pitcher pointed at him and yelled, "Hey, kid, that's my bike! What the hell are you doing with my bike?"

Tryus stood the bike up and sent it rolling in the grass towards the ledge. It went sailing over and landed with a loud plop into the lake.

"What the hell, kid!" the pitcher shouted. "Let's get 'em!" They all started charging towards the steps.

Tyrus took Mostlee's hand and they began running down the other street that was parallel to the shore. They came upon a thick wooded area and turned into the trees before the other kids came around the bend to see them. They stopped for a moment to catch their breaths. Mostlee started giggling. Tyrus put his hand over her mouth and drew her close to him behind the thick trunk of an old tree. The angry kids went running down the street past the woods. Tyrus let out a deep sigh and removed his hand from Mostlee's mouth.

"That was close," she said pleasantly. "What kinda trouble you been getting into this morning?"

He kissed her quickly, instinctually, on the lips, their noses bumping against each other. She didn't say another word as they waited there for a few moments with baited breath before calmly walking back out into the street. They walked down Main Street into Fenimore. Tryus' mind somersaulted back to Mostlee's revelation by Judge's Rock.

"Say, why did Doc Long throw you and your mother out of the house?" he asked her.

"I don't know. Mama said he said she stole something. But we ain't thieves." She seemed to contemplate this for a moment. "I don't wanna talk about it. Take me to a picture show!"

"But I ain't got no money."

Mostlee dug her hand into her dress pocket and pulled out a wad of dollar bills. She smiled and held it up to Tyrus. "Don't worry, I do!"

"You steal that?"

"I just told you we ain't thieves! Mama gave it to me."

They walked to the old movie house in the middle of town to catch the matinee. An *Our Gang* short and *King Kong*. Tyrus didn't tell her that his brother took him to see this feature two years ago when it first played in town. He acted surprised at all the right parts, and Mostlee clung to his arm when things got scary. At the end she almost cried.

"That poor ape," she said shaking her head sullenly as they stepped out of the theater.

"*Twas beauty killed the beast!*" Tyrus said theatrically.

She took his hand. "I better get back to the hotel or Mama will give me hell," she said. "We're supposed to be packing."

"Packing? Why?" Tyrus asked.

"Boy, haven't you been listening to me all day? We got thrown outta Doc Long's house! People think we're thieves in this town. We gotta go. Getting on a train tonight."

Tyrus' heartbeat built into a slow panic. He felt warm and flushed. "Go where?"

"Back to the city I suppose. Wherever Mama can find work."

"She gonna be a singer again?"

"She wasn't ever no singer," Mostlee said in a dejected tone.

"Oh."

"I don't wanna leave. I wanna stay here. I wish we could get married. I wish I could live with you."

"Aww, we can't get married."

"I know."

"I'm gonna marry Myra Long one day!"

"God, you know just the wrong thing to say to a girl, doncha!" She threw his hand away from hers and took a few steps apart, quickening her pace ahead of him down the sidewalk.

"Aww, c'mon – I – I – " Tyrus hurried up beside her, tried to take her hand again but she resisted. "I'm just a stupid kid."

"No kiddin'!"

"I'm sorry. I wish you weren't leaving."

They came upon the hotel and stood at the foot of the walkway leading up to the porch, turned to each other, hopeless.

"Maybe one day you can come to the city, too," Mostlee said.

Tyrus leaned forward to kiss her on the cheek but she pulled away.

She took his one hand and petted it, almost like an old lady would to a little child. She let go and looked longingly at him for just a moment. She reached down in her pocket and pulled out a few dollars. She handed it to him. "Go get yourself some supper before you waste away to nothing."

"I will," he sniffled. "This ain't one of your lies is it? You ain't playing a trick on me?"

"I wish it was." She took a step sideways towards the porch and looked him over one last time. "I hope you find your Myra one day," she sighed and then hurried up inside.

Tyrus walked sullenly to the diner down the road. He felt tired and grimy. He made his way for the washroom. One of the waitresses, a fat young one with rosy cheeks and red hair tied in a bun said with a toothy smile, "Hey there...that's for payin' customers only."

Tyrus showed his wad of dollars to her quickly and dismissively and then made his way into the washroom. He came out with his face and hands washed and his hair wet and parted to one side by his own fingers. He confidently took a seat in the middle of the counter and folded his hands neatly atop while reading the specials on the chalkboard. He had only been here once before with his father, whom he recalled flirted with the waitress. The red-headed waitress came up to him saucily and seemed charmed by his newly refined demeanor.

"How's the meatloaf?" he asked her.

"Just like mom used to make," she said.

"Slap me up some of that, and extra mashed potatoes...*please*."

"Anything to drink?"

"Pop will be fine."

"Comin' right up." She walked away back towards the kitchen, and Tyrus copied the manners of the other men sitting at the counter admiring her plentiful rear-end as it moved up and down rhythmically in her waitress' uniform. He gobbled up his plate and drank his pop in record time. He then regarded the man a few stools down from him reading the evening paper from front to back, neatly folding each section as he was done with it.

"Hey, mister," he said leaning over towards the man. "You mind if I sneak the funnies...if you're done with them, I mean?"

The man eyed him, amused, and slid the portions he was done with down the counter to the boy. Before he was able to open them, the waitress came back.

"Coffee? Dessert?" she asked.

Tyrus examined the pies and cakes behind the counter in their tiered glass display. "How's the cherry tonight?"

"Best you ever had."

"I'll take a piece of cherry pie. And a glass of milk."

He savored his dessert, and when he was finished he perused the paper. Something about a speech from FDR. Talk of Europe. Lou Gehrig homered again yesterday. He lingered on the funnies, but held his amusement to himself. Anything to keep his mind off Mostlee. When he was finished with the paper he folded it neatly for the next patron, paid the waitress, said good evening and left.

Outside it was now darkening, but it seemed from cloudiness as it couldn't be dusk just yet. Tyrus knew it was the longest day of the year and that lately the sun hadn't been setting until what during the school year had been close to his bedtime. Had the day totally escaped him? He felt sick to his stomach thinking back to the early hours of the morning...to those men from the bank...to Ma Abrams...to the rifle he left by the fence. He began making his way towards home.

Indeed it was dusk and the sun was setting, but it wasn't darkness that greeted him as he rounded the bend to where he could see his house and up into the hills. No, it was a heat and bright light...beyond his home, the Abrams' house was ablaze. Completely engulfed in flames dancing wildly from top to bottom. There was a police car at the foot of the driveway and a group of men standing there. Tyrus ran for the fence where he saw Sue halfway up the hill sitting on her haunches hypnotized by the fire. It was the most spectacular thing either one of them had ever seen. He was so enraptured by the inferno he failed to hear the policeman yelling behind him until the man's hands were on his arms pulling him back away from the fence.

Tyrus began flailing around wildly screaming, "No! Let me go! Let ME GO!" He felt like Kong trying to escape the shackles. He wasn't even aware of what his body and his voice were doing. He must've somehow kicked the man in the shin as he was suddenly free and the man was knelt down in the grass in pain. Tyrus stood frozen, his legs spread awkwardly in mid dash, his eyes wide with guilt and shame.

"Son!" the officer said as he stood back up. "Don't make this hard on yourself. Your family's been looking for you."

"Where's Ma Abrams? Where's Duncan?" Tyrus asked breathlessly.

The officer shook his head back and forth. He was a young man, tall and fit, without yet the belly other officers sported. "I could give it to you straight, boy. Man to man, if that's how you want it. Or I could treat you like an animal and throw you in the trunk of my car."

"Man to man," Tyrus said.

"Them old folks...they was in a real bad way. They took the easy way out, son."

Tyrus looked up at the burning house, panting. He corrected his stance and stood now hunched over with his hands on his knees. His hair was soaked. He was sweating. He felt like his skin was burning. "They're in there?"

"I'm afraid so. The fire truck is on its way. They'll take care of it. Best they can. It ain't safe here. Let me take you to your family."

Tyrus straightened his back and looked over at Sue frozen by the fence still hypnotized by the flames. "I ain't leaving without my dog," he said firmly.

"Son, she ain't moving for nuthing right now. The other fellas will keep an eye on her for ya. We'll make sure she gets to Doc Long's. Now you just need to settle down, come with me, and we'll forget about this little scrap we just had."

"Sue!" Tyrus called out. "SUE!" She didn't budge.

Darkness was descending on the hill and meeting with the flames, intensifying their brightness, near blinding now. Tyrus shielded his eyes as he walked over to the policeman. The officer guided him down to his car and into the backseat. There sitting on the floorboards was Duncan Abrams' rifle. The office pulled off down the road back towards Fenimore, the flames shrinking in the distance and Tyrus sat with his arms folded atop the board in front of the rear window watching them slowly disappear. He flipped himself around to face forward and picked the rifle up off the floorboard and rested it on his lap.

'That your rifle, son?" the officer asked.

"Yes, sir," Tyrus replied.

"Heard you shot yourself a bird this morning."

Tyrus' eyes widened, a little bit of pride bubbling up through the sadness, guilt and longing.

"Well, it ain't loaded no more, so don't go getting any funny ideas about shooting something from this moving vehicle. You must've had yourself quite the adventure after shooting that bird."

Tyrus stayed mute. In no time they were parked out in front of Dr. Long's house. The policeman took the rifle and lead Tyrus up the steps to the front door. A frantic Evelyn Kydd opened the door and swept her son up into her arms, Tyrus suddenly feeling so little and helpless again, embarrassed. The policeman stayed out on the front porch just on the other side of the door. He held the door open with his foot and through the opening he propped up the unloaded rifle just against the wall inside.

"Thank you, officer, for finding him," Evelyn said still smothering her son and half-lifting him off the ground. She finally put him down, and he turned around to face the policeman, his hair all tousled and his shirt unbuttoned at the top and crooked.

"Mmm, he found us, ma'am."

"Don't forget about my dog!" Tyrus piped up while straightening himself out.

The policeman smiled and nodded, tipped his cap to them and then turned to make his way back to the car, the screen door slamming shut behind him. Evelyn led Tyrus into the kitchen where she pointed for him to sit down at the kitchen table. She was fixing some warm milk on the stove. Tyrus was still red with rage.

"Now you just need to calm yourself, mister," she said to him. "I don't even know where to start with you. You had us all worried sick." She lost her composure and had to lean on the sink, her eyes teary and turned up towards the ceiling. "And the poor Abrams! Why did they do it?"

"We living here now?" Tyrus asked her harshly.

Evelyn dabbed her eyes with a wash rag and pulled herself together. "The bank took our home," she said.

"How could you leave Sue behind like that?"

"Don't worry, Ty, she'll find her way to you. She always does. I think she just has to say goodbye, ya know?"

Through the hallway and the back door Tyrus heard footsteps out on the porch. Was it the carpenter? He abandoned his mother in the kitchen and ran out back. There in the darkness Sally sat on the steps leading down into the yard facing the lake whose still waters reflected cleanly the full moon beginning its rise overhead. The clear, warm night air was coupled with a tepid wind. It calmed Tyrus as he collapsed exhausted on the steps next to his sister.

"How long you been up?" Sally asked him.

"Since dawn," Tyrus replied tiredly.

"Bet chew think you're a man now, huh?"

Tryus' head fell on her shoulder. He expected her to push him off. Give him some more sass. Cuss. But she didn't. In that moment she seemed to understand him a little better maybe, like she knew whatever trouble he had gotten into today, it was trouble worth getting into. And she couldn't have had an easy day either with all that had happened. She was tired too. And they would be tired together for the rest of the evening, silent, and knowing, until they were ushered up to bed.

The Abrams house started to collapse while the policeman headed back from Doc Long's place. In the frenzy, Sue left her watch and the other officers lost sight of her. Soon the firemen were there battling the blaze. Late in the wee hours of the morning, Sue came sauntering up the steps onto Doc Long's porch where she collapsed and curled herself up by the door for a long sleep, knowing inside that her wards were safe and sound.

EPISODE SEVENTEEN – TROUBLIN' TIMES

E ven in this Podunk town, Doris Welts worried about her husband when he wasn't home before dark. They were young, but they had seen a lot in Philadelphia, and as much as she missed the city sometimes, she was glad they had found someplace quieter to call home...someplace sheltered from the storm that swept the nation. But when he got the call this afternoon about helping the bank "remove" some people from their homesteads, she realized that even in these peaceful hills, money could turn to dust. In fact, she swore she could smell a hint of ash in the air as she bounced their infant daughter to sleep in her arms pacing back and forth in front of the bedroom window. She had taken the advice of her mother, who called from Philadelphia every Sunday, and began drinking brandy after dinner. "Just that little taste...in your milk...will sooth that baby and send her right to sleep." And it did every time, even with the smell of ash in the air.

"These are troublin' times," the preacher had sermonized that week. Doris normally paid it no mind. She went to church because they were new in town, and her husband was the new deputy, and that was the way to get to know people and to give the people the confidence that Welts were of good stock and would fit in and were righteous. Tonight, however, that simple truth echoed inside her head, and she couldn't help but wonder what kind of trouble her husband was stopping.

Doris heard the familiar creek of the front door and her husband's careful but confident steps into the house. She placed the baby down in the crib and tiptoed out into the living room in her nightdress.

"Husband," she said upon looking at him.

"Wife," he said in response.

They enjoyed calling each other this in mocking formality. His parents had called each other, "Mother" and "Father" but that seemed patronizing, old-fashioned.

Doris walked up to him, the top of her head barely reaching his chin, her husband so tall and handsome. She touched the sides of his face and looked up into his weary eyes. "Tell me your troubles, Husband," she said to him, trying to get him to smile at her melodrama. Doris had wanted to be an actress growing up. She didn't want him to know how she really worried. She wanted him to think she was just a bored housewife, which she was, she supposed. His stories soothed her worries and gave her a sense of excitement at the same time.

"I just want to go to bed," he said.

Doris turned away from him and flung herself on the couch, lying back in mock seduction and then grabbing the bottle of brandy on the table and pouring herself another snifter. She held the bottle out to him. He waved the palm of his hand in front of her.

"I'm on fire for you now," she said laughing as she took a few sips.

Pinky Welts rolled his eyes at his wife. "You've had too much to drink."

"What else do you expect me to do waiting up for you?" She took a few more sips and then looked serious, alert. "Do you smell that?"

"There was a fire up in the hills," he said. "They have it under control, but the wind is probably blowing down hill."

"Oh, my dear! Is that where you were?"

"Yes," he said. He slouched down onto the couch by her outstretched legs.

She propped her feet atop his lap. He cradled her feet in his hands, slowly massaging them.

"What happened?" she asked.

"The Abrams – you should remember them from church when we first moved, though they've been absent since the wife fell ill – they were about to lose their farm. And then tonight – there it went. Up in smoke."

Doris had rearranged herself on the couch and was now curled up against her husband, her hand on his chest, rubbing in circles beneath his buttoned shirt. "Arson?"

"It appears they set it themselves, at least that's what the sheriff and the fire chief think...but I don't know. I don't know who could do that to themselves...why anybody would want to voluntarily die in a fire? Hell, in the city people would just shoot or stab each other...or jump off the roof of a tall building if they wanted to do themselves in. But people up here...they have a flare for the dramatic."

Doris's hand became still and her throat stung. She swallowed painfully. "You mean some of what we smell...some of that ash coming down hill...we're breathing in...THEM?"

Pinky kissed his wife sweetly atop the head and wrapped his arm around her shoulder. "I don't want you worrying your pretty little head about such horrible things."

"Don't you dare tell me, Mr. Pinky Welts, what I can and can not worry about!" She pushed him away and backed up against the other end of the couch. "You're telling me our daughter could be breathing   in...*people*...right   now?   Those poor...sick...old...dead...people?"

"Don't be so morbid. It's just the lingering smell of smoke on the wind. We're far away from there."

"But before you came home I smelled ashes outside the bedroom window."

"Now you're imagining things. Don't get hysterical."

Doris folded her arms across her chest and huffed. She didn't like to be dismissed like this, but she did suppose it was all part of the role.

"Have another drink why don't ya?" he said to her, like he was talking to a buddy from back home.

"Don't mock me."

"Oh, c'mon, Wife...it's what we do best to each other."

Doris grew sullen. "Those poor people...the Abrams...they're really dead?"

"I'm afraid so."

Doris edged her way back over to him, and they sat together again side by side touching. "I'm sorry. I was worried about you, like I used to be every night back in Philadelphia."

"I know."

"I thought things like that didn't happen up here."

"There are wicked ways wherever we find ourselves. It's how I make my living, remember?"

"You really think they did that to themselves?"

"I don't know."

"If they didn't do it to themselves, then who did?"

"I don't know. I sometimes get the feeling there're secrets in these hills. Their neighbors...the Kydds...the bank wanted them off their land, too. Mrs. Kydd, when I had to question her about the Abrams, she said Mable Abrams' greatest fear was hellfire...eternal damnation. She said she couldn't believe her husband would set that fire and send her to that fate. And her youngest, he went missing all day...and then he came back and saw that fire...and his eyes...I've never seen that look in someone's eyes like that...he went wild. And I honestly thought I wasn't going to be able to control him, like I was going to have to knock him unconscious...this little boy."

"They talk about his mother in church."

"I know."

"And how his father ran off."

"I know."

"And how his mother used to get on with Dr. Long."

"I don't trust that man. Everyone in this town adores him. But something ain't right about a man like that. That's where they went. That's where I had to take the boy. He really has no one...his older brother is dead...his father gone...the Abrams are gone now, too. His mother is in a sickly way. And what kind of father figure is Doc Long, the way he has women of all sorts in and out of his house? I just wanted to take him home with me."

"You can't save everyone." She kissed him on the cheek and then rested her head on his shoulder.

"But if I could save one..."

"Well, maybe he's not your one. Maybe he'll be just fine."

Doris took her husband's right hand in hers and gently caressed it, his palm, each manly digit and the nub at the end of his pinky finger where the tip should've been. When he was a boy, it was chopped off in an accident with a butcher knife. It's how he got his nickname, Pinky, which stuck with him even into adulthood. She kissed it.

"We all have our burdens to bear," she said. She began to massage his crotch. "Yours right now is an insatiable wife." There was a faux-huskiness in her voice.

Pinky laughed. "You don't have to do this."

Doris sighed and laid her head back on his lap, hey eyes gazing up at him, her hand reaching for his cheek and chin, caressing the prickliness of his unshaven face. "Just trying to be playful...take your mind off things...perform my Wifely duties."

He laughed again. "You don't have to be anybody you aren't. We can just sit here...and talk. The rest will come naturally like it always does."

"That boy really got to you, huh?"

"Nothing about this feels right. The Abrams setting that fire...the kid...the least I could do was leave him with that rifle." He sighed. "Damn...I don't know if the other deputies went back and got his dog. Poor kid...I think that rifle and that dog...that's all he's got."

"Well, you'll just have to keep an eye on him."

"It's the right thing to do."

"And you always do the right thing." Doris closed her eyes...secure...bored. He had that burning smell on his clothes. She breathed it in deeply. Her imagination went into overdrive, but she was too tired. The murmur of his heart and breathing above her head put her fast to sleep. They would make love in the bedroom in the predawn, quietly and gently so as not to wake the baby.

* * *

The Welts went to the funeral four days later. The preacher gave a comforting sermon, waxing about these troubling times and how they could claim even the strongest of the faithful. The church was filled to capacity, and Doris and Pinky stood in the back, with her holding the baby in her arms, it sound asleep after a well-timed feeding, and Deputy Welts standing proudly over them, his arm around his wife's shoulder, both of them looking solemn and dutiful.

Pinky couldn't help but think how even in a drab mourning dress, his wife looked beautiful. Her strawberry blonde hair...her lightly freckled skin...her nicely pointed nose...her plump baby-nursing figure...she was made for the glow of summertime and motherhood.

Doris couldn't help but wonder what exactly was in that pair of coffins propped up by the altar. What could've possibly have been left of the Abrams after that fire? She remembered them being large people...but still. Whatever was in there was probably mingled and indistinguishable from the ashes of their home, as if it too was being buried with them six feet under where no bank would ever take it away from them. She wondered too if her husband noticed how she had allowed the baby's hand to stay where it was, slightly pulling down the collar of her dress which she had left the top two buttons open, revealing just a little bit of her bosom to a man with the right bird's eye view. It was unbearably hot in the crowded church, and there was a little bit of perspiration forming there. It almost made Doris smile, but she held her serious gaze. Keeping up appearances.

At the end of the ceremony, Doris wanted to make a quick exit, but Pinky explained they should wait for the sheriff, who had been up front, to come through. Out in the vestibule of the church, they stood and waited. The baby had opened its eyes and was growing fussy in the heat. Doris bounced it up and down and held the baby's soft head close to her mouth with a soothing "Shhhhh....shhhhhh."

Pinky's attention was drawn to the open door where the bright rays of the sun cast a white glow that made anything beyond the door seemingly invisible. But in the doorway a small shadow of a boy leaned against the frame. It was Tyrus Kydd. Evelyn Kydd...Doctor Long...they hadn't been seen at the church today...but there was the boy standing pensively in the doorway. Pinky moved to go to him, but the Sheriff came up from behind and wanted to talk shop for a few moments. When Pinky turned back around, the angle of the sun had shifted and everything outside was illuminated. The boy was just outside now where the crowd had begun filtering out and lingering in the hot sun.

A man in a dark brown derby hat and dusty suit jacket had his one hand on the boy's shoulder and was leading him away. Pinky recognized the one-handed man immediately as the drifter carpenter who had been working for Doc Long. Like all drifters through that small town, they had their eye on him, and he was rumored to have been involved in a brawl at the bar a few nights ago. The carpenter turned back towards the church, obviously aware of the deputy's gaze, and he made eye contact with Pinky and his wife. He tipped his hat towards them before disappearing into the crowd with the boy.

"Who was that?" Doris asked over their baby's cries.

"Just some carpenter," Pinky replied.

They stepped outside into the crowd. People were milling about, talking about the weather. Women fanning themselves. Men trying to pretend they weren't sweating. Everyone underneath hats, shielding themselves from the unrelenting sun.

"Gonna be a long, hot summer," they said. "Just like the Old Farmer's Almanac said."

"Gonna be one of the hottest on record I bet! Glad we up here by this lake and not in the city!"

But Pinky knew it was no different in a small town then it was in a big city. Rising temperatures meant tempers flaring. Everything comes to a boil. And for some reason, in the pit of his stomach, he had a hunch that carpenter would be in the thick of it.

EPISODE EIGHTEEN – HEAT WAVE

"**S**ay, where'd the carpenter go, Doc?" Tyrus asked as he came running up the back porch red-faced and sweating. His hair was so wet he looked like he had been in the lake.

"He took on work out at Haydon Hall," Doc Long said. He couldn't stand to be out on the porch one minute longer in that heat. It pained him to look at the boy. "You should go swimming. Cool down."

"I thought you was calling us in for supper?" Tyrus said.

Sally came sauntering around from the side of the house, looking far less exerted but ten times as miserable as Tyrus.

Doc Long shook his head. He took off his hat and fanned himself with it. He looked up into the cloudless sky. These long days in this unforgiving heat, he couldn't make heads or tails of what time it was. He just wished it would go dark...though even then he knew the darkness would provide little relief. "Right, yes...supper. Your mother is back from the market preparing supper. You should wash up. After supper, maybe a swim." He turned and shuffled back into the house.

Sally slowly climbed the stairs while Tyrus raced up beside her. "If it's gonna stay this damn hot all summer, you might as well drown me in the lake," she said.

* * *

"I've never experienced a heat like this in my life!" the old bitties muttered to each other wandering aimlessly down the aisles at the local grocery store.

Evelyn thought she might strangle one of the old bats if they said one more damned word about the heat. The town had become over-run with city folk escaping the sweltering metropolises, lured back by fond memories of the little hamlet from when they could afford a holiday on the lake. Tents were set up all along the shore line by locals and visitors alike, seeking respite at night by the cooling waters. In many homes, second floors where unbearable and people took to sleeping on their kitchen floors, on porches or even in their yards. Evelyn couldn't stand the sight of it anymore – people wandering around half-naked, pinching pennies at the local market and diner, crowding out the locals at the lake. It was as if everyone was in a haze, pitiful and with nothing to their name but the sweaty shirts on their backs.

Evelyn picked up cold-cuts, cheese and bread for sandwiches. It was too hot to cook for dinner. She bought ice cream for the children but it was nearly all melted by the time she got it back to the house. The kids didn't care. They drank it like it was a milkshake after eating their bologna and cheese sandwiches. She sat at the head of the table watching them do this, hardly recognizing her own children anymore, the girl and the boy appearing as anonymous poor children...urchins...burnt by the sun, crisping in the heat, sweaty and tired and famished and sick all at once.

Doc Long was resting in his study with a drink and his music. It had been too hot for him to even eat.

"Mama," Tyrus said after he finished his ice cream, suddenly serious. "I'm sorry you didn't get to go to the Abrams' funeral."

Evelyn had had a seizure the night before the funeral, and Doc Long wouldn't let her go in the morning due to her delicate state. "That's okay. I said good-bye to them in my own way. Was it nice?"

Tyrus shrugged his shoulders. "Do you really think – "

Sally cut him off abruptly, "Don't upset our mother with your silly questions."

"It's just...I think Mr. Abrams wanted to be with Ma Abrams, you know, when she...but I don't think – "

"It's not for us to worry or judge," Evelyn said.

"But, Mama, I know you don't think they set that fire!"

"Hush, child!" She took on a bit of Ma Abrams, and it startled Tyrus into silence. "Enough."

Tyrus got up from the table and took his dirty dishes to the sink. He turned sheepishly back to his mother. "Can we listen to the radio?"

"Yes, but quietly. Don't disturb Dr. Long."

"And then can we go swimming?"

"Yes."

"C'mon , Sally." Tyrus walked out of the kitchen.

Sally stood up and put her dirty dishes in the sink. "Do you want me to clean them?" she asked.

"No, run along."

Sally stopped for a moment in the hallway where the large fan stood by the back door and blew hot air all over the place. She leaned against the wall for a moment, letting the air blow up her dress. From the kitchen Evelyn heard her sigh like one of those old ladies in the grocery store. "The whole world is on fire and all we got is this damn fan," Sally muttered before heading off into the living room to listen to the radio with Tyrus.

A panting Sue came wandering into the kitchen. The dog came up beside Evelyn's chair and rested her head on Evelyn's lap.

Evelyn gently scratched behind Sue's ears. After washing the dishes and cleaning up in the kitchen, seeing it was growing dark, she walked out onto the porch and enjoyed a cigarette while leaning over the railing. In the heat of the night, even the cacophonous crickets sounded slow and tired. There was distant splashing in the lake, and it was still light enough that she could see some of the temporary encampments of families along the shore, as if the people had decided to wage war against the heat.

Sue's long hair felt soft against Evelyn's skin as the dog rested on her haunches by Evelyn's bare legs, her snout and panting breath sneaking through the space between the wooden rails out into the hot twilight. Her ears were perked listening intently to the sounds of strangers by the water, moody insects and critters traipsing about the woods.

The screen door slammed behind Evelyn and Sue as Sally and Tyrus came bouncing out into the night. They were laughing and playfully shoving each other, amused, even if for only a few moments, by what they had been listening to on the radio, and their moods improved with the setting sun. Evelyn and Sue watched them as they skipped down to the lake for a swim.

Evelyn looked down at the dog, and the dog looked up at her. "Let's go for a walk," she said to the dog. They walked down off the porch and around to the front of the house. At the sidewalk, Evelyn extinguished her cigarette underfoot. She turned and looked back at the house, the light in Doc Long's study casting a muted glow through the curtains onto the front lawn as the darkness had descended fast. She could no longer hear the sounds of the children down by the lake, but it appeared as if Sue could as the dog looked longingly back around the side of the house into the darkness. "C'mon," she said to the dog, "forget them for a while."

Evelyn walked slowly with the dog close behind, taking in the fullness of the air, admiring the ambiance. On one front lawn two small children grasped at fireflies dancing atop the grass while an old woman sat in a rocking chair on the porch overseeing the affair as if she were watching a ballet. Other people were at work in their gardens or cutting their grass, unable to do such chores during the day under the harsh scrutiny of the sun. Everyone moved slowly, solemnly, as if living at the bottom of the sea where movements were measured and methodical and weighed down by the weight of the world above.

They walked all the way to their homestead and by the time they reached their repossessed home, it was completely dark. The pitch black of night blanketed the once lit hillside where the ashes of the Abrams' house lay mute and the Kydd house now lived in shadows. The pair approached the house with grave trepidation, careful of their steps in the dark up the dirt path and ascending the front porch. A foreclosure notice from the bank was posted harshly on the front door affixed by a thin nail. The door was locked, but Evelyn's key still worked. She stepped inside and the dog stealthily followed. The electricity had not yet been shut off. She turned on all the lamps as she passed through each room, the artificial light casting only the lonely shadows of a woman and a dog upon bare walls and empty floors until she got back into the kitchen.

Evelyn flipped on the overhead light in the kitchen and stood in the doorway staring at the old wooden table and five chairs in the center of the floor. Her throat began to tighten and it felt like a hand was squeezing her heart as she was struck by a memory from last summer...to the last time all five of those chairs were filled.

Just like she had today, she had bought ice cream for the children as a special treat after Edison's baseball game. She dished out hearty scoops for Edison, Sally and Tyrus and even gave a little scoop to Sue in a bowl by her water dish. Between joyful spoonfuls, Edison and Tyrus chattered wildly about the ball game. Sally threw in her two cents when there was a lull in the conversation, playfully busting her older brother's chops about his performance on the field. Evelyn vividly remembered the sound of Tyrus' heels hitting the chair legs as he swung his legs back and forth excitedly beneath the table. Could he have been that small just a year ago where his feet didn't touch the floor? And Sally was still in pigtails. And there was Edison, leaning back in his chair, confidently and proudly, the back tipping over and balanced on just two legs. Evelyn admired the happy scene leaning back against the countertop. She turned to scoop out the last little bit of the ice cream for herself when there was a raucous storming through the front door and galloping down the hallway back into the kitchen.

He always arrived like this. Gone for months, then like a dust storm blowing through the house. The smell of whiskey on his breath – that big, dumb, eager smile of his – grinning ear to ear. The dog barked playfully. The younger children squealed with delight. Edison stood up first and shook his hand. Samuel pulled him for an embrace and then pushed him back.

"Let me look at you!" Samuel said. It had been a least three months since he last saw his family. "Did you win today?"

"Of course," Edison said. "9 to 6. I hit two home runs."

"Oh, Pop, you should've seen it!" Tyrus piped up.

Pop, Pop, Pop, Pop, Pop! Tyrus made his index finger and thumb into the shape of a gun and pretended to shoot his father.

Samuel took Tyrus up into his arms. "You're getting too big!" he said as he put him down.

He hugged Sally. "And how's my beautiful girl?"

"Okay, I guess," she said.

"You guess? Well, there's no guessin' no more!" He then eyed Evelyn standing by the counter.

She was giving him that sly smile, half suspicious, half happy, all her anger falling down to the floor to be swept away when she saw how happy the children were.

Samuel took off his hat and tossed it on the kitchen table. He marched up to her, wrapped his arm around her waist and went in for a kiss. She resisted. He clumsily pecked her cheek. "Aww, Evie, it's so good to be home."

"How long you staying?" she asked him with that look.

"Pop, have some ice cream!" Tyrus yelped.

Samuel looked back at the three children standing eagerly over their half-eaten bowls. "Well don't wait for me!" he said to them. "Eat the rest before it melts!"

The children sat back down in their seats and began to finish their ice cream.

Evelyn reached behind her back and then presented the last scoop to her husband.

"Awww, baby, ain't you havin' none?" he asked her.

"No," she said sweetly. "I don't really like ice cream."

"That ain't true, Ma!" Tyrus yelled.

"Don't sass your mother, you rascal," Samuel said. He grabbed his hat and placed it atop Tyrus' head. The boy smiled. Samuel sat down at the head of the table and proceeded to eat.

Evelyn admired her family, quiet, with full stomachs and full hearts. Happy. Together. Later that night after the younger children went to bed and Edison was outside finishing his evening chores, Samuel presented a stack of twenty dollar bills to Evelyn while she washed the dishes.

"This should tide you over," he said.

"Tide me over until when?" she asked.

"I have to go down to Richmond. My mother is gravely ill."

"Oh, Samuel, you're not lying to me are you?"

"Of course not!"

"I'm sorry to hear about your mother."

"It's a shame you've never met her."

"When are you leaving?"

"In a few days. But I want to take the boys camping down at the lake before I go."

"I think they'd like that, but don't lead them on. They might want you to think they're almost men, but they still have fragile hearts."

"I always give it to them straight. I'll tell Edison tonight that I can't be staying...not this time. But I'll be back. I promise."

"You can say whatever you want to me, but don't make promises to them you can't keep."

She remembered standing by the open window in her bedroom trying to eavesdrop on Samuel and Edison talking in the yard. She couldn't make out what they said. It sounded like two men....plotting...keeping secrets. It made her nervous to think Edison was more like Samuel than perhaps nature had planned.

* * *

"Mrs. Kydd?"

Startled, Evelyn realized she was once again in the empty kitchen. Sue hadn't growled to warn her that someone else had come into the house. She turned away from the table. Deputy Welts was standing in the hallway behind her.

"They haven't locked me out yet," she said sadly with a smile.

"I saw lights on from the road," the deputy said. "I drive by here every night."

"Are you going to arrest me for trespassing?"

"No...no, of course not. You have a right to make sure you left nothing behind. I can understand that."

"Is there going to be an investigation...into the fire?"

"They seem fairly certain Duncan Abrams set the fire."

"And I'm telling you he wouldn't do that to his wife. She was so afraid of all that...fire and brimstone. They were devout people. They didn't believe in cremation. They wanted to be put in the ground, whole body."

"You can rest assured I've brought your concerns to the Sheriff and the Fire Chief."

Evelyn looked down at the floor, then at Sue, then back up at Deputy Welts. "I don't know if I'll ever rest again."

"Let me drive you home."

"This is my home."

"Back to Dr. Long's house."

"Do you think I'm sleeping with him?"

"That's really none of my business."

"What about the dog?"

"She can ride in the back seat. I'm not leaving her behind a second time. I don't want your son angry at me again."

"You don't know anything about my son."

"Please, Mrs. Kydd...if you need a few more moments to look around...gather yourself, a few things? I can wait outside."

"No. This house is empty. I'm finished. Let's go. Thank you."

They rode in silence until he parked the car outside of Dr. Long's house.

"I saw your son at the Abrams' funeral," Deputy Welts said.

"I was afflicted by my condition," Evelyn explained. "I couldn't leave the house that day."

"Oh, I know. I was just wondering...I saw that man with him...the carpenter."

"The carpenter?"

"The one-handed man who works for Dr. Long?"

Evelyn looked at him sternly. "I really don't know who you're talking about." She suddenly felt short of wind. "I must be going.

Thank you for the ride." She opened the door for herself and then the dog and she rushed up into the house.

"Tyrus! Sally!" she called out. She could hear laughter out on the porch. She ran outside. Tyrus and Sally were sitting Indian-style on their towels fresh from the lake, laughing and looking at up at someone sitting in the chair looking out over the children's heads into the dark night.

The children were suddenly startled by both their mother's demeanor and the dog's defensive growling.

"He was just reading us some ghost stories," Sally explained.

"And you find ghost stories funny?" Evelyn scolded them.

Sue still growled.

"Mmm, that's a loyal dog you have there," an ominous voice said. And through a cloud of cigarette smoke, he leaned forward from the darkness and into the light of the moon shining down on the backside of the house. "Mind you, the children here aren't nearly as easily startled as you are, old girl."

Joshua Bloomfield removed his hat and smirked at Evelyn, who answered his smile by fainting.

PART FOUR – BLOOD AND WATER

EPISODE NINETEEN – SMOKE

The boy peered into his mother's bedroom, his left hand leaning on the doorframe, his feet crossed pensively at the ankles as if he was a toddler needing to pee. Sue lay on the bed over the covers, her chin resting on Evelyn's legs beneath the sheets. Evelyn was still, her breathing barely detectable, her eyes closed. It was the most peaceful she had been in the last few days. Tyrus sighed.

Outside an ambulance pulled away with Dr. Long inside. Sally had conducted an elaborate maelstrom of lying that she was even surprised she got away with.

"Mother is sick. She is resting upstairs. We can't disturb her," Sally told the other doctor and Deputy Pinky Welts.

"Who is going to watch you?" the doctor asked.

Withholding her sass regarding the assumption on the doctor's part that she was not old enough to watch herself and take care of her little brother and sick mother, Sally, in a fit of inspired deception said, "Dr. Long's carpenter...Mr. Bloomfield...he's been staying with us while mother is ill."

Deputy Welts raised his eyebrows. "Joshua Bloomfield is staying in this house with you?"

"Since mother fell ill last week. Yes. Oh, he's so very kind and has been so helpful."

"Where is he now?" Deputy Welts asked.

"He ran to fetch some groceries...for supper...just before Dr. Long...*you know*...had his attack."

"My dear, you do realize there is a strong possibility that Dr. Long might not make it through the night," the doctor said.

"I know, I could sense it." Sally shook her head sadly, her eyes glistening. The doctor put his hand on her shoulder.

"Someone must inform your mother."

"Oh, please, let me take care of it. Leave your number. She can call you at the hospital. But she can't be disturbed. She's been so very tired."

"And where is Tyrus?" Deputy Welts asked.

"He's upstairs, watching over Mother with the dog."

The doctor and Officer Welts insisted on going upstairs and seeing Evelyn but they promised not to upset her. Sally calmly obliged. There they found Tyrus in the doorway and the dog and Evelyn on the bed sound asleep.

"I'll be back to check in on her in the morning. If she wakes, please have her call me," the doctor said.

"Of course," Sally complied.

Deputy Welts placed a hand of comfort on Tyrus' shoulder, but the boy stood still. "And you call me..." he said to the boy. "For anything. Anytime. Ya hear?"

Tyrus looked up at him quickly, then returned his gaze to his mother and slowly nodded. "Yes, sir, I will," he said quietly.

When Sally, the doctor and Deputy Welts went back downstairs and out onto the porch, lo and behold Joshua Bloomfield was sauntering up the walkway to the house.

"Coming back empty handed?" Deputy Welts remarked, noticing there were no grocery bags being carried.

Joshua stopped in his tracks to survey the peculiar scene. He tipped his hat to the doctor and to Deputy Welts. "Pardon, officer?"

Sally burst out into to the space between the men. "Oh, silly him!" she exclaimed. "He forgot the list. You went all the way out there before you realized you didn't know what you was to get, didn't you?"

"I sure did, wouldn't you know it!" Joshua grinned. "But I have to ask, what is going on here? Is your mother okay?"

The doctor took him aside by the azalea bushes to explain things. Sally and Deputy Welts remained on the porch and watched as Joshua listened intently and nodded his head after each statement.

"The same goes for you, too, you know," Deputy Welts said to Sally. "I'm your friend. You or your brother...if anything...for anything...whenever..."

Sally nodded. "Uh-huh."

"I'm gonna check in on you kids. Don't you worry."

"We can look after ourselves. Always have. Daddy's never been around. Don't need one now."

"Well, then don't let that man go around thinking he's gonna be your Daddy then, ya hear?"

Sally looked up at him, surprised he responded to her sass with a no-nonsense comment that revealed his power of perception and his respect of her. Maybe he was a friend. "Well, mister, that's probably pretty good advice. Thanks. Thanks a lot."

After the doctor and Deputy Welts left, Sally and Joshua went inside where Joshua poured himself a drink while Sally threw herself on the couch and dangled her feet over the armrest letting one shoe slip off. "Say, ya wanna move in?" she asked Joshua.

"I'm supposin' you told them men that I was livin' here? Lookin' after ya?" Joshua asked her while standing over by the fireplace.

"Supposin' I did."

"Well supposin' you don't seem at all torn up about the Old Doc's predicament?"

"Suppose I thought Doc Long was a dirty old man?"

Joshua grinned and took a sip of his drink.

"You got the gift, girl?"

"Supposin' I don't know what you're talkin' about."

"I knew your mother from a long time ago. And she could always...*see*...things."

"The only thing I see is a man standin' in front of me who needs a place to stay."

"Well, then, I'm supposin' I just might...stay for a little while."

Upstairs Evelyn began to move about. Her eyes remain closed, but she was shifting underneath the sheets and unsettled the dog. Sue jumped off the bed. Evelyn reached her hand out. "Tyrus, come here," she whispered.

Tyrus approached the bed cautiously and took his mother's hand.

"Oh, my baby," she cried with her eyes still closed and her other hand now stretched out fumbling in the air for her son's face. Tyrus took his free hand and guided her hand to his cheek. "Oh, baby, you feel so warm."

"Mama, I'm scared," he said.

"You gotta promise me, Ty, you gotta promise me....you gotta stay away from him. He's gonna...all he wants..." Her breath became labored. Her hands fell down to her own face. Sue jumped back up on the bed and began licking Evelyn's hand and face and neck.

Tyrus backed away. Through the open window a breeze blew in the distant smell of cigarette smoke. Tyrus knew his mother was about to have a small seizure, but Sue was there. And Sue would fetch Sally if it got serious. They would be fine. Tyrus ran downstairs and out back.

The screen door slammed. Joshua Bloomfield knew that in moments the boy's warm presence would be beside him. This had become the summer evening routine. After supper, Tyrus would come out to the edge of the lake. The screen door slamming and the rustling of dirt and leaves beneath his sauntering feet announced to Joshua his approach, while the flickering ashy tip of Joshua's cigarette guided the boy through the dark line of trees to the lonely spot on the shore where Joshua stood away from the people and the tents. And for four nights in a row, they would just stand there and watch the water lap up over the rocks and the shoreline. Not a word spoken between them. Patient. Both.

On the third night Joshua let the child have a drag of his cigarette. The boy coughed, but he was a not a stranger to the ritual. It was not his first time. On the fourth night, Joshua gave the boy his own cigarette.

This night was different, however...somber...both of them supperless. Tonight Joshua held back his offering, and the boy said quietly, "Do you want to go to my hidden spot?" Joshua nodded. They walked through town, staying close to the shore and Tyrus led him down the side street, down those massive stone steps and onto the small landing overlooking the quiet cove and Judge's Rock jutting out from the water offshore. Off to the side was another small flight of brick stairs and an iron railing leading down to a swath of grass stretching along the water. At the foot of these stairs, the water lapped up over the last step and turned a small patch of grass into marsh. They sat down on the steps, Joshua on the top step, Tyrus on the one just below it. Joshua took out two cigarettes and a match. They smoked meditatively, the match flicked into the marsh.

"I used to come here with my father," Tyrus offered to Joshua.

They sat in silence for a few moments enjoying the smoke and the twilight.

"Tell me," Joshua said, "What do you see when you look at the hills across the water?"

Tyrus replied instinctually, knowing the origin of the mountain's name, "I see a lion, asleep."

"Hmmm..." Joshua said through his teeth. "That's where you can tell the difference between a man and a boy."

"Why, don't you see that?"

"I see a woman, asleep, on her side, in the nude." As the boy turned to look at him, Joshua stretched out his arm and traced the curves of the woman with his fingers over the mountain. Tyrus' eyes widened.

"Tyrus, can I tell you a secret?" Joshua said abruptly.

Tyrus tried to wrestle the image of the woman from his mind, furrowed his brow and took a long drag of his cigarette, gazed out to Judge's Rock and contemplated this request. He was used to being asked by adults to keep secrets. He drew the cigarette from his mouth and carefully balanced it between the index and middle fingers of his right hand, lingering in the smoke before turning his face up to Joshua on the step above him.

Joshua shadowed over the boy. "I knew your father Samuel."

Tyrus hardened his face, skeptical. He returned his gaze to the water and the rock.

Joshua took a leisurely drag of his cigarette and blew smoke out over Tyrus's head. "You might not believe me, but it's true. And your mother, too. I knew them both very well...a long time ago. Why do you think she was so shocked when she first saw me?"

"Mother has a condition." Tyrus flicked his unfinished cigarette into the water.

"I know. Look, your father and I were great friends once. When we both played ball."

"How did you play ball with one hand?" Tyrus brought up his knees to his chin and wrapped his arms around his legs.

"This was before I lost it."

"Before those people came to claim the debt?"

"Yes. And your mother and I...you might not believe me, but we were...*very close.*" All the cards were laid out on the table for the boy.

"Did you know my brother too?"

"No."

"My brother's dead."

"I know."

"Does Dr. Long know who you are?"

"No, nobody else knows...except your mother, of course...but nobody else but you. I'm telling you because I feel I can trust you."

Tyrus didn't like what cards divined. "I liked it better when we didn't talk."

"Yes, the silence is good. But sometimes two men need to talk. Need to unburden themselves."

"You sound like Dr. Long."

Joshua placed a hand gently on the boy's back. "You know Dr. Long might not make it."

Tyrus flinched, pulled himself closer, tighter into himself. "He ain't my father, whaddu I care?"

Joshua drew his hand away. "I'm not Dr. Long. You can tell me things if you want."

"Like secrets?"

"Yes, like secrets."

Tyrus relaxed, returned to a normal seating position. "Do you think about secrets when you walk at night...looking into other people's houses...wondering what secrets are inside?"

"All the time."

"You and my father...you were really good friends?"

"Like brothers."

"I think my father hid something...a treasure."

Once again Joshua felt a welling up of self-satisfaction in his gut, knowing that his patience was about pay off. He lived for these moments...these perfect moments when everything he wanted was about to come within his grasp. "You think or you know?"

"I know. He tried to keep it a secret. Him and Edison. But I heard them talking about it. And when I told Edison I knew, he admitted it was true but still tried to keep it a secret. He wouldn't tell me where it was. But now he's dead."

"You knew your brother the best. At one time I knew your father the best. We put our heads together – I bet we could find it."

"We can't tell Sally."

"Agreed. We'll have to be careful so she doesn't suspect a thing."

And they sat there in conspiratorial silence until night had fully descended and tiny points of light appeared amongst the dark woods of Sleeping Lion Mountain on the other side of the lake, definitive reminders of the lives living in the darkness. Their stomachs growled. Tyrus ignored that for the past hour he had to pee.

EPISODE TWENTY – REVELATIONS

S *hit.* Sally couldn't get the image out of her head. Returning again and again. Through the woods. Down those steps. The lake. Judge's Rock. And blood pooling in the water around the rock. Again and again. Woods. Steps. Lake. Rock. Blood. An endless loop. She opened her eyes. Her mind went to the key. She had the key all this time. Pop's key. To the secret box. The key was kept in the drawer of her nightstand. But she didn't feel it was safe there anymore. She fashioned a chain and placed the key on the chain and the chain around her neck, the key hidden underneath her top. Always over her heart.

Meanwhile, Joshua and Tyrus had taken Dr. Long's car out to Haydon's Hill to the Temple Family Crypt. Tyrus had the uncomfortable feeling that Joshua had been here before...creeping...searching...running his hands across Edison's name on the crypt wall. Tyrus went to that loose stone he had first noticed at his brother's funeral and had already checked that day of the Abrams' fire. For show, he loosened it, revealed the nothingness behind it, and placed it back. The man and the boy watched each other suspiciously both of them tracing their hands over the stones, searching for loose ones. There were a few. But behind them was nothing. It was a futile exercise. Tyrus' stomach began to do somersaults. He could see anger welling up in Joshua and coming out of his eyes in his hardened gazes over at the boy while they finished their inspection of the crypt.

"There's nothing her but dust and bones," Joshua said in a defeated tone.

"I'm sorry," Tyrus said. "I thought maybe there was something here."

Tyrus was standing in the middle of the crypt. Joshua walked over to him and placed his hand firmly on the boy's shoulder, his long fingers digging into the boy's neck bone, his thumb anchoring in the boy's shoulder blade. Squeezing.

"It's okay," Joshua said.

Tyrus wanted to wince at the pain. Joshua finally let go, and Tyrus let out a sigh of relief as he remained standing there for a moment while Joshua marched out of the crypt. He quickly followed and caught up with Joshua half-way down the hill on their way back to the car. Joshua took out a gold watch from his pocket and checked the time. Tyrus immediately recognized it as Dr. Long's watch – the same one Tyrus and Edison had coveted as little kids. He remembered Dr. Long mumbling something about it one night not long ago. "Thieves," Dr. Long muttered as he bandied absent-mindedly about his study. And he remembered Mostlee telling him they had been asked to leave by Dr. Long because her mother, Lillian, had been accused of stealing...something.

"Say, where did you get that?" he asked Joshua.

Joshua looked down at him with scornful eyes. "The only thing you need to be worrying about right now is thinking harder about where you father might've stashed that treasure."

"We could go to the farm," Tyrus offered. "But what if it turns out there is nothing left?"

"Tyrus, what did you think of your father?"

"What do you mean?"

"You're a smart boy. What did you think of your father?"

"I dunno. I wish he had stayed put. I wish...he had figured things out better, ya know?"

Joshua nodded. "Tyrus, your father was a stupid man. He wasn't smart enough to know how to spend that money. He was a man who hedged his bets by keeping secrets. And he kept himself hopeful by knowing he could always come back to this secret stash...that part of it, a large part of it, would always be there. That's how some men think. They don't take the time to figure out how the world works and how to take advantage of that. They would rather play games and gamble and let their own family suffer and be sneaky and hide the one thing that could set them free. Do you understand?"

"But Edison said Pop kept the money so we would have an inheritance."

"Your brother couldn't see the forest for the trees. Maybe that's what your father told him. Maybe that's what your brother believed."

"My brother wasn't stupid!"

"But like your father...he kept his secret, didn't he? He was married to the idea of that treasure always being there, too...always hidden...holding it over you...what kind of father and brother were they? Keeping that from you...keeping what rightfully belongs to you hidden."

They were at the car and standing facing each other now, slightly out of breath from their walk. Tyrus was exasperated. He wanted to yell at him. He wanted to demand to know how he came into possession of Dr. Long's watch. He wanted to ask him why he thought he was smarter than everyone else. How did he know so much? But Tyrus was scared of Joshua...of that hand on his shoulder...of that squeezing...of that look of anger in his eyes back in the crypt when they both realized there was nothing hidden there but decades of the dead.

"You're smarter than them, Tyrus," Joshua said, staring the boy in the eyes.

Tyrus turned his eyes from him and took deep breaths, his eyes darting about the hills, wandering about the monuments to the dead...to all the stupid people who died before. Maybe Joshua had simply found Dr. Long's watch laying around the study, and thought there was no harm in putting it to use. Tyrus wanted to believe Joshua. "If I find that money, I'm gonna take care of Mom and Sally."

"You're a good boy, Tyrus. And when *we* find that money, you'll become a man."

They stopped at the diner on the way to the farm. They ate heartily and silently, like men. While eating his hamburger, Tyrus remembered his father, drunk one night, passing through, and sitting down with him at the kitchen table, just the two of them, after the others had finished dinner and left.

"Come closer, son," Samuel said. "Let me get a closer look at you."

Tyrus got up from his chair and approached his father at the head of the table.

"Don't be shy. Don't you love your Pop?" Samuel reached out his arms and pulled Tyrus closer to him. He tousled the boy's hair and shaped his warm, clammy hands around the boy's face. "Your cheeks are cold. Are you cold, son?"

Tyrus shook his head "no."

"When I'm cold, I have a drink. My cheeks are always warm. Feel." He pulled Tyrus' hands to his face. Tyrus vividly recalled the prickly stubble of his father's face, the warm ruddiness of his cheeks, the sickly sweet smell of whiskey on his breath.

"I look forward to the day when can have a drink together," Samuel said with glistening bloodshot eyes. "You're my favorite, but don't tell your brother and sister. It'll be our secret, okay?"

Tyrus nodded in agreement.

Samuel kissed his son on the cheek.

It was warm in the diner. Joshua flirted with waitress, the red-headed girl, the same one who served Tyrus the night of the Abrams' fire. Tyrus imagined a day when he and Joshua would have a drink together.

Outside the diner Tyrus tested Joshua. "You and I, we won't have any secrets from each other, right?"

"I'll always answer your questions with the truth," Joshua said.

"Did Pop owe you money?"

"Your father...he took a lot from me. Not just money."

Tyrus nodded. "When we find it...we split it 50/50?"

"I wouldn't have it any other way."

Satisfied for now, they got in the car.

At the old farm in the hills they started in the cellar. Nothing there. Tyrus gave Joshua a tour of the house. All of it empty now. Hollow. He told them which bedroom upstairs had belonged to whom. Joshua lingered for a moment in Edison's room. Tyrus had the same feeling of being inside the crypt. They checked in closets. There was a loose floorboard in Sally's room. There was nothing there but a raggedy old doll she had discarded years ago. A gloom was beginning to descend outside. Tyrus showed Joshua that great old tree, his favorite tree, along the fence that divided the properties. On the other side of the fence were the charred ruins of the Abrams' place. They shared a cigarette along the fence at a place where part of it had collapsed causing the section snaking further up into the hills to now appear like a crooked spine running up the back of a fallen man. Tyrus' eyes felt red and irritated. He couldn't help but notice the chain of the gold watch spilling out of Joshua's pants' pocket as they stood there and meditated over what remained of the Abrams' homestead.

"You wouldn't play games with me, would you, son?" Joshua asked plainly as he flicked his cigarette far over the fence.

In his mind Tyrus saw that action repeatedly, and he saw the Abrams house appear like a specter and go up in flames. It sent a chill down his spine even though it was a hot August evening. "No, sir," he said.

"I'm a patient man, Tyrus."

Tyrus felt uneasy. "We better go home. It's getting dark."

Joshua nodded and they headed back down the hill to the car. At the curb of Dr. Long's house, Tyrus asked him, "Can you take me to the hospital tomorrow? To see Doc Long?"

"I thought you didn't care about him?" Joshua said.

Tyrus pondered this for a moment. "I'm worried about Mom. I want to see if he's getting better. If he's coming home soon."

"Doc Long is the worst thing for your mother."

"Well, you can't make her better."

"They said things looked grim. That he might not make it. You best get used to the idea of him not being around. All the more reason to find your father's money. That'll take care of your mother...not some old miserable doctor."

Tyrus looked down at his feet, dejected. He suddenly felt exhausted. He moved to open the door and then turned back to Joshua, the gold chain still hanging out of the pocket, taunting him. "C'mon, Sally's fixing supper."

"Just get out. I can't stand to look at you anymore."

"Ain't you staying tonight?"

"I've got some things to take care of...man's things. Now get out."

Tyrus couldn't tear his eyes from that chain. He was frozen.

"I said get out!"

Startled, Tyrus bolted from the car and ran into the house.

Tyrus was up all night in bed. He couldn't stop thinking about the watch. About Mostlee. About Joshua's outburst in the car. The respect and fear he held for the man. The money. His father.

Secrets. Edison. Everything. His mind spun so much that it took flight from his head and rest against the ceiling looking down at him. More than once he got up out of bed, his nightshirt clinging to him in the heat, and leaned out the open window. The night was stale and still. No breeze. And the moon, halved and cloud covered, like his mind on the ceiling, watched him from above.

He finally settled in the dawn, exhausted, his mind descending back into his head with a wicked idea...that loose floorboard in Sally's old bedroom. She held secrets there once. Did she have a secret place now? And he thought of the secret place he had once had with his father – the steps by lake – that he now shared with Joshua. And he thought about the bricks and stones there, by the benches. Some of them had marks. Were there inscriptions? Were there things buried underneath? He fell asleep, deeply, but for only an hour until the sun was bright and the room warm and glowing. When he awoke, that idea was fuzzy and only half-remembered. The room was bathed in gold, and he again thought of the watch.

Tyrus checked the spare room where Joshua had been staying and found it settled, the sheets on the bed unturned. He looked out the window onto the front lawn and the street. Dr. Long's car was not there. He peered into his mother's room. She and Sue were still asleep, though the dog's one ear perked up at the sound of the creaking door, and her eyes opened slowly for just a second to acknowledge the boy. He went downstairs and ate the meager breakfast of toast and scrambled eggs Sally had prepared. Sally had already eaten her share and was reading in the living room with the radio on.

"Have you seen Joshua?" he asked his sister.

"No," she said.

"I wanna go to the hospital to see Doc Long."

"Fat chance of that happening without a car."

"Did you know Joshua has Doc Long's gold watch?"

"Whaddu I care? Geeze, can't you see I'm trying to read here? Get lost!"

Tyrus moped back into the kitchen. He looked over at the phone on the wall and remembered what Deputy Pinky Welts had told him. Call him anytime. For anything. The number was there in the drawer by the phone. He called. It rang a few times before a woman picked up.

"No, I'm sorry the deputy is at work. Did you try calling the station?" the woman said.

"This isn't the station?" Tyrus asked.

"No, this is the deputy's home number. This is his wife, Doris."

"Oh, I'm sorry. Nevermind."

"Wait, who is this? Is this...Tyrus...Tyrus Kydd?"

"Yes, ma'am."

"Is there a message you would like to leave?"

"I was just seeing if he could take me the hospital is all."

"Oh, dear, is there something wrong? Are you hurt?"

"No – no, I just wanted to visit Dr. Long. He's real sick. I just wanted to see him."

There was a long pause. "And there's no one else to take you?"

"No, ma'am."

"Well, look, my husband told me about you. I've a car. I needed to run some errands anyhow. I was just packing up the baby to go out. I could stop by and give you a ride."

"Oh, no, you don't have to. That's okay."

"Please, it would be my pleasure."

"Really?"

"Yes – now are you on Lake Street? At Dr. Long's house?"

"Yes, ma'am."

"Alright then. I know where that is. I'll be there in twenty minutes. You'll be ready?"

"Yes, ma'am. Thank you. Thanks a lot."

"Alright then, you'll see me soon."

Doris had caught a quick glimpse of the Kydd boy at the Abrams' funeral, but only saw enough to judge that he was a bit thin and small for his age. But now she could see he was by no means sickly looking, just tired. As he got into the car, she noted he was a handsome lad by all means and clean and well-dressed, and from what she gathered on the phone, well-mannered and of a sweet disposition. But he had sad eyes, and there were bags under them, the kind you wouldn't expect to find on a child. They lit up a bit, when he saw the baby, and he was happy to hold her on his lap during the drive.

"You're good with her," Doris remarked, smiling.

"Thank you, ma'am," Tyrus responded. "I'm not used to babies. But she seems alright."

"Well. I'm glad you think so."

"She takes after you. She's very pretty."

"Why thank you. You're very kind."

"You look a little bit like the waitress at the diner, do you know the one? I'm a little sweet on her, I guess. Her hair is darker, though. And she's not as pretty as you. I mean she's alright, I guess."

Doris just nodded and smiled. Charmed.

"Deputy Welts must be very happy," he said.

"I hope he is," Doris said. "He's a good man. He makes us happy. And he's always there to help others."

"Like the *good book* says?"

"Well, we're not really religious...but sure. Like the *good book* says."

"I don't go to church neither. But Ma Abrams used to say that. I miss them sometimes."

Doris wanted to change the subject. It made her sad to think of that horrible fire and those poor people, and of how they might have taken care of this boy who was now as good as orphaned. "So are there any little girls at school who are sweet on you?"

"Awww, well...there was one. But she and her mama had to leave town."

"Oh, that's too bad. But don't worry, there are plenty of fish in the sea. I bet a lotta girls are sweet on you...and you don't even know it."

Tyrus shrugged his shoulders and held the baby a little tighter.

"And how's your mother, Tyrus?"

"She sleeps all day and all night. I ain't never seen her this bad."

"And who takes care of you?"

"Sally and I take care of – well, there is Joshua, Dr. Long's carpenter...well, he used to be the carpenter. He's staying with us."

"And is he good to you and Sally?"

"I guess. Can we not talk about this anymore?"

"Sure. We don't have to talk about it."

They rode the rest of the way to the hospital in silence.

At the hospital, Doris waited in the hallway with the baby while Tyrus went to Dr. Long's room. The nurse had said he was awake and would be glad to see him.

"You don't look sick at all!" Tyrus exclaimed upon entering the room and seeing Dr. Long sitting up in bed reading a book.

"Oh, Tyrus, it's so good to see you," Dr. Long said. "It's my heart, boy, you know. Sometimes you can't see the broken bits on the inside, remember?"

Tyrus walked to the edge of the bed. "Who broke it?"

Dr. Long patted him on the head. "Oh, well...many have...but sometimes it's just when you get old...the ticker can't keep up so well anymore."

"Are you gonna die?"

"They're taking good care of me here to see that doesn't happen. Are you taking good care of your mother?"

"Well, Sally and Sue are."

"And then what are you up to?"

"Oh, you know...things. I got a lot going on."

Dr. Long laughed, heartily, but then began to cough. It took him a few moments to recover. When he did, he spoke slower and more softly. "How did you get here?"

"Doris."

"Who's Doris?"

"Deputy Welts' wife. She's real nice. And she has a baby."

"Oh, I see."

"Can I ask you a question about Miss Weathers...and Mostlee?"

"Whatever for? Do you miss them, boy?"

Tyrus nodded, his mood deflated and somber. "Why did they have to leave?"

"They stole from me, Tyrus. And I couldn't abide that."

"What did they steal?"

"They stole something that belonged to you by rights. Something very valuable I was going to hand down to you."

"When you die?"

"Yes."

"Was it your gold watch?"

"Why yes, it was." Dr. Long looked at the child trying to decipher where this was all going. There was a look of sadness and knowing in the boy, like he had just confirmed a great fear.

The nurse came into the room.

"I'm sorry Dr. Long," she said, "But it's time for your exam on the fourth floor." She looked at Tyrus. "Visiting hours are over, young man. I'm sure Dr. Long would be happy to see you another day."

Dr. Long nodded. He coughed some more, and then said. "Yes, run along now. Give your mother my best. Maybe you can all visit another time."

Tyrus nodded and backed out of the room. "Goodbye, goodbye" he said to them both. Out in the hallway he felt dizzy and nauseous. Had Joshua stolen the watch? It couldn't simply have been misplaced all that time and then Joshua had just happened upon it. Did he take it to set-up Lillian and Mostlee? Had that been his plan all along? To get them out of the house so he could move in? Or was it just a coincidence and he was just a thief – taking things that didn't belong to him – like Tyrus' father's money? Was Joshua just playing games like Tyrus' father had been all those years?

"Tyrus, darling, are you okay?" Doris asked him as he collapsed onto the bench beside her. He looked to her like he had seen a ghost. "Is Dr. Long okay?"

"Can we just sit here for a moment?" Tyrus looked her in the eyes. He could see how genuinely concerned she was. A stranger really. Yet she was so pretty and so nice and so motherly and caring to him already. He wanted to burst into tears and cry into her bosom, so warm and inviting, and push the baby aside. He wanted to ask her, "Why does everyone I love leave me, lie to me or die?" But he held it all in, and it exhausted him. He pulled his legs up on the bench as if he was about to lay down on his side and placed his head onto her shoulder. He took the hands of the baby on her lap into his.

"Aww, sweetie," Doris said softly. She felt a bit uncomfortable, this other woman's child suddenly clinging to her, but what was she to do? She could tell he had probably been trying since the day his dad left to appear grown-up and strong, but he was still a little boy who needed a bit of affection. She wrapped her free arm around him and ran her hands through his hair. She kissed him on the top of his head.

Tyrus couldn't remember the last time his mother had done that for him.

And they just sat there like that for a few minutes until the baby began to fuss, signaling it was time to take Tyrus back to the house.

EPISODE TWENTY ONE – THE AWAKENING

The wailing dirge of the horn on the Harlem Hamfats' "Weed Smoker's Dream" was in an endless scratchy loop on the record player. Evelyn's eyes suddenly were wide open, realizing it was only a dream, and it was the endless ringing of the phone that pierced her ears. Back at the farm house, the sound of a phone ringing was foreign to her as the only phone was at the bottom of the hill on the pole. It took her a few moments to orient herself to being in Dr. Long's house. The familiar warmth of Sue lying next to her was replaced with a cold comfort, and as she tuned into her surroundings, she could hear the dog barking downstairs. Quickly she got up out of bed and slipped on her robes and slippers. She felt dizzy. She cascaded down the stairs and into the kitchen where the dog frantically barked at the phone which seemed to be ringing endlessly. She reached for the phone as if she was swimming in thick, murky water and reaching for the edge of a boat or the shoreline to hoist herself up.

The voice on the other line was a bearer of bad news. Dr. Long had had another heart attack last night and passed away. Evelyn collapsed onto the stool by the phone and hopelessly hung her head and arms low. The dog began to lick her hands and nuzzle her. The screen door slammed, and loud feet scampered into the kitchen.

"Mama!" the voices of the children exclaimed in unison.

"You're out of bed!" Sally said.

"What happened?" Tyrus asked. "Are you okay?"

Evelyn pushed Sue away. The dog went to the boy's side. "He's been in this house...hasn't he?" Evelyn said.

"He's been gone for a few days," Tyrus said.

"Just like Pop," Sally muttered.

"He'll be back," Evelyn said as if giving them a warning. "Dr. Long is dead. We have to find Myra."

Later that day Dr. Long's lawyer came to the house. He sat down with Evelyn and informed her that everything had been left to Myra. He tried contacting her in New York City but was unsuccessful. He was planning to take the train there tomorrow to search for her and try to bring her back for the funeral and to settle the Dr.'s affairs. While sympathetic to their unique situation, he told Evelyn she should make arrangements and brace for the worst – that she and the children would have to leave the house sooner rather than later.

"Leave me Myra's number," Evelyn asked of the lawyer. "I'll try reaching her. I'll explain things. She should hear it from me."

The lawyer passed her the piece of paper with Myra's contact information. "Good luck, Mrs. Kydd. I'll be in touch when I return. I'm hoping the search is quick and I'll be back in a few days."

Evelyn spent the rest of the day trying to reach Myra on the phone with no success.

After supper, which was anxiously left mostly untouched, Evelyn sat on the back porch with the children and the dog. She sat on the swinging bench with Sally. Tyrus was in the wicker chair next to the bench. Sue sat in guard dog position by his chair. Evelyn enjoyed a cigarette staring out into the twilight, the crickets and birds draping nervous music over the evening.

"You're all I have left," she said into the thick air.

"Where are we going to go?" Sally asked her mother.

"I don't know."

"Mom, how well do you know Joshua?" Tyrus asked.

Evelyn sighed and took a long drag of her cigarette. Tyrus wished she would pass it to him. "It's not polite for a lady...for a mother...to talk to her children about men other than their father."

"How well did he know Pop?"

"Don't you trust what he told you? They knew each other very well. We all did. If he comes back here..."

If he comes back here, Sue imagined, I would rip his throat out. I told him that when I last saw him. I told him with my teeth. My growl. I will rip your throat out.

"Is he dangerous?" Tyrus asked.

Evelyn didn't respond. "Poor Horace."

"He looked okay when I visited him. He wanted all of us to come back and see him."

"When did you visit him?"

"A few days ago. Doris took me."

Evelyn was struck now by the length of time she had been dead to the world, and by the secret lives her children led separate from her own. *Doris.* She rose from the bench. "I'm going to try Myra again." Even though she knew it was a lost cause. "You both should go back in and try to finish what was on your plates. I don't want you wasting away to skin and bones."

* * *

At the Welts' house, Doris had supper warming in the oven, and she waited out on the back porch for Pinky to return from an emergency call. Before the sheriff arrived to whisk her husband away again, they had been discussing the sad passing of Dr. Long and the Tyrus Kydd situation. Never had something tugged so harshly on both their hearts. Doris envied the baby sound asleep in her crib, dumb to the world of suffering thriving in these mysterious hills. Doris felt for the first time in a long time a bit of a chill in the night...a sign perhaps that this long, hot insufferable summer was coming to a close. She found herself so lost in thought that she failed to hear the footsteps through the house and out onto the porch.

"Wife." Her husband's gentlest of touches fell on her neck.

Doris nearly jumped. She fell back into his quick, smothering embrace. He kissed her on the cheek and the neck.

"Oh, Husband," she almost cried. She breathed heavily, slowly. She held his arms around her bosom with his chest against her back, his warm breath on her ear as he lowered his head near hers. They swayed. He broke the embrace and then took her hand and stood with her side by side.

"What are you looking at?" he asked.

"Oh, nothing," she said wistfully. "Just thinking. Tell me, what happened tonight?"

"I don't want to disturb you."

"You can tell me anything. Everything. I need you to."

"I shouldn't."

"Please. What's eating at you? I can tell this wasn't a normal call."

"I just can't believe some of the things that go on here. I thought it would be so peaceful and quite up here. Away from all the mess."

"Oh, but it is. But there's darkness everywhere. You can't escape it. It's why you are who you are and do what you do."

"We had to go deep into the woods tonight. I couldn't imagine a place farther away from what we knew so well in Philadelphia."

"What were you looking for?"

"There was an old man who had initially called a few days ago to complain about a wolf rustling around the area. Said it was trying to break into the cabin down the ways from his. The Sheriff told him he would send somebody out, but it wasn't a priority. Today the old man called back and said he went down there with his rifle to chase the wolf away, but couldn't find it. What he was really calling about this time was the stench...a smell coming through the open windows of the cabin."

"What kind of smell?"

"Something I hope you never have to experience. A rotting smell. Apparently when the old man described it to the Sheriff, he had a hunch. A bad feeling. We had to go out there. We brought our shotguns. On account of the wolves in the area. The old man pointed us in the direction of the cabin but said there was no way he was going back there to meet that stench again. When we got there, it hit us like a wall. I'm telling you I've never smelled anything like it before. We covered our mouths and noses with our handkerchiefs. We opened the door and that's when we heard it. If ever there was a sound to match that stench...a horrible guttural sound, snarling and chewing and whimpering. And there in the back bedroom, we found them. A wolf...had gotten in...and...this poor woman. She was dead. And the wolf was..."

By now Doris was clinging to his side and had burrowed her face into his shoulder. "Oh, my dear," she sobbed. "Don't say it...*just don't*."

"I'm so sorry. I didn't want to tell you."

"Who was she?"

"A young woman. A waitress. And when I saw she had red hair like yours..."

"Don't speak!" she put her fingers up to his lips to cover them. She held them there for a moment while clinging to him tightly. She then slowly lowered them and loosened her stranglehold on him. She sniffled. "The wolf – had it gotten in through the window and killed her?"

"We're not sure what happened. If she was already dead and the wolf was scavenging, or if the wolf had done it all. We might never know...her body was in such a state..." He shivered thinking about it.

"What did you do about the wolf?" she sobbed.

"We shot it."

They stood there for a few moments and held each other. Eventually they let go. Doris wiped away her tears with her hands and then brushed them on her apron and straightened it. "Well...are you hungry?"

Pinky let out a huge sigh of relief. "Oh, Wife...I'm starving."

Doris feigned a dutiful wifely smile. "Let's go eat that meatloaf then."

* * *

That night, armed with a duffle bag, a spade and her dead brother's flashlight – the one she had held onto as a memento beneath the loose floorboard in her bedroom in the farm house now empty along with a raggedy old doll her father had given her which she had spitefully left behind – Sally snuck out when the other souls were asleep and stole away in the hollow still of the darkness to that secret place – to that place her still living brother had thought only belonged to him and their father. But their father was a drunk and free with his affections. He had taken her there as well, and out of fear for what he thought she was, he revealed to her what he most coveted.

"You got that sight of your mother's, girl," her father told her that night. "You can't fool your old man. I always pictured you taking your gift on the road. Hitching rides with the carnivals and circuses. People paying to have you tell them their futures. Or it could be like a revival almost, ya know? You standing up there. Like a priestess. Wouldn't that be the life?"

No, Sally thought to herself at that moment.

He went on in his drunken rant. "And it's stronger in you because you don't have your mother's other affliction that clouds her sight. Yours is clear. I know that much. I don't trust Edison."

"Cause he ain't really your blood?" Sally asked him. She knew what he feared most.

"I trust you to keep an eye on him, and to know before he knows it himself what he plans to do."

"It don't work like that."

"However it works, just know that you're the only one I trust." In the secret place he showed her the spot and handed her a key.

Sally hated her father. His stubborn stupidity. His games. His fantasies. His fear. With Doc Long dead, this was their only way out now. It was time to use the money. To finally rid the family of it. And to use it to rid this town of them. They could finally be free. Go far away from these hills. What had started as careful stalking in the night through the sleepy hamlet turned into a determined march that removed these thoughts from her mind. Clear, she now felt a presence behind her. She turned around and saw the dog's eyes twinkle in the darkness.

"C'mon on, girl," she whispered.

Sue galloped to her side.

Together they went to the secret place. Next to the stone marker etched with the words JUDGE'S ROCK at the edge of the shoreline, Sally began to dig. The sound of fish breaching the surface of the lake distracted the dog at her side. Sue paced the shoreline, transfixed by the nocturnal activities of a future dinner. It didn't take long for Sally to retrieve the metal box from the earth, unlock its contents and dump it into the duffel bag. She returned the empty box to its resting place in the ground. In the morning, she would show her mother. And then they could leave.

On the walk back to the Long house, she couldn't help but feel another more sinister presence watching her...following her. But the dog was not restless; she did not growl. It must've just been Sally's nerves. Back at the house she panicked trying to find a place to hide the duffel bag. It seemed irrational. She would be giving it to her mother in the morning. There was nothing to fear. She was sure her father was dead. And Joshua was gone...probably already moved onto another town. Besides Sue would stand guard. Yet her heart was racing and her palms were sweating as she stuffed it under her bed. She lay atop her covers in her clothes and tried to sleep but couldn't. She held the flashlight in her unsteady hands and turned it on and off, the orb of light dancing across the ceiling and the walls before vanishing. She finally switched it off and threw it under the bed. Everything under the bed. All the secrets. All the light.

Sally drifted into a deep sleep. She was confounded by the images that flickered before her like the flashing light on the ceiling and walls. But unlike that light which she controlled, these were wild and untamed and blazing. There were those familiar ones that had been haunting her recently that she had hoped would be vanquished by her actions tonight. Through the woods. Down those steps. The lake. Judge's Rock. And blood pooling in the water around the rock. But they were spliced with new images. Rain. Hard, driving, pounding rain. And footprints through mud. A rushing river. Her little brother's empty bed. Sue tied to a post in the clearing behind the house. The dog's body and muzzle moved as if it was barking frantically, but the sound that came out was that of a phone ringing. Sally was suddenly inside the house in the kitchen by the phone. It was ringing. She picked it up. There was a voice on the other line. A woman's voice.

The voice told her. "In the morning, your brother will be gone. This is when you run. But you must go alone. Tie the dog to the post out back. The dog will be safe there. And she will protect him when he returns. And they will meet you at the farm house. And you will run together. For he will be after you. Don't let him find you. You will not be able to protect everyone."

"Who is this?" Sally asked.

But the voice and the image had vanished and she now saw him in his hat and coat and smoking a cigarette underneath the streetlamp along the sidewalk outside the front of the house in the dark of night. All the light was focused on the darkness inside him...the darkness that had devoured his form and left nothing but a black shape. But Sally knew who this was despite not being able to see his face. Joshua Bloomfield was near.

Sally sat up to find herself bathed in the morning light, beads of sweat running down her forehead, her clothes soaked. She jolted from her bed and ran into the bedroom across the hall where Tyrus slept. His bed was unturned; his shoes gone. For a brief moment, she thought irrationally in the mindset of Ma Abrams, and wondered what evil had she unearthed at Judge's Rock last night? Whatever it was, she feared her brother was running towards it. But, Sally, she heeded the voice.

EPISODE TWENTY TWO – THE ROCK

Tyrus' sleep was enshrouded in great multitudes of dust. He could taste it in his mouth and it blinded him. He dreamt he had no clothes on and was standing in the middle of a vast expanse. His naked body was battered by infinitesimal specs of dust and dirt that swirled around in a maelstrom engulfing what he imagined to be the entire world. He felt there was no escape...and eventually he found himself buried. He was suffocating. Choking on dirt. Burrowing and burrowing, he didn't even know which direction he was moving. The dirt became mud. He remembered fantastic stories he had read about heroic soldiers and boys in exotic lands getting trapped in quicksand. He felt as if he was in quicksand upside down. So he swam. He moved as if swimming through mud, heading for the surface. And just as his hand broke the surface of the muck and felt air, he woke up gasping.

Cigarette smoke filled his bedroom in the predawn light. His eyes were watering and his throat convulsing. He took a few moments to collect himself before surveying his space and finding Joshua Bloomfield sitting on a chair in the dark corner smoking a cigarette.

"You came back." Tyrus said in a strained, raspy voice.

"You were having quite the nightmare, boy," Joshua remarked.

"I dreamt I was trapped...drowning...in the great dust storm."

"Mmmm...those problems are far from here. We have our own brand of drowning."

"Why did you come back?"

"I suddenly had a notion...an idea." Joshua seemed to ponder on this for awhile, admiring the dissipating cloud of smoke creeping into the middle of the room, as if it were a ghostly hand reaching for the boy in his bed before disappearing into the ether. "A revelation, you might say."

"About what?"

"Don't play dumb. About your father's...*treasure*. I think you know where it is. I think you have an idea."

"The stones...down by the lake...the secret spot. Some of them are marked."

"I say we go down there and turn over every one. See what might be underneath."

"What time is it?" Tyrus rubbed his eyes.

"Early enough where no one will see us." Joshua stood up and crushed the cigarette butt underfoot on the hardwood floor. "Now hurry up and get dressed. Be quiet. Don't wake the women or the dog. I'll meet you outside by the lake."

Down at the secret spot, they began their excavation. Stone after stone...nothing underneath.

"Are we digging deep enough?" Tyrus asked, his knees and legs starting to ache...the small spade for digging seemingly useless.

"It's here...somewhere...I know it..." Joshua said.

"You have the gift like Mom?" Tyrus smirked, wiped his brow and stood up. He moved towards the stone engraved with JUDGE'S ROCK.

"Don't sass me, boy. You better not be playing games with me...leading me on."

Tyrus was surprised how easy it was to kick the stone over with his foot, as if someone had loosened it before their arrival. Closer to the shoreline the dirt underneath was moist and muddy. Tyrus knelt down and began to dig. The spade hit something. Metal against metal. Tyrus looked to see if Joshua had heard the noise. The man stood still staring out over the lake. Tyrus placed his hand in the mud, palm down, fingers spread. He let it sink until he felt the cold metal hit his palm. He found a handle. With his other hand he cleared mud away from the edges. He pulled it out with a great force, almost falling back onto his spine. A bit of the tide lapped up just inches from his shoes. He stood up with the dripping box, triumphant...beaming.

Joshua rushed over to him. "Gimme that!" He grabbed the box from the boy's hands and went over the bench and sat down with it. He cleared off the mud as best he could. He discovered the key hole. It was locked. "Where's the key?"

"How the hell should I know?" Tyrus said while kneeling down by the water and washing his hands. He stood up and looked back over at Joshua.

"You know where that damn key is, don't you?"

"Maybe Mom has it."

"You have it...I can see it your eyes. You're lying to me." Joshua stood up from the bench and walked over to the boy, towering over him, eyes flaring.

"You're crazy. Why don't we just take a hammer to it?"

"I'll take a hammer to your skull if you don't stop lying to me."

"I've never lied to you. I've always wanted to help you."

Joshua took a few steps back and the turned out towards the lake with a deep sigh.

Tyrus was near panting, anxiety rising up in him, the feeling of mud still on his hands. He felt like he was in that nightmare, suffocating. He looked out over the water. He wanted to give Joshua a few moments to calm down, return to reason, but then he blurted out, "Say, where have you been all this time anyhow? How do I know you ain't playing games with me? Lying to me?"

"I told you I had man's things to take care of. Needs to satisfy."

"Like what? I thought you said I was becoming a man. Why can't you tell me what you've been doing?"

Joshua stood there silent for a moment, a grin starting to trace itself across his face, his head slightly bobbing in agreement with whatever thought had crossed his mind. "You really want to know?"

"Yes!"

Joshua kept his eyes fixed on the lake, refusing to look at the boy inquisitor. "Okay. I went to find that waitress. You know, the one you like? The ripe, sassy red-headed one. And I found her. And I fucked her. For days. Rotten. We fucked like animals, senseless. I fucked her like I fucked your mother." He calmly took out the gold pocket-watch to check the time. "I'm beginning to lose patience with you, boy."

Tyrus, his anxiety now anger blowing up his heart to where it was about to burst out of his chest and his face swelled red, realized now it *was* Joshua who had stolen Doc Long's watch and was responsible for Mostlee and her mother having to leave town, lunged for the watch in a violent strike. He successfully ripped it from Joshua's hand and threw it out into the lake towards Judge's Rock in one fluid fit of rage.

Joshua responded in due fashion by grabbing the boy by the back of the neck and his shirt collar and dragging him out into the shallows. Tyrus kicked and flailed and screamed but Joshua's grip was unrivaled. Joshua stopped by the rock where the water was knee deep. The boy's legs splashed as he kicked and he twisted himself in frantic contortions trying to break free. Joshua threw Tyrus down face first against the rock. Realizing he had been holding his breath the hold time, Joshua suddenly gasped for air and took a few steps backs almost falling backwards into the water. The boy's body floated lifelessly face down in the shallows with a trickle of blood pooling around his head.

What was this strange feeling he felt? Panic? He had never felt this way before after trying to kill someone. He could barely move while he took deep, labored breaths. Looking down at the boy he felt...remorse? The gold watched glimmered against the rock floor under the shallows in the space between the boy's body and Joshua. He reached down and grabbed it, stuffing it into his pocket. He breathed heavily through his nose. There wasn't a lot of blood. It was already diluted in the water. The boy must've just nicked his forehead. He thought about Edison and how he died out on this very lake, out on the ice...his head dashed against it. His son. He continued to look down at Tyrus, and the boy's body seemed so tiny floating there face-down, like a discarded doll. He thought about how he had killed this little boy's father in the shallows of the James River, smashing his head against the rocks until nothing was left but a bloody pulp. Was Samuel Kydd his friend? Had Joshua ever had any true friends? This child, Samuel's child, had only wanted to help him.

Joshua stepped closer to the body, reached down and lifted it from the water. He carried the boy to shore as gently as he had done that afternoon when he found the boy passed out with the little colored girl in Doc Long's study and lay him down in the damp grass next to where they had been digging. The boy wasn't breathing. He rolled the child onto his side and then patted his back until the child began to cough water. He pushed the child onto his back, his eyes still closed, his mouth making strained gurgling sounds, a few coughs still releasing the last trickles of water. Joshua brushed back the wet hair from the boy's forehead to reveal the gash covered now by clotting blood. The child seemed to be struggling to open his eyes. Joshua regarded him with a torrent of mixed feelings...remorse, sympathy, anger.

Samuel Kydd was a snake who deserved to die. He had robbed Joshua of what was rightfully his...a fortune that had belonged to

Joshua's father. And then he stole away with Joshua's woman and son, a son who then died out here on this lake in a freak accident while that scandalous slut of a woman still slept soundly in the house of another man she had seduced and used, also now dead. And here was this little boy, this misbegotten fruit of lust and betrayal...Samuel's only true son. The apple didn't fall far from the tree. Joshua would be duped by *these people* no longer. Yet he couldn't quite find the strength to wrap his fingers around the boy's tender throat and squeeze the last bit of life out of him. With his stump, Joshua punched the boy in the face twice, knocking the child fully unconscious and leaving him with complimentary bloodied lip and nose.

* * *

There was a late summer buzz of insects and haze both outside and inside his head, a hum. He opened his eyes but the light hurt. He closed them again. His head ached. He felt like he had no face. The hum. For a moment, to relieve the pain he imagined the hum turning into the sweet lullaby hum of his mother, and he thought of himself as an infant cradled in her arms, protected and cherished. But the hum and the buzzing and the haze had a life of their own and would not let him rest. He opened his eyes again.

Tyrus sat up, heavy-headed and sore all over. He rubbed his eyes, and his nose felt like hell when his fingers brushed against it. He couldn't bring himself to touch it. He felt the rest of his face. He tasted the blood on his lip and could feel it swollen. He felt the pulsating bump on his forehead, sore like something angry and alive was living beneath his skin trying to burst out. He looked around and for a moment everything appeared in double and titled and sliding. He realized he had half fallen over and his hand was trying to hold his body up but it was slipping in the wet dirt. He struggled to balance himself and tried to stand up, but his feet slipped too and he felt dizzy. He sat back down and straightened himself. He closed his eyes so the world would stop spinning.

"Don't fall asleep," a voice in his head announced.

He opened his eyes again, wide. Taking it all in. The sun high in the sky glistened atop the gentle ripples of the lake. He breathed in deeply the air. Things began to come into focus. He felt a sudden surge of energy. Still scared to stand and fall, he crawled to the shoreline and splashed the cold, clean water on his face. He cupped some of it in his hands and drank it, his parched bloodied mouth relieved. He ran his wet hands through his hair and around his neck, the coolness counteracting the painful throbbing even if only for a moment. He stood up. He bent over and puked into the water, his throat stinging now from the rushing bile. But it felt a great relief, as if some of the pain and wobbling went out with it. He wiped his mouth, turned and marched up the great steps, careful but confident. He headed to Doc Long's house.

He could hear Sue barking from a block away. As he approached the house, he veered around to the side yard where the dog was tied to a post. She stopped barking when she saw him. The dog looked up at the second-story window to Tyrus' mother's room and then back down to her boy. She yelped. Tyrus' heart began to race. He ran around front and up onto the porch through the screen door which rattled on its hinges as he passed through. The dog began barking again. The phone in the kitchen beckoned him as he passed through the main hallway. He rushed over to it and dialed Deputy Welts' number. The phone rang and rang, but there was no answer. He put the phone down and walked back out into the foyer and took a long gaze up the staircase. He gulped, his throat still soar from the puking. With great trepidation, he made his way up, his hand on the rail, his feet begotten by the wobble again. At the top of the steps he had a clear line of sight down the hallway and into his mother's room, the door open wide.

Tyrus approached slowly trying not to make a sound, the rubber soles of his shoes near silent against the carpeted floor. As he came closer, a wider expanse of the room came within his sight, and he could see the end quarter of the bed. He could see his mother's bare legs and feet, twisting in odd contortions, struggling under the hem of her dress. He thought for a moment she must be having a seizure, and surely that's why Sue was barking frantically outside. He stopped in his tracks pondering briefly the idea of running back outside, untying the dog and letting her back in to tend to his mother as she had done so loyally for years. But there was something odd about the way his mother's legs and feet were moving...something about it felt sinister. He heard some manly grunting, which despite the overwhelming fear he felt, caused Tyrus to step closer and closer, almost inside the threshold to the bedroom.

His mother's legs twitched and then stopped moving. He peered in and saw a dark figure on the bed over his mother. For a moment the hum returned, he felt dizzy and went blind. But then everything came back into focus in a flash of red.

It was Joshua. And he had with his one hand strangled the life out of Evelyn Kydd. Satisfied with his handy work, Joshua turned and regarded the boy in the doorway with a smile.

"Why did you do it?" Tyrus cried. "Why did you do it?"

"Don't you see, son?" Joshua explained calmly. "When I saw your mother sleeping so soundly, I couldn't help but place my hand around her neck thinking of all they ways in which she had betrayed and disappointed me. I just couldn't help myself. You can't stop instinct, boy."

Tyrus backed away from the door. He turned and went for the closet in the hallway where his mother had kept the rifle.

Joshua loomed now in the doorway. "Looking for this?" he said holding the rifle.

Tyrus backed up against the wall at the top of the steps. He was dizzy with anxiety and slid down to his knees.

Joshua pointed the rifle squarely at the boy. "I should've finished the job out by the lake. But I am glad you were able to see your mother one last time." He fired.

Tyrus rolled over, the shot hitting the wall just above where his head was a split second ago. He sprang to his feet, still tottering, and he stumbled down the precarious steps, skipping the last three and landing with a running start on the ground floor. It knocked the wobble out of him, and he sprinted out the door. Sue was sitting stoically on her haunches, eagerly awaiting him. He untied her and they ran. Another shot rang out through the bedroom window. Who would've thought a man with one hand would be such a good shot? It grazed the dog's rear right haunch. She yelped but remained undeterred. The two ran through the back yards of the other houses. An eerie quiet peacefulness rushed past them in a blur of graceful stillness like a breeze through wind chimes hanging from a back porch that Tyrus knew he would never fully sense again. He had this unshakable notion that we he would never stop running. They turned into the woods at the end of the block. Sue sprung forth into the lead. And the boy blindly followed.

Bloodied, wounded but unshakable, they ran all the way home to that empty house on the hill.

* * *

Pinky Welts was making love to his wife in the afternoon when the phone rang the first time. It woke the baby, and the two lovers sweaty and wanton in the stale sunlight streaming in through the yellow curtains, rushed now to finish. Pinky held a hand over Doris' mouth as he finished his thrusts and almost brought her to scream. He collapsed fully onto her warm pillowy body while she let out a gentle muffled laugh, her legs still wrapped tightly around his waist, her womanliness still flexed passionately around his generous but shrinking manhood.

"If it's not one thing, it's another," he said breathlessly while the baby's wail in the other room increased in desperation. He propped his torso up and he pushed his hands into the bed on either side of her.

Doris smiled and gazed lovingly up into his eyes. Her tickly fingers tiptoed through the light pool of sweat that formed in the spinal ridge of his arching back and when they found their way down, playfully squeezed his buttocks just before her legs let him lose and he rolled off of her. In the doorway he turned to look at her as he threw his robe over his still quivering body. She rolled over onto her side, her head propped up on the pillows, her womanly hips and shapely bust more beautiful than any mountain gently rolling in the landscape outside their door. She was positively glistening. It was times like this he wished he were a painter or a poet.

"The princess of the kingdom awaits, my king," she said.

Pinky nodded and went to tend to the crying infant. After quieting his daughter and lying her back down in her crib, they both got dressed. Doris made some coffee. The phone rang a second time. Pinky picked it up while his wife tended to the stove. Doris watched as a paleness draped over her husband. "Uh-huh, okay. I'm on my way," he said before hanging up.

"Husband, what is it?" Doris asked gravely but wishing to sound playful.

"There's trouble down at Doc Long's place. Neighbors reported shots fired."

Doris placed her hand over her mouth.

"You don't think that was the kid trying to call me, do you?"

Doris put her hand down. "Oh, don't think of it. Just go. Go."

Pinky arrived on the scene with the coroner and the sheriff already there. The two children and the dog were nowhere to be found. The house was empty spare for the corpse of Evelyn Kydd at rest in her bed, bruises around her neck.

"Crushed her throat with a single hand," the coroner remarked.

"Wonder then what...*I mean who*...the shots were for," the sheriff said.

Pinky went to the open window. He traced a finger through dust on the window sill and brought it to his nose. Gun powder. He looked out the window onto the backyards of the neighbors, everything green and peaceful and still, expanding into a darkness around the bend into the woods. The white drapes fluttered around him in a breeze carrying with it a smell of fear.

Dusk fell.

* * *

"Sally!" Tyrus cried out as he entered the house through the kitchen, panting and flushed with adrenaline. Sue sniffed about. They both heard feet running down the hall and into the kitchen. It was Sally. She stopped in the doorway, her one hand gripping the door frame. She regarded the bullied boy and dog. She then ran to him, arms open. They embraced, lost in a communal sense of relief, but not for long.

Tyrus pushed her away from him and looked at her with tearful eyes. "Did you know this would happen?"

"I left Sue there...for you," Sally said.

"He shot her!" Tyrus motioned down to the bloody, matted patch of fur on the dog's haunch.

"But you both made it, like I knew you would."

"How could you leave Mom behind?"

"I didn't. She stayed."

"To wait for me?"

Sally started to tear up. "No, you idiot. For him."

"What are we going to do now?" Tyrus kneeled down and petted Sue who was nuzzling up beside him, whimpering, a little unsteady now on her paws.

"I have the money, Ty. And supplies. Some food. What I could grab. A flashlight. A knife. A blanket. We have to leave here and never come back. The three of us."

Tyrus nodded and stood up. "Okay. I trust you."

They retrieved the two bags from the other room and left the house behind for good. Tyrus turned his head to look at it one last time, his entire life up to this moment seemingly packed neatly away between its dead walls, his past slowly peeling away like the chipped paint beneath the exteriors of the windows from which he used to stare out into those hills and dream of where this life would take him. And the trio ventured up further into the hills, beyond the rambling fence that separated the land once owned by their mother and the Abrams, past the Robinsons' place, past Gorey Pond, beyond where they had feared to tread as the children they no longer were, deeper into the woods and into the descending darkness that came down to meet them on the mountaintop.

EPISODE TWENTY THREE – ON THE LAM

"**A**re we runaways?" Tyrus asked his sister.

"We're only runaways if we have parents to run away from," Sally said.

"We're orphans."

"You're my little Oliver Twist." Sally tousled her brother's hair.

At night they sat atop the hill in a clearing. The wind was strong but warm and it carried the comforting cadence of insect songs. The dog, exhausted but still alert nestled between them on the blanket, her one ear perked up, her eyes straining to remain open.

"I'm hungry," Tyrus said.

Sally ruffled through her sack. "Here's a candy bar. We'll find someplace to buy more food in the morning."

"Somewhere down there?"

They looked out at the small spectacle of lights down at the bottom of a series of gently rolling hills. It was a small village, probably not unlike Milton or Fenimore, but it seemed a strange and foreign land to them from way up there. On the horizon below there were even more lights, but they grew faint and far between. Tyrus ate the candy ravenously. His eyes scanned the horizon and then traced their way skyward like they were connecting the dots of light up into the sky where the stars looked down on them in an impossibly infinite ever-expanding sphere. He laid back on the blanket with his hands behind his head and he imagined soaring up into the night sky and getting lost, forever...and he found solace in the idea as amongst the great multitudes of points of light, how could Joshua...how could anyone...know which one he was? He closed his eyes.

"That's west down there," Sally said.

"We should head east and then south," Tyrus said. "To the city. We can find Myra."

"The river snakes back around this mountain. We can head down into town and then follow the river east."

"We should follow the railroad tracks. Hop a train. Like hobos."

"We can buy first class tickets, stupid."

"Oh...I forgot. What are we going to do with that money?"

"Spend it. It's the only way to be rid of it."

"He's after more than that money though. He's after us. He won't stop until he finds us."

"Well, then we won't stop moving. Now go to sleep."

"And if he finds us?"

There was no answer. Tyrus opened his eyes and took a quick glance at his sister who was shifting around getting ready to lay her head down on the duffle bag full of money. The dog shifted beside him and rested her head on his chest. He closed his eyes again.

Tyrus awoke in the predawn, his body aching all over from sleeping on the hard cold ground. His sister was already awake. She gave him some bread and water.

"You look like hell," she said.

Tyrus almost choked on the bread he swallowed it so fast. He gulped down the water. He stood up and had to pee. He walked over to the tree line for some privacy while Sally packed up the blanket. It was still dark as night in the woods. He heard rustling which made him want to hurry. His heart quickened. He thought of wolves. He thought of Joshua. He quickly finished and then ran back out into the clearing.

"Where's Sue?" he said. He suddenly had this notion that his sister woke up before him and found the dog dead...or worse...took the dog into the woods and killed it thinking it was beyond healing and would slow them down.

"She's two steps ahead of us," Sally said while looking down the hill at Sue who was already making her way and impatiently looking back at her charges to follow her.

It was late morning by the time they reached the tiny but bustling town in the river valley. They walked into the center of town and found an all-purpose oasis – GAS, BREAKFAST, LUNCH, DRY GOODS.

"You wait out here with Sue," Sally said. "I'll get us some provisions."

Sally walked into the store and casually perused while the lady behind the counter eyed her suspiciously. Sally flipped through some road maps by the counter.

"Say, girl, you ain't from around here, is you?" the counter lady said.

"No ma'am. We're from out west."

"Out west you say?"

"Yes ma'am. Cattaraugus County."

"Cattaraugus County! My dear, you've come a long way, haven't you?"

"Mama drove us all night." Sally continued to make her way leisurely down the aisles, picking up a few things here and there, responding softer or louder depending on her distance to the counter.

"And where's Mama now?"

"Aw, heading back to Cattaraugus County I reckon."

"Say, girl, you ain't lyin' to me now, is you? You ain't runaways?"

"No ma'am. We sendaways."

"That your little brother out there? Look like somebody did him no good for what?"

"Yes ma'am. See, after Papa died last year, Mama took up with this real mean man. He beat up on my brother and the dog, see. But he ain't never touched me now no way no how. I told him I'd cut 'im, see?"

The counter lady was flabbergasted. "You don't say!"

"Oh, but I do say ma'am. So you see, Mama just couldn't stand it no more but she still crazy in love with him. Says she's gotta choose. Him or us. So for our own safety, she says you see, she gotta send us away to our Auntie's out in Saratoga County. The dog, too, wouldn't you know it! Mama always had a sweet spot for dem dogs couldn't stand seein' that dog get whupped for nothing neither. But you see that old jalopy just wasn't gonna make it all the way from Cattaraugus to Saratoga. Heck, ma'am, I don't even know but how far that is but know enough to know it's far! So she drop us off here. Said take the bus the rest of the way."

"*The bus!*"

"Yes ma'am, gave us money for food and tickets and all. Wrote down our Auntie's address. We pretty resourceful. And it was such a beautiful day and this here seem like such a niiiiice town, well we just took to strollin' around." She brought an armful of groceries up to the counter and plopped them down.

"That seems an awful lot for just a bus ride out to Saratoga County."

"My little brother, he's real hungry."

"You ain't find no bus depot, did ya?"

"Well, funny you should mention that, ma'am. We got so struck up by just how nice everything is we plum near forgot to look!"

The lady began to ring up the items on her register. "Well, there ain't much lookin' to do cause there ain't no bus depot here. Your Mama didn't know that?"

Sally leaned in close over the counter and lowered her voice to a whisper. The lady leaned down to listen. "Between you and me, lady, Mama's been takin' real hard to the drink. Only way she can handle him I guess. I drove most of the way so she could sober up. She said for us to go on and git out here and then she drove away."

The lady's eyes went wide. She backed up, finished ringing the items and began to put them in a paper sack. "Well I'll be! You poor sweet dear things!"

"How much, lady?"

"Why I couldn't charge you for this!"

"Heck, lady, I got the money." Sally peered up at the register and saw the total, "$4.37". She pulled a five out of her pocket and slapped it down on the counter. "Keep the change." She grabbed the bag off the counter.

"Where will you go?"

Sally turned around half way out the door. "Oh, right! Say, you don't know if the train comes through here, do it?"

The lady shook her head. "No dear. But if you follow the river it will take you to the next town over and you can pick up the tracks from there. That's about a full day's walk. Then you just follow them tracks into the next town and there'll be a station there. But oh, dears, won't you stay? Let me fix you lunch."

"Thanks, lady, but kids are spoiled these days. We gotta learn to be industrious." And with that she was out the door.

From the storeroom behind the counter came the lady's old man.

"Did you hear that?" she said to him.

"I sure did!" he said.

"Well, I'll be!" she said.

Outside, Tyrus was in a white hot panic.

"The hell is wrong with you?" Sally asked.

"I just saw Doc Long's car," Tyrus said dumbly.

"The hell dya mean?"

Tyrus pointed out to the row of houses across the street. "Going right down that street all slow."

"Are you sure it was Doc Long's car?" Sally was busy stuffing the newly bought food into her sack and discarded the paper bag.

"I swear it was."

"Lotta people drive cars like that."

"But it was *him*."

Sally stood back up and surveyed the surroundings. "Well, did he see you?"

"No, I dove behind the trash can."

"Why would he come all the way around to this side of the mountains to this Podunk town? Why would he ever imagine that this is where we are?"

"He's tracking us. He knew we would go to our old house. And he followed us from there up into the hills. He's gonna kill us. Just like Mom."

"He would've had to have tracked us by foot through there. You need to calm down. And we need to get moving." Sally threw her sack over her shoulder and handed the duffle bag of money to Tyrus. "Here, you carry it."

Tyrus took the bag and glanced nervously at the pay phone outside the door to the grocery story. "Let me call Deputy Welts," he said.

"What? So he can drive out here, pick us up and bring us right back to where Joshua will be waiting for us? Even if Joshua is gone, they'll take the money. They'll put us in an orphanage. Is that what you want?"

"Doris wouldn't let him do that."

"You're off your lid, kid. Now let's go before the old folks inside get any more suspicious and have a mind to come snatch us."

They marched off down the road towards the river.

As the sun set, it felt colder than it had any night earlier in the summer. The children and the dog stayed along the river on the outskirts of what appeared to be a ghost town. They listened closely for a train in the distance to try to ascertain where the tracks might be that they could then follow to the station in the next town over, but they heard nothing but the birds and the insects…a few distant howls. Sally was beginning to doubt that the old lady behind the counter knew what she was talking about, but she didn't want to let on to Tyrus that she might not know where they were headed.

"I'm beginning to think we should've stayed in Mitlon. We could've followed the tracks out of town and to a closer station. We could've been in New York City by now," Tyrus prattled on.

"Don't you think that would've been the most obvious path? Joshua could've gotten on the same damn train." Sally said. "You think the tracks will be close to the water or should we head into the center of this town here?"

Tyrus stopped to catch his breath and ponder this for a bit with Sally behind him and Sue continuing on ahead. He stared off down a dirt road into the dark quiet town. He felt the chills. "No thank you, I'll stay right be this river. At least we know where we're at with this water by our side."

Sally looked around. There were hills encompassing them, some more distant than others, but she couldn't tell from which hills they had come. "I think we might still be heading west."

"I thought you said this river snaked around the mountains back east."

"Aw, hell, I just wanted to sound like I knew what I was talking about. I glanced at these maps at the store. I shoulda bought one."

"Well it sure is a swell time to realize that now, isn't it?"

"Shut up. You have any better ideas?"

"Yeah. Follow Sue."

They both turned forward but had lost sight of the dog in the darkness.

"Sue!" they called out in tag-team, running along the river. They came to a bend and a dirt road slopping up onto the edge of town. Sue was wandering up this road away from the water. She turned around to look at them and waited for them to follow before continuing.

They both had heard the stories from Ma Abrams – religious stories about great pilgrimages...to some old cathedral in Europe...to the Holy Lands (wherever they were). How the thing...the place...the object of the journey would suddenly appear and the kids always imagined church bells playing, like the charming old bells of Ma Abrams' pastoral church. When the old woman would tell these stories and describe these great cathedrals or grand ruins so vividly, the familiar bells would get bigger, and it was like they were up there in the sky...*ding...dong...ding...dong.* Calling them home.

The great billboard framed back fence rose first along the right ridge of the road, elevated on a small grassy knoll. And it appeared greater and higher than it was in the darkness with nothing but the moonlight and the stars shining down. The trio traced their path along the back of the billboards until Sue sensed a breach point and sprinted around the curve of the structure to an opening in an actual fence. They slipped through the opening instinctually and found themselves in the outfield of an abandoned ballpark. The dog ran around in the open field as if she had been set free for the first time, as if there were sheep grazing out there and she had died and gone to heaven.

Sally pulled out their flashlights and she tossed one to Tyrus. They shined them all over illuminating in quick flashes slivers of the infield, the grandstand behind home plate, the dugouts. Behind the grandstand there was a faint hue of light from street lights in the town beyond the field. Indeed this town was alive, and this field its heart. And both children, though they spoke not of it out loud for fear of ruining the illusion, thought they heard church bells ringing.

The beam of his flashlight tripped fantastic as Tyrus bounded for the dugout. There he threw down the duffel bag and flashlight, picked up a bat and made his way to home plate. Sally stepped up to the mound, put down her sack and mimicked lobbing him a ball. Tyrus swung, dropped the bat, raised his fists in triumph and began circling the bases in a homerun trot, the dog playfully nipping at his heals.

They tossed some balls around. They chased each other. They laughed. Tyrus stood at the plate and pretended to be his heroes. Lou Gehrig. Edison. They spread the blanket out in centerfield. They tossed more balls for Sue. They ate. Bread. Canned sausages. They shared some with the dog. They drank soda.

They cried. They cried like they were alone. Like no one was watching. They cried for Edison. They cried for the Abrams. They cried for their mother. They laid back and stared up at the stars, tears still streaming down their cheeks. The dog settled in again between them. Licked their faces and their tears with her course tongue. Their only comfort. They fell asleep.

The sound of a honking car horn awoke Tyrus in the early dawn. He sat up and could see beyond the grandstand entrance into a partially obstructed view of the street. A police car circled around. Sue was up and alert.

"Sally, get up," he said.

No response.

He jostled her shoulders frantically. "Sally, get up!"

Sally moaned and slowly brought herself to sit up. She rubbed her eyes and looked out into the street. The police car circled again. Passing by the entrance of the ballpark appeared what looked like

Doc Long's car. With a shot of adrenaline she was wide awake now.
They quickly packed up their things. In the light of dawn, the old
ballpark looked like a ruin. The grass was overgrown in some
spots, dead in others. A part of the grandstand was collapsed.
Looking out at the billboards they were weathered, worn down or
peeling.

Maybe it was all a dream last night.

Like thieves on the lam from the law, they snuck through the
opening in the back fence, Sue leading the way, and they headed
back down to the river.

But there was something else they heard...something more real
than the great big church bells in the sky from last night.

A train whistle.

EPISODE TWENTY FOUR – HELL'S BELLS

Sally, Tyrus and Sue had been following the tracks for hours. They were on an elevated path with the tracks to their right and then about twenty feet of grass on their left before a sloping descent to the river's edge. Morning was met with clouds and distant rolls of thunder, then rain. By afternoon it was a downpour that soaked them to the bones...warm, thick sheets of rain. They could hear the river rushing and swelling to their left. They could hardly look up and see in front of them. Sally tried to put the blanket over her head for cover, but it just became a heavy suffocating weight. Sue was tiring, limping more. The area on her haunch where the bullet was lodged appeared swollen and infected. The weight of her long, wet fur was dragging her down, and panting she lagged behind the children now.

"I'm worried about Sue," Tyrus cried out.

Sally turned around to look at her brother. She couldn't tell if it was tears or rain running down his face. He was in a sorry state, looking like he was just about to topple over and sink into the mud at the river's edge...as if that would provide him rest.

"We might have to leave her behind," Sally said.

"You're crazy!" Tyrus screamed. "If you think I'm leaving that dog behind...I did it once already and I'm not about to do it again, not this time! There's just about anything I would be willing to do right now, but leaving that dog behind ain't one of 'em!"

"Okay, okay, calm down." Sally looked forward again. In the distance there was a road that crossed the tracks and became a small bridge over the river. "Look, we just have to make it a bit farther to that bridge, see it over there? We can take cover under the bridge and think things through."

"I ain't leavin' Sue behind!"

"C'mon, let's go."

The children continued their trudge through the rain, but Sue just stood there. Tyrus turned around and pleaded, "Please, girl, just a little bit further. C'mon now!" The dog struggled but eventually followed. At the bridge the children took shelter underneath on the concrete ramp that went down into the water which was increasingly tumultuous and rising. Both children breathed heavily, their wet clothes clinging to them. The bags were soaked through, too, the rest of the bread ruined, the money wet. Sue remained out in the rain at the edge of the bridge above them.

"Girl, come in out of the rain," Tyrus pleaded with the dog.

"I think she's scared she'll slip," Sally said.

"She ain't scared of nothing!"

Sue looked down at the children and whimpered. She stayed put and looked out over the road and the tracks as if keeping guard. Her paws began to sink into the muddied earth, and she lay down with her back to the children.

Tyrus was crying uncontrollably now. "Sue, please! Come down here! C'mon, girl."

"Leave her be," Sally said.

"We can't just let her die."

"It's not our choice. Let her keep her eyes out for Joshua while we rest."

They sat there and said nothing to each other for some time, laid back against the concrete slab. Only the sound of the rain and their own shallow breathing. A car rattled across the bridge. It seemed to shake them to their bones.

"I'm cold, we can't stay here," Sally said. "We need to keep moving."

"Shhhhhh..." Tyrus muttered.

Another car rattled over the bridge. The rain was drawing down to a drizzle. Tyrus stood up, stealthily climbed up to the edge of the bridge and crept towards the dog still lying in the mud. He reached out for her, his hand near her wound on her back haunch. Sue's head whipped back and her snout lunged at his hand. At her quick bark, Tyrus backed away. He was fighting back more tears, but he had this new determined look on his face. He turned back to his sister who was sitting up now.

"You're right," he said. "She won't even let me touch her. She's done. I seen it before with the Robinsons' dogs when they was old and bitter and ready to lay down for good. But she can do us one last thing. She can be a part of the decoy."

"The hell are you talkin' about?"

"Joshua ain't gonna stop till he finds us. Lots of cars pass over this bridge here. Maybe one will be him in Doc Long's car. We'll let Sue stay here. We'll make it look like we slipped in the mud and fell into the rushing waters. Look at this long track of mud here. I'll walk back up onto the grass and back track the way we came some, and then make it look like I stepped down into the mud...maybe heading for cover under this bridge. And I go right down to the edge there by those skinny trees before the bridge and I make like I got washed away by the rising current. Gimme that blanket. I'll drape it on the branches, make it look like it got caught and I tried to hang onto to it before being swept away."

"What about me?" Sally asked.

Tyrus pondered for a moment. "You go back up and then come right down that mud path the dog is lying in. Right down to the edge next to the concrete slab. First take the money and put most of it in your other sack. Leave just a bit in the duffel bag. And then it will look like while I was slipping, you came running down to help, but you got caught in the current too...and the bag got caught in the branches there and torn open while you tried to pull yourself up with it and the money came pouring out into the river."

"What if Joshua ain't nowhere near here..."

"Well someone will come across it then. Find the dog, the blanket and the bag caught in the branches along the water. Piece things together. Think we're dead."

Sally nodded. The children got into their places, Tyrus with the blanket back up along the road and Sally with the money bag now near empty, just a few stacks left inside. Tyrus came down to the river's edge and left deep footprints in the mud that was stabilizing now in the light drizzle as he walked along the surging waters. He came upon the first tiny naked tree bent over as if about to be uprooted and taken by the current, and he draped the blanket over the branches trying to make it look like it had been tugged upon. He got it to rip a little, a sharp branch poking through as he tugged down tightly. He stood there, his feet sinking in the mud, the water lapping up oh so close.

"Whuttarya gonna do now?" Sally called out from her spot at the top along the bridge by Sue. "They're gonna see your prints in the mud beyond the tree coming back up here."

Tyrus looked forward at the raging river, then back at his tracks in the mud. Carefully, with his arms used for balance, he stepped backwards through each track in the mud, deepening their imprint, until he had stepped backwards all the way to the beginning. Once free of the last footprint, he scrambled up the grass to the train tracks and made his way back to the bridge along the rails so as not to leave any sign of footprints along the way.

"Who knew you were so acrobatic," Sally said sarcastically as Tyrus took a tiny jump off the iron rail and landed onto the concrete road.

"Would you have jumped into the river after me if I went in?" Tyrus asked.

"Absolutely not!"

"Well, hurry up then."

Sally traipsed down the mud track along the concrete slab under the bridge. At the river's edge she jumped onto the slab, and from there she was able to secure the strap of the duffel bag to the branch of another small tree losing its grip on the ground in the surge. It was perfect. From where Tyrus stood he could see the open bag and the one stack of bills. Sally had taken the other stack and unbound it, letting the bills fall like wet leaves onto the slab and into the water to be washed away downstream.

"We should throw all the money in the river!" Tyrus yelled excitedly.

"Are you some kind of idiot?" Sally yelled back at him. "We gotta pay our way to New York City, don't we?" She shook her head and then crossed over the slab to the other side and climbed up onto the bridge.

Tyrus took one last look at Sue, who was still lying in the mud, her chest heaving up and down. She perked her head up at him and their eyes met.

"C'mon, girl, one last chance...prove me wrong." He knelt down and reached his hand out to her head.

The dog growled vehemently, barked and snapped her teeth at his fingers. Tyrus slowly backed away.

"C'mon, she don't want you to see her like this," Sally called out from the other side of the bridge. "It's time to go."

Tyrus made his way across the road and to the tracks where his sister was waiting. The drizzle had all but stopped now. They made their way along the tracks and an hour later finally reached town and the station.

"Ain't you children got slickers or an umbrella?" the station agent asked them.

"No, sir," Sally said.

"And what in blue blazes happened to him?"

Sally had almost forgotten about Tyrus's nose and lip. They seemed to be healing a bit, but still must've looked a shock to strangers. "Oh, he fell."

"Tried to save my dog, she fell right into the river. Mister," Tyrus piped up.

Sally elbowed him to shut up.

"Well ain't that the saddest thing I heard today," the man said, though not quite believing it. "The next train to New York City ain't until tomorrow morning. You just missed the last one today."

"Thanks, mister," Sally and Tyrus moped away from the station.

"Whuttarwe gonna do now?" Tyrus asked.

Sally turned to him and smiled as they stepped out onto the town's Main Street full of shops and people bustling by in the late afternoon under the fresh sheen of the day's earlier rain. "Ain't you sick of people lookin' at us like that? Let's get us some new clothes."

It was 5pm when they finished up at Harry's Department Store and stepped back out onto the street. It must've been a factory town as there was a five o'clock whistle in the distance announcing the end of another day's work. The children strolled off Main Street into the quaint tree-lined residential neighborhood full of rows and rows of brick town homes. As they walked up the slopping street, Sally took notice of the milk bottles out on the all the porches. It must've been the dairyman's delivery day. At the end of the street at the top of the hill there were some larger homes with generous yards and big front porches. There was one at the end that didn't have any milk bottles out on the porch. A few cars and straggles of sauntering men from the local factory started pulling into some of the row homes down the slope. Lights were on in the other big houses, and the sweet smell of pies and supper wafted through open windows indicative of housewives preparing for their menfolk to be home for the evening soon. But all was dark and still at the house without the milk bottles on the porch.

"These people must be away," Sally said.

The children walked up to the front door. It was unlocked. Into the quiet, safe house they slipped. Tyrus walked over to a lamp to turn on a light.

"No," Sally said, "We don't want anyone seeing lights on in the front rooms."

The house smelled of fine woods, and in the dusky unlit gloom, it all appeared so dark and beautiful. They put their bags down at the foot of the steps and walked around from room to room, running their dirty fingers across the smoothness of the polished furniture, the thickness of the rich drapes, the plush couches and chairs. They felt as if they had been out in the wilderness for years and this was their grand return to civilization. In the kitchen they found some cold cuts and cheese in the ice box. Some stale bread on the counter. They gorged themselves and drank seltzer water.

"What if they come home tonight?" Tyrus said, his mouth full of bologna and cheese and bread.

Sally shrugged her shoulders and laughed a little. "It's the chances we take now."

They took their bags upstairs and found the master bedroom in the back of the house where they turned on a small lamp. There was a huge four-poster bed in the middle of the floor adorned with an inviting fluffy white comforter over clean white sheets. Tyrus dropped his bags and moved to jump on the bed, but Sally held him back.

"Not like this," she said, looking down at their still wet dirty clothes.

They found the bathroom with its big porcelain tub and huge sink and vanity and mirror.

"You go first," Tyrus said.

While Sally took a bath, Tyrus took his flashlight and explored the rest of the house. He held the light up to the pictures on the wall in the grand hallway downstairs. From the pictures he ascertained the house was owned by a wealthy older couple, pleasant looking, and they had five children all grown (three girls and two boys), some married and with children of their own, one of the boys in the military. He figured they must've been visiting one of their children who had moved out of town. Despite the seemingly welcoming smiles on the faces in the pictures, he felt uneasy in the house, like an intruder. This wasn't the same as when he played house with Mostlee.

When he came back upstairs to the bathroom, Sally was sitting at the vanity wrapped in a towel brushing her hair. Fresh hot water was filling the tub. She looked refreshed, relaxed, at home.

"How can you just sit there like that?" Tyrus said.

"What do you mean?" Sally said, continuing to methodically brush her hair.

"When everyone is dead. When we left Sue behind. And now we broke into this house."

"We didn't break into anything. The door was open. They should've locked their doors if they didn't want any visitors."

Tyrus threw his hands up. "Is this how we're going to live now? Like *him*?"

Sally threw the brush down on the vanity and turned angrily to her brother. "The hell do you mean by that?"

"Isn't this what he did...to Doc Long? Just came into the house like it was his. Isn't that what he's done all his life? Him and Pop.

Wandering around. Leaving loved ones to die alone. Going from town to town."

"Ty, you need to calm down. Take a bath. Relax. We're just staying here for the night. Tomorrow we take the train." She stood up and walked past him to the master bedroom.

Tyrus stood there watching the steam rise off the top of the water in the tub. He waited until the tub was about three quarters full and then he turned off the faucet. Sally had laid out soap for him. He peeled off his filthy clothes and slowly dipped into the warm water one leg at a time. He laid back and slid his body down flat against the floor of the tub, his head completely submerged, the warm water soothing his aching bones. He closed his eyes, holding his breath and counting in his head.

One...two...three...four...five...six...seven...

But the counting in his head became drowned out by the sound of Ma Abrams' church bells. In the morning Tyrus awoke lost under the sheets of the giant master bed. All the world was white. He climbed out from under the mountainous soft pillowy fabric into the warm light of the sun coming through embroidered white drapes. He emerged to find his sister sitting on the floor counting out the money.

"Did you sleep well?" Sally asked, still focused on her counting and careful stacking of the money.

"How much do we have?" Tyrus asked.

"One thousand five hundred and sixty seven dollars."

"Is that all?"

"It was a lot more once. But every time he went away, Dad dipped into the box."

"And you knew this all along?"

"Don't be mad at me, Ty. How was I to know it would end up like this?"

"Don't you have the gift like Mom did? Don't you know everything?"

"You know that's not how it works. Mom didn't know everything. And neither do I. What I do know is the train leaves at 9:25 this morning. It's 8 now. So let's hop to it." She snatched up the money and stuffed it in her sack.

Tyrus climbed out of the bed and his feet hit the floor with a thud. As Sally was standing up, he kicked the sack out into the middle of the floor. "Some inheritance!"

And coming through the window now was the sound of real church bells. It was Sunday. They dressed, packed, made the bed and cleaned up what they could. They went to the station and bought their tickets. The man, a different one from yesterday, went through the rigmarole of explaining the multiple transfers further down the line as they got closer to the city. "Going to spend a few weeks with our Gran in Manhattan!" Sally told the man. "Daddy dropped us off on his way to church." And the two of them were dressed all nice, like they could've been going to church, and the man didn't seem to question two children their age traveling alone.

After all, it was an era of sendaways.

EPILOGUE

The lunch counter by the train station had been busy that morning with people grabbing breakfast before church, and it would be busy again with those without Sunday suppers simmering at home when church let out, but it was dead hour now. Ethel, frumpy and middle-aged with nary a smile for customers, smiled now slightly with a cigarette dangling from between her lips after her ritualistic wiping down of the counter with her dingy white rag. She lingered in the still smoke of the empty diner while watching the train rattle by on its way to the Big City. She thought about the time she spent there as a young girl, and it made her all tingly until Clyde came clopping out of the back kitchen in his dirty apron to disrupt her brief reverie.

"Did you hear old Chuck telling that tall tale this morning?" Clyde said while leaning on the counter, sweat on his brow, his underarms stained, trying to lead her on into gossip.

"I never pay Chuck no mind," Ethel said.

"Apparently he went to the river like he does every Sunday morning at the crack of dawn for a little fishing. *One man's church* he always says. Anyhow, said when he went down there this morning he found the damndest thing. Now remember, he was in the trenches during the Great War, so he's no stranger to odd scenes and the macabre...you know...but this one, *this one* took the cake he says. Apparently washed up on the shore was the body of a man...and guess what *beast* was with him?"

Ethel took another drag of her cigarette and continued to gaze out the window. Her raspy voice said, "Jonah's whale?"

Clyde laughed. "Nah, Ethel, wouldn't you know it, a dog had its jaw clamped right down on this man's throat..."

"What kind of dog?"

"Now, Ethel, I didn't see fit to ask him that. Would you just let me finish the story? I didn't even finish the story yet."

"Wonder if it was a wolf."

"Well, hell, Ethel, if it was a wolf Old Chuck woulda said it was a wolf, wouldn't he? Don't you think a sporting man like him would know the difference between a wolf and a dog, and wouldn't a wolf make it a completely different story now?"

"Well, how would I know if it would make it a completely different story, I haven't heard the whole thing yet?"

Clyde slapped his hand on the counter. "Gosh dang it, Ethel, that's what I'm trying to do here."

She took another drag of her cigarette. "Well, I ain't stoppin' ya. I was just trying to picture this scene in my head and it would help if I knew what kind of dog it was."

"Let's say it was a German Shepard."

"Well, ain't that strange? You don't see many of them around these parts. Most folks up in the hills have border collies. Much nicer disposition I hear."

"Well, okay, Ethel. It was a border collie."

"But you just said it was a German Shepard."

"I said *let's suppose it was*...for crying out loud, woman, it was a domesticated animal!"

"But you said earlier it was *a beast*."

"Ethel – there was this dog, and its jaw was clamped down on this man's neck. And the man had a knife that was dug into the dog's chest, like it had leapt for his throat and he pulled out a knife in self defense and then they fell into the water, all tangled up like one monstrous being. But the strangest thing was..."

"Now why on earth would a border collie leap at a man's throat like that?"

"Well, hell, Ethel, I don't know...but the strangest thing was the man had one hand."

"Well, that's funny, innit? So did Old Chuck catch anything good?"

"Well, yeah, he caught a few decent herring, enough for Sunday supper for him and Gertrude, but dang it, woman, that's not what I'm trying to tell ya..."

"Okay, okay, calm your ill humors, Clyde. So after he caught his catch of the day..."

"So after he did what he came down there to do and got himself a nice supper for him and Gertrude, he naturally went to the police. Turns out they think this may be a man wanted for murder back in Milton-Fenimore. Sherriff out there had put out a notice to all surrounding areas to be on the look out for a one-handed man. Old Chuck, you know how he gets and how he has such a way with people, he got the Sheriff here to spill even more beans over a cup of coffee right here at this counter this morning, I can't believe you missed it!"

"We was busy Clyde, and what in samhell were you doing yappin' out here with the muckity-mucks at the counter instead of slingin' hash back there? No wonder we got so backed up."

"Nevermind that now, woman. Look, so anyways...Sheriff told Old Chuck that they were on the look out for some missing kids, too, kids who this dog mighta belonged to, see? But they're worried they might've been swept away in the waters, too. Yesterday it got pretty bad down there by the river with the swelling and the rushing and all."

"Well, that sure would be a cryin' shame. Two little kids you say?"

"Two youngins – a girl and a boy."

Ethel smashed her cigarette butt into a saucer plate on the counter. "There were two nice lookin' kids in here this morning. A boy and a girl. Dressed all nice for church I thought. Well mannered I'd say. Real nice. Boy looked like somebody had been beatin' on him, but that wasn't too odd. Saw 'em hop that train just moments ago."

Clyde stood up straight and his eyes went wide. "Hell's bells, woman...you don't think?"

"Naw, kids pass through the station all the time."

"There was money involved the Sheriff said. Them fellas from Milton-Fenimore are coming out here. You gonna tell them what you saw?"

"Well, them kids had money alright, but I ain't seen a damn thing."

* * *

On the train Sally and Tyrus sat in the back row of the car, Sally at the window, Tyrus on the aisle. There was a great sense of relief in the feeling of the train hurling down the tracks and rushing them ahead of all who may still have been after them. The sounds and the rattling brought comfort to their minds. His stomach a tad upset from the greasy breakfast they grabbed in a hurry before the train pulled in made Tyrus pull his legs up onto the seat and lay his head down onto Sally's lap. Watching the familiar landscape of the hills roll by outside the window, Sally ran her hand gently through Tyrus' hair like their mother used to do to both of them. It felt soft and clean, and she thought of the days when she was small and he was a baby.

"I miss the hills already," Sally said.

At the thought of this she closed her eyes and fell into the rhythmic propulsive cadences of the train. She drifted into sleep. There she found herself walking down from Doc Long's back porch in an autumnal twilight, through the grass and into the thin line of woods bordering the water. As she passed through the trees, the lake and Sleeping Lion Mountain revealed themselves. So too did loved ones passed. They stood on the shoreline looking back at her with welcoming smiles. Pop. Mom. Edison. The Abrams. Even Sue. They were all there.

"C'mon, sis," Edison said, holding out his hand to her.

Sally's heart was bursting. She had never felt so much warmth. She took her place on the shoreline between Edison and her father. Samuel placed a gentle hand on her back.

"Pop," she said. "Where have you been?"

"Hush, girl," he said.

She looked passed Edison to her mother and the Abrams. "Mom," she said. "I'm so sorry."

Evelyn smiled. "It's not your fault," she said. She looked back from where Sally had come and then turned back to her with a more pensive look. "Where's Tyrus?" she asked.

"I don't know," Sally said, suddenly feeling a gust of cold air. She shivered and her father's light touch fell from her back.

"Look!" Edison said pointing out to Sleeping Lion Mountain. "Can you see them?"

Sally strained her eyes, but she couldn't see anything beyond what was before her eyes, that familiar tranquility of the mountain and its dark reflection on the clear lake forming a pointed arrowhead west.

"Listen," Edison said.

There was a rumble. From above. In the air. Over the mountain. Something falling from the sky. Loud whistling booms and great splashes into the water. Planes soared violently overhead. Bombs dropping on the mountain and the lake. Then the rumble came from the ground. The others all seemed calm and just stood there and watched. Sally's heart was like a hot iron against her ribs. She was positively frantic. The ground rumbling continued, and then the most amazing thing occurred. The mountain seemed to move, rise, as if the lion was getting up from a long nap. And it was angry. And it roared.

Sally felt her mother's hands on her shoulders. "Not yet," Evelyn whispered hotly into her ear. "Not yet."

Sally burst awake as the train came to a stop. Tyrus was sitting up, staring forward plainly. They sleepwalked through the transfer. The second train was more crowded. There was a third transfer after a short ride. In the third train they stood. Finally. Grand Central Station. They moved amongst the streams of rushing people through the cavernous cavity of the building, the late afternoon light streaking in from the high-set arched windows casting sepia palls across their faces. They flowed with the other souls out into streets. Sally felt like she was still in a dream. The noise, the towering buildings, everything all-encompassing as if the rest of the universe outside the manmade skyscraper walls of this city did not exist. There were no mountains here. No sleeping lions. All were alive and encaged and enraged.

On Madison Avenue they stopped at a busy Automat, walls of people lined up in front of walls of looking-glass meals. Money in. Grubby-hands grabbing grubby food through tiny windows opening and shutting. Meals rotating. Next! They ate like robots on hard metal stools at a hard metal counter. They didn't know how to speak to each other in this foreign land. Yet all around them people talked, yammered, yapped and yelled. Nothing they could've read about or seen in the picture shows could've prepared them for this. How would they ever find Myra in this sea of noise and people? There was a collective, unconscious feeling of hopelessness they shared as they traversed the streets. Sally reached out to take Tyrus' hand as they crossed 57th Street, but Tyrus walked out ahead of her, already adapting to the "throngs of people" mentality of navigating the streets and dodging honking cars in groups and hoards. Power in numbers. Moving forward. Always.

Dusk. A park. Central Park. On the greener paths, things were quieter but still murmuring. Kids at play in the grass, unshackled by the distant calls for supper time. Couples strolling along holding hands, secret kisses shared before going home for the night. You could even hear birds. Looking up into the trees and beyond along towering window ledges, Sally realized there were perhaps even more birds here in the city park than in the hills back home and it made her shudder to imagine an angry swarm set off by the discordant sounds of the cityscape enclosure.

Finally, her voice. "Let's sit," she said breathlessly as they came across a row of benches that seemingly stretched out forever along the winding path at the edge of the park. They sat. The ham sandwich from the Automat wasn't sitting well in her stomach. She felt cramps from the physical exertion of walking during the attempted digestion of unbalanced food. She felt a little feverish. "There's a letter," she said. "In my bag. From Myra. With a return address. We'll find her. I just have to rest for a moment and then get our bearings."

Tyrus said nothing.

Sally placed her bag as a pillow at the end of the bench, curled up and laid down.

Tyrus waited patiently for her to fall asleep. He looked up through the trees into the emerging night sky. He could see no stars. All around the park checkered patterns of light appeared in the windows of the tall buildings, an eerily unnatural night brightness. The sounds of the city were relentless. The birds and their songs seemed defeated against the ghastly cries of the haunted metropolis.

Tyrus took off his sport jacket, all delusions of the decorum needed to complete this trip seeming to melt away with this action, and bundled it into a make-shift pillow. He stood up and then knelt down by Sally's head. Ever so carefully he lifted her head and replaced her bag with his jacket. She seemed not disturbed and instead curled up even tighter. He brushed the hair away from her forehead and gave her a light kiss. He walked over to the adjacent bench, sat down and began ruffling through the bag. He pulled out the bundle of money and counted it out. He figured half, counted that again, folded it and stuffed it in his shorts' pockets and then returned the other half to the bag. He placed the bag at Sally's feet on the bench and walked away.

Lillian and Mostlee Weathers were in Harlem. Tyrus had his own letter. He would find them. He walked confidently through the park, his hands jammed into his shorts' pockets, the cool night breeze bristling against his bare arms in his short-sleeves and blowing through his hair. He came upon a brick archway over the path and walked into its shadows undeterred, eager for the city to open its mouth and swallow him whole.

Made in the USA
Middletown, DE
16 November 2018